THE GOLDEN MOMENT

by

Benjie Meleras

FOREWARD

This book has been a labor of love, though frustrating at times. I'm really not sure where the idea originated but I do remember the first words were put down on paper in October of 1992 on a Paris Métro. I was inspired by the magical city of Paris where I was lucky enough to have spent time growing up visiting my Dad's family and later during my College years and beyond by playing baseball and traveling Europe doing so. And second, by the then recent World Series victory of the Toronto Blue Jays, my employer at that time.

I started to let my imagination wander and began to weave a story in my head that I finally finished a decade later, interrupted by the real world of marriage, children and a job.

I guess most will call this a baseball book and it is, but I hope you will find more. There is love, friendship, perseverance and hope.

In this book I have used many real people from the world of baseball to lend more authenticity to the story. Many of them I have been lucky enough to meet during the seven years I worked in professional baseball as well as the years I played in Europe. Please note however that the words I have given them are purely fictional and the places, circumstances and actions that I have put them in are simply a result of my imagination and desire to tell a compelling and interesting story. I have though, where applicable, used facts that are in the public domain.

You will soon come to meet Jeff Williams, the main character of this book and a pitcher. The character is in no way based upon the Australian pitcher who was the hero of the 2004 Olympics. This was pure coincidence.

I would like to acknowledge those who helped inspire the story: The Paris University Club and French National Baseball teams from the mid 1980's, Hobart College in Geneva, NY and the students of the classes of 1982-1987, and the Toronto Blue Jays organization.

A big thank you to my wife Trish who has always believed in me and was my number one proofreader and cheerleader. To my parents Carolyn and Simon-- I thank you for always believing in me and loving me. To my brother Jeff and sister Michele for always being there and showing me how much fun life can be. And to my children Abigail and Alexander who put smiles on my face each and every day of my life.

Now I hope you enjoy The Golden Moment as much as I have enjoyed creating it....

"I wanna do it all
Visit Paris in the fall
Watch the Yankees play ball."

Terri Clark
Written by Tim Nichols,
Rick Giles & Gilles Godard

PROLOGUE

Jeff Williams sat high on Montjuic and stared into the beautiful Barcelona night amazed at what had become of his life since he first played on this historic field. It was even difficult for him to fathom what he had accomplished and to reflect on all that had happened to him.

"What are you doing here?" A security guard bellowed at him in Spanish.

"Nada," Jeff replied in a tone more of bewilderment and surprise than of anger. As the guard approached, he suddenly realized who the man in front of him was and simply said "Good evening sir."

From his perch near the Olympic rings he looked down into Olympic Stadium and saw the frenzy and the fireworks, the dancing, singing and uncontrolled celebrations. When he first dreamt about the Olympics, when he was just eight years old, this is how he envisioned them. He remembered Franz Klammer's gold medal run at Innsbruck, Nadia's perfect tens in Montreal, the *Miracle On Ice* in Lake Placid, the Opening and Closing Ceremonies in LA, and the gut-wrenching saga of Dan Jansen in Calgary. He had always hoped and dreamt to one day be included in this festival which united the World, and now, in his own special way he was. Tears streamed down his face as he made his way to the stadium for the Closing Ceremonies.

ONE

"Un Ricain" yelled the first baseman using the French slang word which refers to Americans. The players glanced as the stranger approached. Jeff had been observing from a distance for about ten minutes, before he decided to move closer.

During his Junior year at small Hobart College in upstate New York, few scouts took notice of his twelve wins and 1.17 ERA. All they saw was a short right-hander with a decent fastball and a good curve. Jeff thus came to Europe during the summer of 1985 to visit relatives in Paris and take a class in International Law at the Sorbonne. He had been there many times during his youth, always discovering something new in this magnificent city. His Dad was born in Paris so Jeff was lucky. He saw the city not only as a visitor but as a resident--he loved it. Yet during all those visits, he never saw what he did that sunny June afternoon as he returned to his aunt's apartment on his way home from class.

There, in the Bois de Vincennes, a baseball practice was taking place, in organized fashion and with decent players. If not for the location, the language, the hookers and the old men playing bocchi, you could, with a little imagination, mistake these guys for a decent high school team back home. Jeff had finally decided to approach the young man who seemed to be the coach. He was a strapping 6'3" with rugged good looks and an athletic body. Of all of them, he was the only one who really looked like a ballplayer. He had what baseball scouts called "the face." There was some intuitive feel and belief by scouts that baseball players had a certain face and look, almost a fire burning inside of them, a way to hold oneself, a way to move. Scouts liked to use terms such as "reminds me of," when describing players. Jeff knew that this young man had "the face."

As Jeff began talking to them what he quickly found out amazed him. He was watching the French champion Paris University Club Baseball team also known as the PUC. They were really just an affiliated organization of the University with only a couple of the players actually being students there.

The coach was in fact an American and his name was Pete Moggle. He had played at Yale with Ron Darling and was later drafted by the Cleveland Indians and made it to double AA quickly before being released. He had learned about baseball in Europe through *Collegiate Baseball*, an amateur baseball newspaper and figured that it would be a great experience if he could hook on to the right situation. He found that situation in Paris.

Not only was Moggle the coach of the PUC but also of the French National team. The PUC, as a club team was allowed to use foreigners while the National team was made up of only French citizens. With these two positions Moggle was able to make a little money and see Europe. Not bad for a poor boy from Hell's Kitchen in NY, who was blessed with both athletic and intellectual prowess. He had just turned twenty-five and would be starting a Master's program in International Relations at Columbia University in September. This was the ideal summer job.

At Yale, Moggle was viewed as a contradiction. Even Ivy League schools had their pure jocks and Moggle appeared as such at first glance. He had been offered football and baseball scholarships to over fifty schools including the University of Miami, Florida State, UCLA, Stanford, and Georgia Tech. But when it was time to choose a school, he narrowed his choices to Amherst College, Yale, Brown, The University of Virginia, and Cal-Berkeley. He also decided to solely play baseball.

In the end, he chose Yale because of its proximity to New York City and its program in International Economics and Politics. In addition, while not a national power, Yale did possess a strong baseball program that traveled extensively and played a national schedule with trips to Florida, California and Hawaii. He knew that he would not get lost in the shuffle and that he would get a chance to play from the start.

Moggle's paradox became evident when you took into account his fondness for folk music and tie-dyed shirts, Jack Kerouac and science fiction, baseball statistics and existentialism. He probably would have fit in better at Berkeley, but at Yale he stuck out and was different from all the preppies, just as he was different from the gang members back in New York. But that's what he enjoyed, and that's what inspired him to be the best, on the field as well as in the classroom. He was a little different and a little off-center yet he excelled at whatever he did and could adapt without problems.

So often the Ivy League Universities were the domain of the privileged, which he was not. Pete would love to preach, expound, and outduel his classmates with his mind. He enjoyed showing the prep school girls and boys that a kid from The City knew more than they did. He managed to do this in a manner that did not offend, nor in a tone of contempt. It was not revenge or one-upmanship which motivated him, but simply the fact that he enjoyed being smarter than others. It was this same single-mindedness and intensity which made him the top high school linebacker in New York State.

Winning these intellectual duels and games often gave him more satisfaction than pitching a shutout or hitting a home run. Pete was always a little ahead of his time. In fact ten years before Jack McDowell and Mark McGwire grew goatees in the Major Leagues, the entire Yale team grew them before a series against Harvard and went on to sweep the Crimson three straight.

It was this enthusiasm for life, will to succeed, ability to bring out the best in others as well as himself, his love of challenges and sense of adventure which brought him to France.

While the PUC was the best team in France with nine straight French Championships, Pete's big challenge would be with the National Team which had not had any type of success in over fifteen years. After the "great debacle of eighty-three" as it was known, the French Federation decided to concentrate on identifying and developing young talent.

In 1983, at the European Championships in Italy, France lost all eight games they played and was outscored 153-18 including a 32-0 loss to Holland, 36-0 to Italy and 25-0 to Belgium. It was time for a change and Pete Moggle was brought in to find and develop young players and pump some new life into a program that had stagnated for the past twenty-five years.

The PUC was preparing for the European Cup of Champions that was to be played in Grosseto, Italy in a couple of weeks. The National Team composed of many PUC players would be playing in the European Championships in Barcelona in early August some six weeks later.

"Why don't you come out and practice with us?" We could use an extra arm, plus you might enjoy it, and maybe even get to play in a few games." Moggle's tone was one of forceful and friendly persuasion. Jeff was curious and intrigued even though he had somewhat soured on baseball after not being drafted. Not knowing what to expect, he told Pete he'd be at practice the next day.

At this point in his baseball career Jeff thought that he would be riding the buses of the Northwest or New York-Penn Leagues, not playing ball with a bunch of Frenchmen in what was little more than a playground.

TWO

Jeff always felt that he had something to prove. At his French Lycée back home in Washington he did poorly. This was more a reflection of the strict and uncaring French system than of his true intelligence. But being the son of a French diplomat meant going to school with sons of other diplomats from Europe, the Middle East, Asia, Africa, and Latin and South America.

After school activities included fencing, gymnastics, and team handball. Jeff found his release away from school; he excelled in lacrosse, baseball and football, while playing for his hometown team in Alexandria, Virginia. He was not a rebel or a troublemaker, yet he would show up to class, on occasion, with an Orioles hat or Notre Dame T-shirt, just to piss off his European teachers who could not understand what made him tick.

His fellow classmates looked up to him for his skills and leadership, and his unwillingness to conform. They knew what the teachers and administrators did not and that was that Jeff was special, special in ways which, for now they could not understand. On the one hand, he was very intelligent, yet his grades were relatively poor. His teachers were confused by his high IQ scores and stories from students about his athletic prowess, as if the two could not go hand in hand. They did not seem to realize that growing up in the United States meant that there was more than Moliere and Rousseau and that Louis XV and Charlemagne were not quite as important as the Declaration of Independence, Abraham Lincoln, Jim Palmer, Bert Jones, the Congress and the White House.

Jeff could not understand why he was learning about Napoleon and not about the Constitution and the government of his country. However deep in the back of his mind, he knew that one day his Dad might end up back in France and this was a way to ease the transition.

School was not always as miserable as he made it out to be. He did have a few friends who made his life there tolerable and at times enjoyable. One was Bernard Deniger who also had a French father. Bernard had lived in the States for about six years and was relatively entrenched in the North American way of life. Even though he was slight of build Jeff would get him to hold the ball on field goal attempts in the school yard and even on occasion, Jeff would bring him a catcher's glove and throw Bernard slow curves. But the most fun they had was in the library and in class where they would often sing the theme songs to *Gilligan's Island, The Brady Bunch*, and *The Partridge Family*. They were somewhat of an odd couple. It's funny how things are, but once Jeff went off to college, they never talked again.

Jeff came from a loving family of five. His father, Pierre, grew up in Paris during the war years. His parents were Lithuanian immigrants who arrived in France in 1929 with no money or possessions. Pierre's father was killed in Auschwitz near the end of the war and Jeff's Dad grew up with nothing. His three brothers and sisters all lived in a two room, nineteenth century wooden apartment building with a stand up bathroom three floors down in the courtyard. Pierre was the lone member of his family to get any formal education and after University he went on to graduate school to become a translator and interpreter. During his mid-twenties, while finishing his studies, he toured Europe as a Bee-Bop dancer. His free-spiritedness would show up in all his children.

Finally, after a few years of little work in Paris, he got a job as a translator and interpreter at the World Bank in Washington, DC. He had never been to North America and even though he would be leaving his family behind, he felt that it was important for him to go, so he did. Though he felt somewhat bewildered and homesick, there were many other French people working not only at the World Bank, but throughout DC. It was at a gathering at the French Embassy, where Pierre met his future wife, Jennifer, who was the date of a fellow interpreter. She immediately caught his attention with her jet black hair, green eyes and youthful exuberance. In some ways, she reminded him of Parisian girls with her elegance and presence, but she was definitely an American.

She had grown up in Brooklyn, NY, in a middle class family. Her father was a policeman who died of a heart attack when she was sixteen. After finishing a Political Science degree at Brooklyn College, she moved to Washington and got a job as a Research Assistant at the Brookings Institute. Just a year out of college, Jennifer married Pierre six weeks after they met.

Jeff's brother Marc was almost three years younger and just as talented and just as smart. He was much more imposing physically at 6'2" and two hundred and fifteen pounds. He was heading to the University of Michigan on a baseball scholarship as a pitcher/thirdbaseman. Their sister Louise was fifteen and had grown up somewhat in the shadows of her two older brothers and their athletic success. Around Alexandria, she was known as Jeff and Marc's little sister but that wasn't fair. As talented as her two siblings were on the ball field, she was even more so intellectually, mastering French, English, Spanish and Russian by age fourteen. As smart as she was, she was even more beautiful.

Jeff grew up in a loving and nurturing environment. He traveled and was encouraged to read, to think independently, to question what people presented as fact and to be suspicious of the conformity which existed in American society. He possessed a sharp mind and a sharp wit. He loved being around his friends and having a good time, he just never felt quite at home at the Lycée.

When it came time to choose a college, Jeff figured that with his interesting background, language skills, high SAT scores and a strong right arm, he would have no trouble getting in to the University of North Carolina or the University of Virginia. Just in case, he also applied to the University of Delaware. He applied to Hobart as an afterthought as one of his Mom's friends had gone there many years before and loved it.

He soon came to realize that many kids had better academic records and a few, even better arms. His unique background did pique the interest of both admission counselors and baseball coaches, but his marks just were not good enough to get him into his first choices.

When the admissions office at Hobart invited him to their school for an interview, he fell in love with the beautiful campus and the close-knit atmosphere. Jeff decided that upstate New York would be a better place for him than the University of Delaware. Just as important, the Dean of Admissions and the baseball coach were equally impressed with him. The match was made.

Hobart was a small Liberal Arts college situated in Geneva, NY, on Lake Seneca in the Finger Lakes, about half way between Syracuse and Rochester. While Hobart was technically an all-male school, it shared classrooms, dorms and facilities with their coordinate partner William Smith College, their female counterpart. The eighteen- hundred students were equally split between the two schools. Geneva was a small town with about twenty thousand people, with old houses and big willowy trees, neighborhood bars and Hobart and William Smith.

The campus was beautiful, nestled right on Lake Seneca with plenty of greenery and old architecture. It felt like home and the students were like one big family. The academics were highly regarded as both rigorous and innovative. Hobart was at the forefront in teaching interdisciplinary studies and nurturing students, giving them as wide a field of knowledge as possible and the tools to think independently and critically.

At Hobart, Jeff blossomed. As a seventeen-year-old freshman, he was younger than all his classmates. Nevertheless he excelled in the classroom proving that he was not only smarter than all his Lycée teachers made him out to be, but that he could truly accomplish great things. He was exposed to, and became interested in subjects and situations which were new to him. He concentrated on economics and political science, as well as, American history and literature, subjects that he had never studied before. Playing it a bit coy, he made sure that all his professors were aware that he had never studied nor written in English before, and though his work was well above average, it no doubt helped him achieve his three-seven grade point average.

He was lucky enough to get a roommate with whom he really got along well. Tim Sanders was from Syracuse and was a running back and a high school All-American lacrosse player. Their backgrounds were quite different as Tim came from a lower middle class family and had been outside New York State on only a few occasions. Also, he was black which enhanced the development of their relationship. They became an almost inseparable pair on the small campus. They complemented each other in many ways, as Jeff played the role of the worldly pseudo-intellectual and Tim filled him in on the ways of the street. Though both freshmen, Tim was almost two years older than Jeff and guided him through his social adaptation. The college social atmosphere was a bit different than the Lycée, which was not well known for its Friday night bashes. On the other hand, weekends at Syracuse's Henniger High would often get a little out of control.

Tim nursed him through his first beer and helped him survive those first-term fraternity parties. One thing was for sure; that first Miller High Life pretty much turned Jeff off of beer for good. Vodka was his drink of choice, though he did learn to down a few beers if that was all that was around. Jeff made it through his first Toga party, sampling the upstate New York delicacy of "Dog Dew" which is a mixture of Mountain Dew and Mad Dog, a cheap wine usually consumed with a brown bag around it. He also enjoyed and perfected the fine art of gatoring which was sliding on the beer-drenched floors of Kappa Sigma fraternity. He finally saw the movie *Animal House*, and became fond of doing 'The Worm', when the song *Shout* was played.

Not only did Jeff love being in college, and doing well, but he also found new challenges on the ball field. Fall practice proved quite enlightening as he had to compete against players three and four years older than he was. However, most of his doubts were erased when he struck out nine straight hitters in his first intrasquad game. After that he knew he belonged. as his curveball had them flinching and his fastball had them swinging at air.

The coach of the team was John Brown, an old man who graduated from Hobart in 1932. He later went on to scout for the Cubs and Astros. In many ways he was lovable, yet he was not well reputed for his baseball strategy or his handling of pitchers. As Spring rolled around, Jeff began to realize that his strong pitching in the Fall would not get him much mound time. Unfortunately, this concern became reality. By the time the season was over, he had pitched just fifteen innings. His record was one win and one loss with a save. In his innings of work, he gave up only ten hits while striking out nineteen, to go along with an ERA of 2.40. The team finished with a 12-20 record.

When the season was over, Jeff went to talk to Brownie. He knew that he had to be straightforward with the old man, and did not mince his words. Jeff had to get his point across. "I know that I am the best pitcher on this team. I was a freshman this year and I kept quiet and did what was asked of me, but next year I want to pitch, and if I do, we will win. I guarantee it."

Brownie liked Jeff's fiery attitude and agreed with him. He knew that he held his young pitcher back and did not have a valid excuse for doing so. Jeff had the best stuff of any pitcher on the staff and could no doubt win at the college level. His sophomore year, he would pitch, and pitch a lot. The old coach knew that most of his thinking was antiquated and that he often narrowed his thoughts to that traditional hierarchy which left freshman with the least playing time. He had finally realized that Jeff was a special player and person, one who could transcend small Hobart College and pitch at a higher level. In some ways, Brownie viewed him as a throwback. He was not flashy, but gutsy and efficient with the big breaking curve that had become more and more obsolete with the newfound fascination with the slider and split finger.

"Son', the old Coach said in his scratchy voice, "Every once in a while, I need one of my players to give me a kick in the butt and let me know when I made a mistake. Unfortunately, it doesn't happen often enough. I don't think that I have ever coached or even seen a player at Hobart with pitching instincts and tools like yours. Keep working hard and make me regret my mistake."

Jeff left the coach's office with a new appreciation for the old guy as a human being and as a coach. Even with his outdated methods, Brownie knew more baseball than most men forgot. Eventually as their relationship developed, Jeff would look forward to his conversations with the old man. The old man who would teach Jeff to work hard and how to win and what it really took to succeed beyond Hobart.

THREE

Jeff spent the summer back home working as a busboy in a local restaurant, hanging out with his friends and trying to get into good shape. He worked out with Marc, who had become one of the top high school hitters in Virginia. Jeff would talk to Tim a couple of times a week. His "roomie" was back home in Syracuse working in lacrosse and football camps. They did manage to visit each other on a couple of occasions over the summer, and they were both glad to realize that their friendship existed away from Hobart. In fact, it became stronger than before.

When it was finally time to return to the Finger Lakes, Jeff was pumped. While he enjoyed his summer, he missed what he had at Hobart. He was looking forward to rooming with Tim again, playing ball, going to parties and even hitting the books.

Jeff and Tim had one of the large rooms on campus in Hale Hall. It overlooked The Quad and was the center of the campus. Almost every student would walk by at some point during the day. Some would toss lacrosse balls or Frisbees, co-eds would sunbathe and music would blare out of the windows; it was a great place to be. Tim had been on campus for a couple of weeks for football practice and had already fixed up their two-room suite. Classes were to begin in a couple of days, but today was Jeff's birthday, and for now, it was time to celebrate.

About fifty people gathered in the common room at Hale Hall. They were mostly familiar faces, but the boys didn't discriminate as they invited freshmen and freshwomen alike. A couple of kegs, some vodka and Hale Hall was rocking. The girls all looked healthy after a summer of fun and relaxation. They had lost their "Freshmen Fifteen" while the first year youngsters were out to have fun with their freedom. Jeff and Tim played gracious hosts replenishing the beverages and mingling with the guests and trying to get a take on the new crop of William Smithies. The famous "Pig Book" had not come out yet, so the quality of the new students was still unknown. "The Pig Book", as it was referred to was a booklet with the pictures and hometown of all new students. Both sexes used this as their first tool in targeting the young men and women to plan their attack.

Suddenly, Jeff's eyes fixed on the girl he had always wanted, Robin Palmer, a 5'7'" blonde with a perfect body; a cutesy girl, from Columbia, South Carolina. Her accent and smile had him hooked from the first time he saw her last fall. There may have been prettier girls but no one lit up a room like she did. During their freshman year Robin and Jeff had kept their distance, but no one could truly understand why, including themselves. It was apparent that they liked each other, yet something kept them apart. She would show up with friends to watch some games from the hill which overlooked Alumni Field. They would talk on campus and at parties from time to time, but that's about as far as it went, so Jeff was surprised, yet pleased to see her there.

"Welcome, and hello," Jeff said with his boyish shyness.

"Nice to be here," Robin replied with her Southern accent that created pictures of debutante balls and the girls who went to Alabama football games in gowns. Oh, was she special.

Jeff already had a buzz on and after about twenty minutes of small talk and staring at her magical smile, He was forced away for some birthday kamikaze shots which he proceeded to down much too quickly.

The combination of the ten Kamikaze shots, the Voodoo punch and the Clash's *Rock the Kasba* started to make him a little queasy and he soon found himself stumbling to the bathroom for his first encounter with the porcelain. After five minutes with his head in the toilet, his stomach was cleansed but his head was still spinning out of control. While the rest of the partiers moved on to a fraternity party, one stayed behind to help Jeff.

Robin washed his face and helped him change. She held him as he sat in a chair while his head spun out of control. Jeff had never felt that way and every time he tried to get up, the dizziness overcame him. Finally, Robin put him to bed and left, not sure of what made her want to take care of him.

Jeff had been sleeping for seven hours and would sleep for another eight, when Tim came in at 5:00 a.m. At 1:00 p.m., when Jeff finally rolled out of bed he was surprised that he didn't feel worse, as he recalled in his mind the events of the previous night. He reached for the Tylenol and a Mountain Dew and started his nineteenth year.

At 2:00 p.m., while Tim was still sleeping, Jeff showered, got dressed and went to the Student Union for a grease fix. The two hundred-yard walk in the brisk fall air rejuvenated him. The Quad was full of students enjoying themselves and it was at moments like this that he realized how lucky he truly was.

The lunch rush was over and the Student Union was just about empty as Carla worked the cash. She was a little lady in her mid-sixties who had worked at the Colleges for thirty years. She was a friend and a mother. All the students, past and present were hers and she looked out for them and was there for them when they needed to see a friendly face. She lectured Jeff as he ordered his favorite, a rare burger with onions and mayonnaise, a large Coke and fries, all of which his system needed and craved to get his body going again.

He munched down with pleasure and joy as he read *USA TODAY*; first Sports, then Money, then the purple section and finally the front page. It was his daily routine. Finally, at about 3:00 p.m., he was ready to start the day and the first order of business was to find his guardian angel from the previous night and thank her.

In the lounge at Hirshon Hall, Robin was quietly reading. Classes hadn't started yet, but she was deep into her philosophy book.

"Ah, if only they were all as smart as Descartes," Jeff said, hoping to break the ice. In fact, he didn't really know what to say.

"Actually," Robin answered with a big smile on her face, "I think Jack Daniels said it best. Enjoy, but don't overdue it. That's philosophy."

"Touché." Jeff answered back with a wide grin and a hint of embarrassment.

"How you feeling, big boy?" Robin asked playfully.

"For some reason, not too bad." Jeff responded. "Maybe it's your beautiful smile," he fired back half sarcastically and half seriously.

A little girl "thank-you" was all she could muster, but in reality, she had made it easy on him--no guilt, no scorn, and no judgment. She was indeed a special young lady.

"I really wanted to thank you for helping me out last night. I guess I got carried away," Jeff said with embarrassment.

"I guess you owe me one, and I definitely plan on collecting. I'm filing this one away," Robin said.

"That's fine with me, and as a show of goodwill and in the spirit of paying back my debt, how about dinner one night," Jeff asked with anticipation.

"Tomorrow night would be fine," she said.

"Great" Jeff answered.

Jeff left the dorm and was pumped while Robin felt goose bumps all over her body. What looked like a sure-fire romance, actually led to one of the greatest friendships of their lives. Right from the first dinner at Mario's Italian restaurant, a certain chemistry and openness developed. After two weeks of hanging out together, they knew all there was to know about each other, and then when they kissed each other for the first time, they both broke out in laughter. They had reached the point of no return, when friends could not be more. They quickly became confidantes and advisors. They were two young people with different pressures, uncertain goals and a world of promise in front of them.

Robin, the Southern lady, was not sure what was expected of her, and more importantly, less sure of what she wanted. A great student, she loved the sciences and wanted to pursue her love of nature. Her mother wanted her to go to college to find a husband and start a family. Her father owned three furniture stores in Columbia and wanted his only child to follow in his footsteps and take over the business. She wanted time, time to find out on her own what was best for her and what she really wanted out of life. And Jeff was no different from her, or most of the other students at Hobart and William Smith for that matter. They were really still kids, uncertain about their abilities and not knowing, either what they wanted to accomplish, or what they could accomplish. Yes, he loved playing baseball, and he thought he was pretty good, but was he good enough? Would he be forced to be a lawyer or a banker? Would that be so bad? He just didn't know.

Just as he had done with Tim, he helped open her eyes to the World that was out there, as he knew it. There was more than South Carolina and the small isolated and safe campus. There was a world full of different cultures, social backgrounds and ways of thinking, Why were Americans looked down upon in many countries? Were the Republicans and Democrats really two different parties, or just two sides of the same coin?

Did Americans have political choices, or were they just like the Soviets with one party and one ideology? Why did the French love Jerry Lewis? The inner city black athlete, the Southern Belle, and the almost intellectual jock sure formed an interesting trio.

Jeff and Robin's friendship continued to develop, but no one could understand, nor believe why such a beautiful relationship could or should remain simply a friendship, but it did.

Spring rolled around and Jeff felt in great shape, throwing harder and better than ever. In class, he kept his grades up and was once again on the Dean's list. When the season finally started, Jeff started seeing results. Hobart fielded a young team and the hope was that they would grow and mature together. Jeff felt that the turning point came early in the season on the long bus ride back from Canton, NY. They had just swept Clarkson and St. Lawrence to up their record to seven wins and three losses. Jeff had already won two of his three starts. The ride back was full of aimless banter and kidding around, baseball trivia and campus gossip, dirt and locker room talk, and stories of the famous "red one", the William Smith red head who screamed a lot and loud when she was entertaining.

When they arrived back in Geneva, they all headed to The Oaks, the campus bar famous for fifty-cent mug nights. You could bring in any size mug and have it filled with draft beer for fifty cents. The Oaks was every student's home. It was already a little past midnight when the guys headed in and got smashed quickly on rye, beer and Long Island Iced Tea. It only took five or six dollars to get the job done at The Oaks. They were finally a team and it felt good.

This feeling carried them through Spring and resulted in Hobart's best season ever as they turned around their record to twenty wins and twelve losses. Jeff accomplished what he had set out to do, but knew that he could do more. He finished the season seven and one with a 1.83 ERA and two saves. In seventy-one innings, he allowed fifty-nine hits with eighty-three strikeouts and forty-seven walks. He was named a first team New York State All Star and a third team All-American. Hobart's baseball turnaround and his personal growth and maturation had begun.

FOUR

Jeff returned home after Spring term with energy and a true desire to cultivate the entire person, mind and body. He firmly believed that this would be a truly important year in his life. Intellectually, he knew that his mind was growing and becoming a sharp and dangerous instrument. He continued to read and to think. He wanted to know what was out there far away from his surroundings. He read about the tribal customs of the Aztecs, the Japanese business culture and the *Diary of Anne Frank*. He read Tom Seaver's Art of Pitching and Ted Williams' book on hitting, looking for that one edge that made players, and people, stand out.

His body continued to mature as he added some bulk to his frame, and for the first time he believed that he had a special talent, one that could take him to a higher level. He trained himself not to let his mind get in the way of his pitching. Yes, intelligence was useful, but over-thinking was not. This was the year to give it his all, to let it all out and see where he stood. His junior year would be his draft year, his coming out party and the beginning of his trip to the Major Leagues. He hoped to live every boy's dream.

Jeff spoke to Robin and Tim every week and as the summer progressed, they also looked forward to returning to Geneva. They all missed the time they spent together and the feeling of peace and belonging which engrossed them all on the small campus in upstate New York. Tim had become the second person in school history to be named an All-American lacrosse player as a freshman and a sophomore. He still played football, and even though he was a starter, he looked upon it more as a pastime than with the seriousness with which he displayed in lacrosse. He had become a Dean's list student and now planned to study for an MBA and work with minority businesses in Syracuse.

Robin spent the summer arguing with her parents and trying to figure out what she wanted to do. It became clear to her that South Carolina and the family business was not the place for her. All summer long her parents wanted to fix her up with young men from Columbia's upper class, but she did not want anything to do with them. Her heart had suddenly become a quagmire of unknown feelings and she was not sure what had caused it. She could not confide in the one person she wanted to, because Jeff was the problem. While they had always been so open, the thought of pushing him away was something she could not bare.

She now felt love in her heart for her best friend and did not know what to do. He had done nothing to give her the impression that their relationship had evolved beyond a friendship to a romantic one, but she knew that this did not matter as her heart continued to cry. She did not know whether this love could ever be attained and that made her heart break even more. Between her family, her studies and Jeff, she did not know what would become of her. She did not see what everyone else saw; that she would become whatever she wanted.

The junior year seemed to get off to a little less of a bang than the previous year. Jeff, Tim, Robin and her two housemates, Karen and Ariel went out for dinner at Mario's where they munched on pizza and wings and toasted Jeff's birthday while quaffing down cocktails. After a couple of hours, they moved the get-together down to The Oaks where friends and familiar faces were getting re-acquainted.

Robin had hoped that being back at school would somehow change the feelings she had experienced all summer, but it did not. Deep down she felt that Jeff was hers, and she could not stand the constant flirting between Jeff and the girls. That was actually the lone area they rarely broached-- what each of them was doing in the bedroom and with whom. It was not easy to hide things on the small campus, but Jeff and Robin just did not talk about it. Tonight Jeff and Karen continued the suggestively flirtatious relationship that had gone on for about a year. Tonight it seemed to be getting a little out of control as Karen kept on saying how hot she was as Jeff kept rubbing ice on her thighs and legs. It's a good thing they kept on drinking so their supply of ice never was dry.

It was after midnight when Robin slipped out of The Oaks. Everyone was feeling the effects of the alcohol and no one noticed. The jukebox which had entertained students for years was blasting Marvin Gaye's *Sexual Healing*, which only fueled Karen and Jeff. Meanwhile, Ariel met up with some other friends and Tim played pool.

Karen was a tall blonde with long legs and shoulder length curly hair. Like Tim, she was from upstate New York; a small town called Cortland which apparently had one of the highest percentages of inbreeding in the country. It was evident that Karen was not part of this percentage. She had a certain look which gave her the image of a wild woman and Jeff really liked it. You wouldn't really describe her as either cute or beautiful. She sort of reminded Jeff of Tatum O'Neil and Kristy McNichol and Jeff had always loved Kristy.

She loved to talk dirty and tease Jeff and she was in prime form tonight. She had always believed that her friendship with Robin would prevent anything from ever happening, but it seemed evident that Jeff and Robin continued to be just friends and that there was no reason to deprive herself of what she wanted. Jeff had always pictured a quick romp with Karen, but felt that it would end up causing more harm than the pleasure he would receive. However, as often is the case in university, hormones and alcohol took over and Jeff made good use of the single room he now had.

They went at it like animals, all night, until dawn, time after time as though they had been waiting all their lives for the moment. And then when it was over, they realized that it would not happen again. For some reason, the guilt was suffocating. They did not believe what they had done was wrong, but it sure felt that way. It was just after 6:00 a.m. when Karen left.

Jeff felt that he had betrayed Robin even though he really hadn't. They had been friends for a year and that is all they were; yes great friends, but friends. Karen was not the first girl he had been with since his friendship with Robin, but this one was probably too close to home. He showered and went to meet Tim for brunch. As usual, after a night out, everyone felt as if all eyes were staring at them for something or someone they had done the night before. This morning Jeff felt those looks even though it was all in his imagination.

"How's it going?" Tim asked.

"Well, to be honest, not so good. I had a little adventure last night that I sort of regret," Jeff answered.

"Karen," Tim shot back matter of factly.

"Yeah, man. How did you know?" Jeff said.

"Well, I probably could have told you at dinner that something was going to happen. There was just that feeling and the looks. I think it really got to Robin, especially at The Oaks," Tim answered.

"That's what I'm worried about, I shouldn't feel guilty but I do. My feelings toward her have not changed. You know I wouldn't hurt her for the world, but I cannot live my life looking over my shoulder. I don't know what to do," Jeff finished.

"You better get this out in the open before it messes both of you up so much that you will be wrecks," Tim concluded in a convincing and determined tone.

Jeff spent the afternoon alone, reading and thinking. He enjoyed time on his own. It was early evening, when he decided to take a walk. He crossed The Quad and walked along Lake Seneca. It was a peaceful Fall night and Jeff looked up to the clear and beautiful sky. He wished that he was asleep, dreaming and taking a night flight. He then closed his eyes and pictured himself circling over the campus and then hovering over Robin, trying to figure out what she was thinking. He always loved his night flights, they made him feel good and special, and it felt so real. From almost as far back as he could remember he would fly in his dreams, never really fast like Superman, but always peacefully.

Jeff took Tim's advice and talked to Robin, but not much was accomplished. She did admit that what happened with Karen bothered her, but only because it was Karen and not because she was jealous. She told Jeff that their friendship was as strong as ever and that no romantic feelings had surfaced, but appearances were deceiving and an uneasy tension mounted.

Robin's feelings for Jeff were hard for her to disguise and he either was not ready, didn't want to, or felt that there was no reason to confront the possible evolution of their relationship. On top of this, he was becoming more and more focused on the baseball season and did not want any distractions from his pitching. He wanted to be prepared like no other pitcher had ever been.

He went from class, to the library and to the gym. He kept his grades up and took relish in and enjoyed the challenge of trying to excel in every facet of his life. In the dead of Winter, he would spend one hour running in the morning, while in the afternoon he would put himself through grueling workouts on the treadmill and mix in some weight training, focussing on his legs. He was not a really big pitcher, and he would need the strength of his legs to gain velocity. He knew that if he ever hoped to make it to the next level, the hard work was only beginning.

Under Brownie's guidance, Jeff worked on improving his game. He tightened his curve, worked on a slider that would put less strain on his elbow and made sure his arm speed and motion were the same for his change as for his other pitches. And then the things which made the difference between a thrower and a pitcher like holding runners on, a quick release to home, knowing when to change speeds and knowing the importance of location.

"Any good hitter can hit a 90 mile per hour fastball, and yours is only 83 right now, so you better put it where you want it." Brownie would lecture to him at every session. Three times a week, Jeff would throw to the strings. It was a drill which the old coach had learned from the Cardinal's great instructor George Kissel. Attached to two wood poles were strings with a knee level target and opening the size of the strike zone. It helped pitchers focus on throwing low and hitting the corners. By the time March rolled around, Jeff felt like a new and improved pitching machine, both mentally and physically.

FIVE

Hobart was embarking on their most ambitious schedule ever, starting with a ten game Southern trip which included four games against Division I schools and four against Division II teams. The bus left Bristol Gym early on the Monday morning following Winter exams and the twenty players settled in for the long bus ride to Charlottesville, Virginia for their opener against the University of Virginia. With the snow and freezing temperatures, it was hard to imagine that tomorrow, they would be playing ball outside. Some players read, but most fell asleep listening to tunes on their walkmans.

Jeff followed suit and quickly drifted off. He was scheduled to pitch three games on the trip; the opener against the University of Virginia, one against national power University of Miami and another Division I team, either Northeastern University or New Hampshire. These games would be his, as well as the team's big test. If they could stay close, then they would be ready and confident for their Conference schedule, and a chance for the playoffs. To their advantage, the unheralded Hobart squad would be taken lightly. They felt that this was the year to prove that they could play and they were ready.

Jeff knew that there would be scouts at the games down South. If he pitched well, he would get some second looks up North, but if he struggled, it would cause a major problem in his dream of playing professional baseball.

The bus finally rolled into the Holiday Inn in Charlottesville at about 8 p.m.. This would be their home for a couple of days, before they continued on to Florida to play the bulk of their schedule. Here in Virginia, they would play a single game against the University of Virginia and a doubleheader against Division III Roanoke College.

Most of the team headed to a small college hangout called the Varsity Club, which was recommended by the girl at the front desk. They ordered burgers, wings and fries. Jeff sat with freshman pitcher Rick Stevens and Joe Sherman, the catcher. Stevens won the number two spot in the rotation behind Jeff. He was 6'3" out of James Madison High School in Brooklyn. He had turned down some partial scholarships with Division I schools to come to his Dad's alma mater.

Sherm was a stubby little linebacker-bodied catcher who had rotted away in the bullpen with Jeff when they were freshmen. Now he was the starter, and along with Jeff a co-captain; an honor rarely given to juniors but, for the first time in recent memory, there were no seniors on the team.

The three talked about everything and nothing, but the two co-captains had a motive for their little conversation. While Jeff and Joe were looked up to as team leaders, Rick was informally the leader of the six freshman who were going to have to play big parts on the team. It went further though because Rick was admired by the entire team, not for ability, but for his humility and hard work. Without realizing it, he was also a team leader.

"You know" Jeff said, "there's been quite a change the last couple of years. Remember when our Southern trip was to Pennsylvania and we got snowed out of one game and played a doubleheader in the frozen tundra at Bucknell. We then sat on the bench all year. That is not baseball. What we are doing now is baseball."

Rick listened intently as the two teammates exchanged stories. He wanted to turn out like they had, to lead like they led, and to work like they worked. Finally Jeff addressed Rick.

"Ricky boy," he called him playfully. "When we were freshmen, we were made to feel somewhat equal, but separate. We are not, and will not have a team like that. Everyone, whether they play or not is a part of this team. We need everyone to pull together to win. We will let the other guys know how we feel, but we need you down in the trenches helping us."

"Don't worry, you got me," Rick said.

At about 10.30 p.m., they all headed back to the hotel. It had been a long day and the game was at 1.30 p.m., the next afternoon.

"I think we got him," Sherm said "He has the fire in his eyes, the rest of them will follow."

Jeff had a good night's sleep, and after a 9 a.m. team breakfast, the bus headed to the Virginia campus. UVA was beautiful and historic with its' old buildings and mansions. Spring had already come to Virginia and the morning sun accentuated the elegant campus. By 11.30 a.m., the players were getting ready to hit the field for stretching and batting practice.

The air was crisp, but for early March, this Virginia day was great. The sixty-three degrees felt like ninety to the Northern boys who had been cooped-up in the gym all Winter. It was opening day, a new beginning full of hope and anticipation. The rye grass had just come in and the field was lush and perfect. The bounce in the legs against the turf felt wonderful. For many, the small three-thousand seat stadium was the first real stadium that they had played in, as opposed to the more modest diamonds of upstate New York.

The fact that Jeff had wanted to attend UVA was not lost on him as he walked on to the field for the first time. While this added an element he could draw on, he was happy where he was. Virginia would be a very solid test for the young Hobart team. In fact, Hobart would probably be outclassed by the Division I school from the powerful Atlantic Coast Conference. Virginia had already racked up five wins in seven games, while Hobart hadn't even been outside yet. A mismatch was looming.

As game time approached, Jeff took some extra time to run and stretch before he began to warm up. Sherm then joined him in the bullpen with a brand new ball, which Jeff rubbed down. It had high seams, just the way he liked it, so he could break off his big hard curve ball. He felt good as he finished his warm-ups with the back-up catcher as Hobart went to bat to start the first.

Virginia's pitcher was a freshman making his first college start. It was in games like this that the big schools gave their less experienced pitchers a chance. Hobart took advantage of his nerves and after a couple of walks and a double by Sherm, Hobart was up by two before you could blink. The Virginia players were surprised, but figured it would be an easy comeback-
-they were wrong.

Jeff pitched a masterful game, giving up only three hits; one a solo homer, while striking out eleven and walking four. He used all his pitches and was most excited about the movement and location of his fastball. His velocity was not where he wanted it to be, but he knew that it would come as he got some innings under his belt. It was the start to the season that the team was cautiously hoping for, and they got it with a 3-1 victory.

The following day, they split a doubleheader with Roanoke. Stevens plugged through five innings before leaving with a 5-4 lead. While he struggled at times, the guts everyone knew he had really showed. Sophomore closer Mike Delucia came in and pitched the final two innings for the save. In game two, Roanoke struck first, often, and hard on their way to an 11-1 romp. Hobart headed to Florida with two wins and most of their work ahead.

The eight-hour drive to Jacksonville seemed even longer through the night. The bus finally pulled into the Best Western at about 2 a.m. and the boys finally hit the sack.

The players felt a little groggy at the team meal at 11 a.m. The single game against the University of Jacksonville was at 3 p.m. and Brownie was going to get a look at how deep his pitching staff was. In Virginia, he got what he expected from Jeff and Stevens, his number one and number two guys, as well as from Delucia whom he wanted to keep in the bullpen. In the loss to Roanoke, he used three pitchers for a couple of innings each and while they all got hit hard, the work was needed as they were all going to pitch again on this hectic Southern trip.

Today Hobart would go with a junior, technically the number three man, Pete Samuels. He hadn't thrown much his first two years, but the junkballer needed to pick up his game this year and give some depth to the young pitching staff.

By the third inning, a couple of things were evident; physically, Samuel's game was not up to par as he got hit hard, but he did battle and gave the team some needed innings. He left trailing 9-6 after five innings. Delucia came in to pitch the sixth and seventh. He gave up a run, but Hobart scored five against the powerful Cougars, including a grand slam by sophomore center fielder, Todd Whalen.

With a one-run lead in the eight, Brownie went to Jeff. He had thrown one hundred and twenty four pitches two days before and had planned to throw a little on the side anyway. They were all hungry for the win and knew that the game could be theirs. His arm did feel a little tired, but it gave him more movement on his fastball and sharper break on his curve. It took him just seventeen pitches over two innings and it was over.

Hobart was now 3-1 as they headed to Clearwater where they would play two games against Eckerd College and one each against the University of Miami, Northeastern, the University of New Hampshire and the University of Tampa.

They were staying at the Rodeway Inn, on the corner of busy US 19 and route 60, with the mall and restaurants within walking distance. Spring Break in Clearwater is pretty far removed from Geneva. The streets were full of Michigan and Ontario license plates with snowbirds and tourists enjoying Spring Training and the beaches. They were in the middle of a baseball hotbed with eight Major League organizations holding Spring Training within fifty miles and many College and University teams playing. At the Rodeway, they were happy to find out that the Michigan and Notre Dame swim teams, as well as many spring breakers were staying there. The atmosphere would be a little more festive than if they would be surrounded by retired snowbirds.

After four games in three days and fifteen hundred miles of bus rides, the team had a day off to rest some tired arms and bodies and enjoy a little bit of Florida. For lunch the entire team headed to Hooters, a chicken wing and burger joint famous for their perky and busty waitresses, dressed in tight shirts and shorts. For the locals, it was somewhat of a family restaurant while tourists flocked to see the wholesome suntanned, attractive servers.

The boys enjoyed the break from baseball and the friendly flirting with the "Hooters Girls" who were obviously pros at it—it was all innocent fun.

After lunch some guys went to the Clearwater Mall while others lounged by the pool. A couple of hours later, Jeff and Sherm grabbed Stevens and another freshman pitcher, Brian Reed for an afternoon visit to the Tampa ballet. Apart from being a spunky catcher, Sherm had a knack for finding out where the action was and had already mapped out the day's entertainment.

He had rented a car for the afternoon for a mere nineteen dollars. The four teammates jumped in and took the ten-minute drive across the Courtney Campbell Causeway toward Tampa. Sherm pulled into the parking lot adjacent to the house-like building as he saw the sign he was looking for: Tanga Lounge--Nude Girls. The parking lot was half full, even in the middle of the afternoon. They paid the five dollar cover charge and were immediately accosted and grabbed at the crotch by naked girls of varying degrees of beauty and age asking them if they wanted a private dance. The four young men barely had a chance to get their bearings.

In contrast, to the beautiful Florida sun, the inside of the Tanga was dimly lit with tables around a stage where girls danced. The walls of the establishment were surrounded by couches where customers, for twenty dollars would get a private dance, also known as a lap dance. Lap dances did not exist up North. A lap dance consisted of a naked girl dancing and grinding on your lap while you were free to do what ever you wanted to her. A young kid's budget could disappear quickly at such a place. The boys guzzled down a couple of drinks while gawking in bewilderment.

It was only three in the afternoon but about twenty girls were working, and a beautiful blonde cheerleader type came on stage for a dance, followed by a girl who barely looked sixteen. She was followed by a thirty-year-old librarian, who gave Jeff and his friends quite a show. Finally the boys could not resist as they each picked out a girl and went for the "Two Dances for thirty" special. They thoroughly enjoyed it as the dancers encouraged them to feel at home and grope. After ten minutes of grinding, Sherm, was happy that they did not accept credit cards, because this could become addictive. They decided to chalk it up as an adventure and go find some women and fun that wasn't quite so expensive.

They drove a little further into Tampa and quickly arrived at the Yucatan Liquor Stand. The after work crowd was starting to mix with the spring breakers in this huge two floor night club with a big tiki bar terrace where frozen drinks, beer and cocktails all flowed freely. The music was varied with a party theme--from country, to disco, to rock and roll. This was their first outing in Florida, and they could barely keep their tongues in their mouths as they drooled over the sun-tanned girls of all shapes and sizes, decked out in tight shorts and shirts or short skirts and heels. These were not the William Smith girls of jeans and sweater fame, these were movie babes, more likely to find themselves in a rock video and in a young man's dreams.

Rick and Brian took a stroll around to gawk at the Happy Hour crowd while Sherm and Jeff sipped their Seven and Sevens with a Kamikaze shot and enjoyed the late afternoon buzz. "Man this wouldn't be such a bad place to be," Sherm said.

"Yup, I think I could get used to hanging out here and just watching the sites. For awhile, I could probably deal with just watching." Jeff replied.

"That's right bud." Sherm said. "I think this little escapade, getting away from ball for a day is just what we need, you can't be wound to tight to play the game and this should loosen us all up."

"Hey, hey." Jeff shouted. "Look what we have over there, I guess we know who the real men are on this team." As he looked over to the dance floor and saw the two freshmen doing their best to dance with two gorgeous young ladies who they had obviously just met. It was quite a show watching them grind it out. Sherm and Jeff raised their glasses and toasted their two teammates who had shit eating grins on their faces, basking in their glory.

After about fifteen minutes of this, the four boogie machines left the dance floor and came over to Jeff and Sherm. "Don't wear out the boys, they're not used to such a high level of activity." Jeff said.

"It's ok, we didn't mind," Rick shot back with big smile, still not sure if the girls in front of him were real or just a dream. "We have to get our workout in somehow today," he continued as the two girls giggled.

Proving that he wasn't mute from excitement, Brian opened his mouth. "Heather and Kelley," two perfect Barbie doll names, Jeff thought. "are from Clearwater," Brian continued, "and know a great bar right near the hotel that's the place to be on Thursday night. Why don't we head on over in a bit and be back near base."

Finally, Heather, the taller of the two girls talked. "I think you guys will like it. It's Ladies Night and some of our friends will be there."

Well that was all Jeff and Sherm had to hear. They were sold. Brian and Rick went with their new friends as the two elder statesmen followed them back to Clearwater.

Joe Dugan's was nestled in behind the Rodeway Inn, in a small commercial center. It was only 8:30 P.M., but a line was already forming. After a short wait the six got in to an almost packed bar. The decor was rustic, with tables where people drank and ate with a raised bar area that was packed.

There was a small dance floor in the back which was still empty. Several other team members had obviously found out about this place and were well on their way to enjoying themselves. In a far corner, at a table, Jeff noticed Mike Schmidt and Larry Bowa of the Phillies with Buck Martinez and Rance Mulliniks of the Blue Jays but the customers were too busy enjoying themselves and didn't have time to worry about the big leaguers among them. At Dugan's it was a common occurrence, and they were left alone.

On Ladies Night, young and old ladies alike could drink all they wanted for five bucks. They got a plastic pink glass and matching bracelet and could thus consume. At 9:00 p.m., there was electricity in the air as the music was turned up a notch and the party kicked into a higher gear. The people were there to have fun, and it became apparent that they did.

Jeff and Sherm wandered around and let the foursome get better acquainted. They squeezed their way up to the bar and got another round of drinks and once again took in the scenery. It was easy to tell apart the pale Northerners, like themselves, and the natives. With a quick glance, it appeared that the natives outnumbered the tourists.

After a couple of pops, the two now buzzed co-captains met up with a few of the guys from the team and filled each other in on what they had done during their day off. By about 10:30 p.m. the second wave of drinkers had arrived and the place was packed. Jeff sensed the night just getting going and ordered another round for himself and for Sherm, as they watched their partners in crime, on the dance floor with the two Barbie dolls, having more fun than pigs in mud.

"Enough standing around. Let's get on with the hunt or we'll never hear the end of it from those two." Sherm said to Jeff with determination. The rugged catcher, did not usually have problems finding girls and he planned on good hunting in this fertile yet competitive battleground. They took a couple of laps around the joint to scout out the talent, stopping at the bar for another round. Jeff could tell that his buddy's mind was working on overdrive, calculating odds and determining which young girls they had the best chance of taking home with them.

"Ah, if only you used your mind for good and not evil." Jeff uttered in his best Maxwell Smart imitation.

"Hey man, I don't hear you complaining about all the panties this mind has gotten you into," Sherm fired back. "And by the way, I think I found our two, right over there sitting at the bar, just make sure you've got your broken English and French accent Pierre. It's showtime."

Jeff, a.k.a., Pierre, the French exchange student/baseball star was now on display and Jeff enjoyed this little game. It was fun to pretend and tonight Sherm had picked out the two sexiest women in the joint for them. It was time to perform. They looked a little older than their usual prey, probably somewhere around twenty-five, which for the two boys made a big difference. One was blonde and buxom in a tight black mini dress which hugged her tight body, and a pair of four-inch heels. The other a red head was wearing the same dress in white with heels just as high. Jeff couldn't stop salivating at the simple thoughts that took over his mind.

Their first move was to get into striking distance as they camped a few feet away from the two targets without looking or paying any attention to them. The two buddies just kept talking and drinking while the two girls did the same. While the high-heeled babes realized what was going on, they were enjoying it and they did not see through Jeff's French accent. The two girls had also been drinking and were in the mood for fun. Out of the blue they got up and grabbed Jeff and Sherm and led them on to the cramped dance floor, where they pressed up to and danced with the musically challenged athletes.

Finally after about four dances, they left the dance floor and went back to the bar.

"Hey Pierre," his blonde dream girl asked. "Have you ever done it on the beach?" She didn't wait for an answer as she grabbed Jeff's hand and led him to the parking lot where her convertible was parked. The red head grabbed Sherm letting him know that she had plans for him also.

It was a little after 5:00 a.m., when the red convertible pulled up to the Rodeway Inn and left young Jeff off in front of his room. When he entered, he could see that Sherm had as good a time as he had. The mattress was on the floor as Sherm slept on top of it snoring away with a tiny pair of white thong panties clenched in his arms and a wide smile on his face. He'd be good for a couple of hits today Jeff thought as he hit the sack for a short two and a half hour sleep. He loved his team, but he did not regret the night.

At 7:30 a.m., the front desk rang with a wake up call as the two co-captains struggled to get up. Though, they were not in top shape, their hangovers were mild as they had managed to sober up a little before they actually went to sleep.

"Thank you God", were the first words out of Jeff's mouth as he let the beautiful Florida sun into the room. The stubby catcher wasn't sure if his roommate was thanking God for what had transpired the day and night before or simply for the fact that he was awake and alive to tell about it. They each showered and grabbed a Mountain Dew to get the day started before breakfast and their noon game against the University of New Hampshire, which Jeff was happy he did not have to pitch in.

At breakfast, they ran into Brian and Rick, the two freshman pitchers. They had big smiles on their faces and kept on singing that they had met the girls they were going to marry, amidst the merciless teasing of their two mentors who tried to divulge as little information as possible about their women.

"At least we have some class," Stevens shouted "we got their phone numbers and remember their names."

"Well sorry stooge one and stooge two but remember who made it possible for you two social Neanderthals to get it last night." Sherm shot back in a tone which seemed less amusing and somewhat vengeful.

"Easy," Jeff said as they finished breakfast just as they had been yesterday afternoon---four college friends having fun, being young and looking forward to playing ball.

SIX

When the bus rolled in to Geneva, the team was happy to finally be home. The most ambitious trip in Hobart Baseball history was over and the tired arms, bodies and souls needed rest. The most ambitious trip was also the most successful. After the 3-1 start, they beat the University of New Hampshire and Northeastern. They split with Eckerd College and lost a surprisingly tight game against the nationally ranked Miami Hurricanes, as well as, the University of Tampa.

Jeff continued his outstanding pitching, shutting out Northeastern on a four-hitter, pitching an inning and a third against Eckerd for the save, and pitching seven strong innings against the Hurricanes before leaving, down 4-0 on one unearned run.

Heather and Kelly cheered on their new favorite college team at every game, inspiring strong performances from their boys. As if transformed by a newfound self-confidence, Stevens and Reed started pitching like seasoned veterans. First Reed, after his adventurous night, pitched five strong innings against New Hampshire for the win, and then Stevens went seven against Eckerd before Delucia and Jeff came in to shut the door. His next start against Tampa was also strong though the team lost 8-2.

The 6-4 trip was nothing less than a huge success as the upstart Hobart team embarked on the most important part of the season and the drive to their first ever play-off appearance. Jeff felt good and was confident in both himself and the team. He realized that he had ability and talent. He felt that he was demonstrating the type of performance that would rank him with some of the top pitchers in the country. He would have to continue to work hard, fine tune his skills and to grow along with the rest of the team. There would be five days before the Northern schedule started at Rochester, against the University of Rochester, and the team had to remain focused.

Tim was back on campus after the Lacrosse team's California trip and he was just as fired up as Jeff. Spring was always tough on their friendship as they were both off with their teams, either practicing or playing, but they made time for each other and did not let the love of their sports interfere with their relationship. There was always time for a meal, a few drinks or a movie crammed between sports and classes. They both continued to push themselves in the classroom. They became almost obsessive, in a good way, about excelling in all they did.

And then there was Robin. Jeff slowly felt her drifting away right before him. It hurt. He knew that it must be hurting her too. At times, it was as it used to be and at others she seemed distant and confused, unsure of where she was going and what she wanted. Robin had a big important place in Jeff's heart, it just wasn't the place she wanted to be in and that became painfully clear to her. Accepting this became difficult though.

The friendship, almost a kinship, meant so much to both of them that they could not, and would not let the imperfections and somewhat unspoken problems and troubles interfere with their relationship. They both knew that they needed each other and would be miserable apart, yet they were still somewhat sad. This apparent conflict would remain not only throughout the end of the school year but for years to come.

While his life off the field was somewhat muddled, on the diamond, he became more focused than ever. Through ten northern games, Hobart won nine. Their only loss was a 1-0 fourteen inning affair against Division II power Lemoyne College of Syracuse. Jeff had pitched 10 shutout innings, stifling his opponents' bats. With their six wins down South, they were on track to set a school record for wins and already cracked the National ranking at number twenty-one in the nation, another first.

The team's power became evident. It was the pitching and Jeff, Stevens and Reed became the big three, responsible for eleven of the fifteen wins with Rick Delucia earning seven saves. Division III baseball in upstate New York had always been ruled by two teams, Ithaca College and Oswego State. Ithaca had last won the National Championship in 1980 and Oswego was always close by. As the schedule would have it, Hobart would have to play a doubleheader against Oswego on Monday, followed by one against Ithaca on Friday and a single game against the Rochester Institute of Technology on Saturday. Five games in six days against three top fifteen teams and a chance to show the baseball powers that there was a new team to reckon with, and to a certain extent, they did.

Jeff overpowered Oswego in game one pitching all seven innings which is the standard length of College doubleheader games, allowing four hits, two runs, and twelve strikeouts. Sherm hit a three run double on the way to Hobart's 5-2 victory. In game two, Stevens struggled but battled through five innings, before leaving with the score tied at five. Delucia came in and pitched a brilliant one and two thirds before giving up a two out solo homer in the bottom of the seventh which gave Oswego the victory. While the loss hurt, the day proved what the young Hobart squad already knew and that was that they could compete with anyone. It gave them the little boost they needed as they prepared to play the number four team in the nation, the Ithaca Bombers.

Alumni Field didn't have more than forty bleacher seats, but the hill along third base was packed with students, fueled by the three kegs of beer the team had bought in an attempt to attract their fellow students to these most important of games and the battle for national recognition.

About three hundred students had already gathered at noon for the 1 p.m. start and a few hundred more approached as Jeff took to the bullpen with Sherm to start warming up. He felt strong and loose, and a bit nervous, but he didn't mind that. He started breaking off curve balls and sliders as the Ithaca players watched from afar. Ithaca was countering with their number one, a tall hard throwing lefty, Jim McNair, who had shut out Hobart in each of the last two seasons, out-dueling Jeff the previous year. Jeff wanted the cocky son of a bitch this year and would do all it took to win.

As Jeff finished his warm ups, he noticed Robin and Karen in their Hobart Baseball t-shirts and caps, each holding a cup of beer, as they took their position on the hill. Robin's smile was all he needed for that extra energy. He knew that whatever inner conflict existed, they would always be connected in a special way.

Peas at the knees and ungodly curve balls was all the Ithaca hitters saw for the first three innings as Jeff struck out six of them, with a single and a walk mixed in. McNair was almost as sharp allowing only a double, but the Hobart hitters were not intimidated, saw his pitches well and knew that they would be able to hit him. They just needed a little more time.

Their time came in the bottom of the fifth, with the score still tied at nil. Mike Fox, the freshman leadoff hitter battled for a walk and was then sacrificed to second. Todd Whalen who had been a hitting machine lined a single to left center which scored the speedy Fox as Whalen took second on the throw. Sherman came up and doubled in Whalen. It was all Hobart would get, but it was all they needed. Jeff struggled with his control, walking two hitters in each of the last two innings, but he pitched out of it. Seven innings, four hits, ten strikeouts and an ugly seven walks, but a beautiful win. That was one of Jeff's strengths that would follow him for the rest of his life. He always found a way to win.

In game two, Brownie went with Reed, saving the stronger Stevens for the single nine-inning game against Rochester and allowing him one more day of rest. The two teams, whose bats had been silent for the first game of the doubleheader, erupted in an old-fashioned college slugfest. It was tied at seven after three innings. The gallant freshman Reed just could not stop the powerful Bomber attack as he had managed to do with other teams. Brownie brought in Pete Samuels who had found himself in the bullpen after being shelled down South. The junkballer pitched a strong three innings, shutting out the opposition in the fourth, fifth, and sixth. Hobart had gotten a run in the fifth and took a one run lead into the seventh. Samuels got a quick first out, but then gave up a double, before Delucia came in. He was greeted by a single which tied the game at eight and it remained that way until the top of the tenth when Delucia, in his longest outing of the year gave up back-to-back doubles as Ithaca took the lead.

But Hobart would not give up with the top of the order due up. Again Fox walked and was sacrificed to second. It was then up to Whalen, and he delivered. On the first pitch, the left-handed slugger smoked a powerful line drive homerun off the Student Union beyond the right field fence. Hobart had swept the mighty Ithaca Bombers. The following day Stevens disposed of Rochester Institute of Technology 8-2 and when the next ranking came out the Hobart Statesmen had catapulted all the way to number seven. They were 13-2 up North and 19-6 over all. With six games left, five wins would guarantee them a playoff spot while four should be enough to make it.

At 5:15 p.m., on May 11th, the news finally arrived--Hobart had been seeded number one in the New York Regional of the College World Series with an overall record 24-7 and a number six rank nationally. In the double elimination format, they would have to face old foes in Ithaca and Oswego, as well as, John Jay College. Two days to get ready and plan as the Statesmen would host their opponents and welcome them to what the campus paper had dubbed "The Hell Hole" because of the sunken field surrounded by "Keg Hill."

It was a cliché-filled glorious spring weekend. The sun was shining, the grass was green and the air smelled sweet as the sun beat down on the most beautiful of sports fields, the baseball diamond. "Keg Hill" was full of exuberant fans enjoying the warmth, the fun, the beer and baseball. And oh, what baseball did they have to enjoy as the hometown team put on a display of the great American pastime that even they could not have scripted.

It took them but four games to dispose of the rest of the field. First Jeff shut out John Jay 5-0, then Stevens and Delucia combined to beat the once almighty Ithaca 6-4 as Sherm and Whalen each drove in a pair of runs. Brian Reed started against Oswego and held on long enough for Delucia and Jeff to each pitch an inning in a 7-6 win. And then with Ithaca having to beat Hobart two in a row, Jeff didn't even give them a chance. Once again the score was 2-0 but it really wasn't even that close. The control which Jeff lacked during the regular season was there as he out-classed McNair one more time.

The young Hobart squad was almost home. They were now off to Marietta, Ohio for the finals of the College World Series. For the first time since being down South, Jeff had noticed the scouts behind home plate with their radar guns and stopwatches. Jeff hoped that he had shown them what they had wanted to see in his outings. David Karl of the Cardinals had come after him to let him know that St. Louis was interested in him. He got the same dance from the Mariners and the Astros. What that meant, he wasn't quite sure, so he asked Brownie.

"Well, to be honest," Brownie said, "It probably means that somewhere in the draft, if they need a pitcher you will be on their lists, probably not early on enough to make it interesting for you to sign, but don't rule it out. Remember, you are young, because if it doesn't happen this year, you still got time, and that's very important."

Jeff felt a little discouraged by the reality of his immediate professional chances but the joy of what had been accomplished could not be dampened by the temporary dashing of his dreams. He felt, and knew deep down inside that he would live more dreams than most people could imagine before his time was up. He would not be held down, because within him burned a flame, a mystical power of hope and accomplishment. What he later would understand to be *THE POWER OF ONE*. The ability and the magic which each person possessed inside and which each person must find deep down in order to fulfill all they could and all that they wished for.

In the book *THE POWER OF ONE*, written by Bryce Courtenay, a scrawny young white South African boy named Peekay becomes the lightweight boxing champ of the World and a great fighter of human rights in his home country. It inspired Jeff so, that it would guide him to find the fire, drive, and enlightenment which would open his mind and his heart, his sensibility and his desire, in his effort to live a complete life.

Jeff saw the clock turn 8:00 a.m. when the wake-up call came through. He had not slept well in the strange room at the Holiday Inn in Marietta, Ohio. Sherm stretched and yawned and stumbled out of bed, five hours away from the biggest game of their lives. The final game of the College World Series, an event even they could not have dreamt about a mere two years ago.

They had swept their first three matches; all hard fought. First they battled Johns Hopkins to win 3-2 behind Jeff and Delucia's right arms. Then Stevens pitched seven scrappy innings against Cal State San Diego in a 9-7 slugfest and Reed did the same against Plymouth State, before Jeff shut the door in the ninth for a 6-5 win. Today they would face Marietta, the host team, in a one-game battle for everything.

It was one of those rare days when you just knew everything would be perfect. From the time you pull up the blinds and get that natural high and energy from the sunlight that burst upon you, to that first glass of cold juice which tingles and refreshes you, Jeff knew it would be, that it had to be, one of those perfect days.

The uniform felt extra good and he could feel the bounce and the life in his right arm. Yes, he had pitched a lot lately, but his pitch counts were low and he believed that the more he threw, within reason, the stronger he got.

The field looked perfect in the mid-day sun. The week of games had not damaged the beautiful little field on the small Midwest campus. The weather was warm with a touch of humidity. Jeff would have no problem loosening up.

An hour before gametime he tossed around with Rick Stevens, the freshman pitcher who would back him up, in the event Jeff got knocked around. This had not happened all year. A half-hour before gametime Jeff jogged around the field a couple of times and then stretched. At twelve minutes to game time, he took his place in the bullpen and started to throw to Sherm, just as he had done all year. Sherm knew his pitching better than anyone. He knew when he was on, which pitches would work and when he was unbeatable. Sherm also knew that today would be a perfect day, and indeed it was.

It was like an instant replay. Fox led off the game with a bunt single and was in turn sacrificed to second before Whalen drove him in with a single to right. Jeff was masterful. Through five innings, he had given up only one single while striking out eight and was getting stronger with each pitch. His fastball had had more zip on it, and his often elusive control was pinpoint and his curves fell off the table like a bowling ball. The opposing hitters had no clue what was coming or how to hit it.

In the seventh, still trailing 1-0, Marietta let their best chance slip away with a one-out single and walk, but Jeff would not break as he recorded strike outs ten and eleven. In the top of the eighth, Hobart got the insurance run that they had been looking for since the first. Whalen singled with two outs and the stubby little catcher, Joe Sherman, doubled down the left field line. Six more outs and it would be over.

Jeff took the mound and sensed victory. It was almost there, almost his, all he needed was six outs. The eighth inning took him only ten pitches: a pop out, a groundout, and strikeout number twelve. In the top of the ninth, it was as if the Statesmen didn't even want to hit, they just wanted back on the field, they wanted their three more outs.

It was with confidence, pride and determination that Jeff jogged out to the mound. He briefly thought back to his first days at Hobart, the friendships he had made and his early lack of playing time. All the hours of hard work and practice would now mean something to the short right-hander with the average fastball, the good curve, and the fire and fight of ten bulldogs.

As he finished his warm-ups, he looked over to his coach, the old man whom he had once held in contempt, who, more than anyone had contributed to his development, and now would be able to celebrate like a kid, with his kids. Because for all the players had to put up with, one thing they all knew was that John Brown cared about them like each and every one of them was his own.

Jeff knew he would have to reach deep down inside to finish the game. The invincibility and strength was still there, but some of the zip was gone and the past few weeks would take their toll if he didn't concentrate.

The first hitter helped Jeff, who hung a first pitch curveball, but even a Williams' hanging curveball had enough break to fool a college hitter and he feebly popped up to the firstbaseman. Two more outs. Jeff quickly jumped ahead of the next hitter with two fastballs at the knees. He would not waste a pitch, he would go right at him with his curveball. Oh, it looked good to the hitter but by the time he finished the swing, he had missed the ball by about a foot, as Sherm caught it just off the ground. Thirteen strikeouts and one out to go.

Suddenly, Jeff remembered waking this morning and how he felt. He knew it would be a perfect day, the game was destined to be his. A curve ball for a called strike, a swing and a miss on a slider and a called fastball at the knees and it was over. Hobart had won and Jeff had led them to victory.

The Finger Lakes Times, the Geneva newspaper, would describe the baseball team victory as "the greatest sports achievement in Hobart's athletic history." Quite a compliment when you consider that the Lacrosse team had just won its fifth straight National Championship, but then again, that was expected. And then, they talked about Jeff.

"...There is no doubt that the heart and soul of the young squad was junior pitcher and co-captain, Jeff Williams. Not only are his personal achievements worthy of All-American status: twelve wins-one loss, four saves and an ERA of 1.17. In eighty two innings, he allowed sixty hits, thirty-nine walks and accumulated one hundred and twenty one strikeouts. But when you talk to teammates, and those close to the team, you learn that his greatest contribution may have been his ability to bring others up to his level, and ultimately to victory. Opinions are divided on whether Williams will get drafted by a Major League organization in a mere ten days during the annual amateur selection. The young man probably deserves it, but understands that many scouts are worried about his size and velocity. "All I can do is wait and hope." He recently said in a tone that gave away the disappointment he expected. For us, here in Geneva, there could be worse things than seeing Jeff Williams return in September."

Back on campus, the celebration was short and intense. A one night blowout in the true sense-booze, music and women. The team had arrived back on campus at 1:00 a.m. after the game and mobilized the next morning to plan the festivities. The more the merrier. Kappa Sigma fraternity made their house available and even kicked in a few kegs and a couple of bottles of booze. By 4:00 p.m., the first keg was tapped and the first Screwdriver poured as the music blasted. Some of the players had obviously started the party earlier as Pete Samuels and Todd Whalen stumbled in with big mugs full of some alcoholic concoction.

It was a beautiful Spring day and the party spilled outside. The students enjoyed the last hours of warmth and fun before the final push for exams which were a mere two days away. Jeff sat outside with Tim as they caught up on lost time. Tim had now been through a National Championship celebration of his own three times, including one five days before. The two friends drank and laughed, as others would join in from time to time.

"What's up with the draft?" Tim asked.

"It doesn't look too good." Jeff answered with resignation. "About five teams have talked to me, and they all seem to say the same thing. I'm a little small with a body that probably won't fill out too much. My fastball at 82-83 miles per hour is a little short and that if they need to fill out a roster, I would be high on their list, if I was willing to sign for a small bonus.

"Tim," Jeff continued, "that's not the way I want to go to the pros. I know that I can make it and part of me says if the chance is there take it no matter what and the other part is saying wait, watch me grow a bit, pick up a foot on my fastball and make you all eat shit. Right now I just gotta get through exams and wait it out a week or so.

"Just relax man," Tim said.

"You're still young, you still got next year."

"Yeah, I know, " Jeff said meekly.

Then from behind him, he got a big hug and kiss on the cheek. He immediately knew that it was Robin as he got a faint smell of her perfume. The perfume which always made him weak at the knees but could never remember the name of. No matter what his true feelings toward her were, that enchanting smell would always be with him. Boy did that hug feel good to Jeff and it came at the perfect time.

"Did you ever know that you were my hero?" Robin sang mockingly to Jeff, as the two were now face to face and exchanged another hug and a kiss.

"Thanks, toots," Jeff answered as a smile returned to his face. She always had that ability with him.

"Let's go dance," he said as he grabbed her affectionately by the arm and led her to the make-shift dance floor in the basement of the old fraternity house where they rocked to Eddy Grant's *Electric Avenue*, and the Clash's *Should I Stay or Should I Go*, as well as many other party favorites.

The party went on well into the night. Samuels and Whelan had passed out. Reed and Stevens were still mesmerized by Heather and Kelley's magic, two months later, but nevertheless basked in the attention of the co-eds and their new stardom. Sherm was holding court to whomever would listen with his fisherman's hat, cigar and huge mug of beer, which he would only put down to take a shot of Jack Daniels. He was in Heaven.

Jeff and Robin spent the night like long lost friends. It hadn't been that way or felt that good in months and the smiles on their faces, brought joy to the friends who noticed. They danced, they drank, and most importantly they talked. For the first time Robin opened her heart to Jeff, letting out her true feelings, telling him all that he meant to her and all she wanted and needed from him. Jeff knew that one day this moment would come, when he would have to decide deep down inside what he truly felt and what and how he would say it. He had always hoped that it would come out right.

He glanced into her puppy dog eyes and started. "Robin, when I look at you, it brings sunshine into gloomy days. You have, and will always mean so much to me. In many ways, you are probably the best thing that has ever happened to me, and I don't know if it's because I don't want to lose what we have, or because my feelings are strong, but not in the same way as yours. I just don't think we should change our relationship."

The tears started rolling down her cheeks as he hugged her inhaling her perfume as though it was for the last time. He continued. "You are the most special girl in the World, and it hurts me to say what I just did, but I just think that right now it should be this way."

His heart ached as he held and hugged her. He didn't really understand why he felt that way. Was he scared and immature or was his gut feeling right, as it had almost always been? Only time would tell.

"Let me walk you home." Jeff said as he grabbed her hand and held her tight. It was a short walk back to her apartment and when they got there she asked him to come in.

"I need you to hold me," she said. Soon she fell asleep in his arms as all Jeff could do was look and admire her and wonder what he had just done. It was not fair for a nineteen-year-old to make such decisions.

At 5:00 p.m., on June 5th, back home after exams, the phone still hadn't rang and Jeff now had confirmation of what he had feared. He had not been drafted. One day he would show them all.

SEVEN

The PUC met at the Gare De Lyon for the eighteen-hour train ride to Grosseto for the European Cup of Champions. It had been less than three weeks since Jeff had stumbled across this rag tag team of ball players, but he was now part of it. It felt strange but he felt at home.

Moggle had quickly realized that Jeff was good--very good and since he was French he would not take the place of any of the two foreigners allowed on the team, namely himself or Mike Earl, a pitcher, who had played at Merced Junior College in California.

As they settled into their compartments, Jeff found himself surrounded by an almost uncommon group of characters. There was no Sherm, no Stevens and no Reed or Samuels, but in the short time that he had known them, he had found friends. There was André "Dédé" Lhebar, born in New York to French parents. He moved to Paris when he was twelve and found baseball, the game he played on the streets of Queens. He had always been a middle infielder but Moggle had converted him into a catcher and a fine one at that. Jeff enjoyed throwing to him. He took charge, worked hard and knew what to do behind the plate. He called a great game.

Luc "Chiche" Chicheportiche was a slightly round ex soccer goalie and Déde's cousin. He had cat like reflexes at third and solid line drive power. He was a bon vivant who loved to eat, drink, smoke, fart and hit a baseball. He worked at the market selling ladies dresses. He found a clientele after practices at the Bois de Vincennes selling to the prostitutes who worked out of their minivans. Thiery "X" Xuereb was a tall, lean, athletic outfielder. He had a rifle arm , but he wasn't a natural. His grasp of the game wasn't perfect, but he made up for it in athletic ability. He also told the best stories as he worked in one of Paris's peep shows on Rue St. Denis near Les Halles.

Gilles Thomas was the best pitcher France had ever produced. He was now twenty-eight and somewhat past his prime but he still had a nasty two-seam fastball and split finger. At first Jeff felt some tension and anger vented his way, but they soon became friends and tried to help each other improve. Thomas had lingered many years in the obscurity of PUC and French baseball with the weight of any important game always resting on his shoulders. He now had some help and a chance to finally show something to the European Baseball World.

After a meal in the dining car and a few beers, it was almost 2:00 a.m. by the time they went to sleep in the cramped quarters of the train. Jeff was a little overtired and had trouble falling asleep. He thought back to a few weeks ago and how he wanted to get away from baseball and the pressures, to sit back and think in another environment, to develop his mind and let his arm and body rest. Yet he was back on the field, ready for another adventure; seeing Europe and re-discovering baseball as it might have once been. Playing for the love of the sport and no other reason. He realized then that he would never be able to get baseball out of his life. The unplanned nature of this odyssey gave him more enjoyment and more reason to believe that it was meant to be.

He wondered what his teammates and friends would think if they knew where he was playing. Sherm would wonder about the European babes and their liberal sexual morals. Stevens would want to know if there was room for him on the team. Brownie would want to make sure he wasn't throwing too much, and Robin would probably want to be with him experiencing life away from upstate New York and South Carolina. She would want to stroll down the Champs Elysées and have a café and a croissant, but she wasn't there and Jeff felt badly. He was still somewhat confused and wondered if she was ok after what he had told her.

Finally, after a long time of mind rambling he fell asleep on the small, hard bunk. He did not have a good night's sleep. It was a little after 8:30 a.m. in the morning when the train finally rolled into Grosseto. Grosseto was not one of Italy's biggest or most well known cities. Tucked away about two hundred miles south of Florence, not far from the Mediterranean Sea, it was famous for its pork dishes and the passion for baseball, rivaled only by Parma.

At the station, they were met by a representative of the Italian Baseball Federation and a beautiful young girl in her early twenties named Maria, who would be their interpreter for the tournament. It didn't take long to load the bus and get going to their temporary home. Lavish, elegant and central it was not. On the outskirts of Grosseto, the PUC was staying in what was once an orphanage, but was now used to house groups like themselves. In itself, the place was not so bad, but it was isolated, and since the host Italians were paying the bill, it was hard to really complain, so the PUC would make do.

The rooms were clean and nice, though a little bare. Jeff and Moggle would share a room for the week and they headed there for a pre-lunch nap, to catch up on the rest that they had lacked on the train. Within minutes they were fast asleep.

While it was not the Hilton, it was home and the two old ladies who cooked and cleaned had prepared a home cooked Italian feast of salads, pastas and meats. It was delicious and every meal would top the previous one.

The squad spent the afternoon playing ping-pong and relaxing. They took about forty-five minutes in the courtyard, to go over some defensive plays and signals. At 7:00 p.m. , they headed into town to catch the opening game between the two Italian teams, the host Marbre of Grosseto and the defending European Champions Parma World Vision. They were each led by a former big leaguer. Grosseto's slugger was former Montreal Expo outfielder Bob Pate, while Parma had former Ranger, Cub, Met and three hundred hitter Lenny Randle who had become a bit of a hero and a rock star in Italy with a number one record entitled *"I'M A BALL PLAYER."*

While most of the team was sitting down the baselines, Jeff and Moggle had managed to get two scout seats behind the plate. With the way the schedule was set up, Jeff would be facing one of the two teams towards the end of the round robin. The game progressed rather slowly as the real show was in the stands where the crazy Grosseto fans rooted on their team with a variety of cheers, songs, music and firecrackers. It was a combination rock concert, fraternity party, and ballgame. Then during the seventh inning stretch baseball cheerleaders resembling the Dallas Cowboy Cheerleaders in every way came on the field for some gyrating. It was just what the fans needed, more reasons to make noise.

Finally after three and a half-hours the game ended with Grosseto winning 4-3 on a three run homer by Pate.

"How good are they?." Jeff asked his new coach and friend.

"Well it's a little hard to tell and probably depends who's pitching," Moggle answered. "But in general, it's probably low A ball or rookie ball."

"Just the challenge I need." Jeff responded. "But first let me take on those Spaniards from Villadecans tomorrow."

Villadecans was the Spanish equivalent of the PUC, Champions the last five years and the best Spain could offer in their attempt to catch up to the European Baseball elite. They were a scrappy team of contact hitters with good speed and decent defense and one big star: Jose Felix Caño. He was a twenty-year-old stud, 6'3" and two hundred and ten pounds, who could pitch and hit. Years later *USA TODAY* would call him the Spanish Babe Ruth, and in three outings, the PUC had never beaten him.

The Italian heat was already almost unbearable at 11 a.m. when Señor Caño took the mound against the new and improved PUC. After two quick strikeouts, Moggle doubled, but was left stranded on second when Earl popped out.

Jeff now took the mound in his first real game since he won the National Championship. He looked around at the team behind him. Dédé catching, Phillippe Bonnery at first, Jean Michel Cy at second, Moggle at short and Chiche at third. The outfield had Phillippe Gommy, Earl and Xuereb from left to right. All-Stars they all were not, but they did form a nice little team.

Europeans were generally good fastball hitters so he used his breaking pitches to set up his hard stuff. The strategy worked as he cruised through the first five innings allowing only a pair of hits, but Caño was equally effective. The PUC players had all been psyched out by him, that is all but Moggle and Earl who in the sixth rapped back to back doubles after Dédé had beaten out a bunt single. The PUC led 2-0. In the bottom of the eighth, Jeff gave up a leadoff homerun to Caño, and after a one-out walk, Moggle brought in Earl.

"It's a long week we're gonna need you soon." Moggle said. "You threw a lot of pitches with your strikeouts. Let's give the lefty a chance to finish it up."

"No problem." Jeff said with obvious disappointment, as it had been a long time since he had been taken out of a game. Earl came in and the lanky Californian closed down the Spaniards with high fastballs that they couldn't lay off. It was a great victory for the PUC and gave them some momentum as they embarked on the rest of the tournament.

"Jeff, man, great game," Moggle said to him on the bus back home. "You showed me a lot, more than I expected. You've got great stuff and know what to do out there. Demain, I'd like to suggest a few small things which I think will make a difference and boost your velocity a bit. Nothing major mechanically, but enough to fool the hitters."

"Sure, Pete. No problem," Jeff said. "I know I have some room to still do better. I want to know how good I can be."

"Great." Pete responded. "Gilles is going tomorrow against Bagamossen. Earl against Haarlem and you will probably go against Parma. As for the last game against Grosseto we'll see what we have left."

The game against the Swedes from Bagamossen proved to be just as much of a struggle as the previous day's game. Moggle wondered if he should have not started Earl against the lefty hitting Swedish line-up. Thomas struggled with his fastball and by the fifth inning it was 8-6 for the Swedes. With few arms and at least three more games, Moggle brought in an up-and-coming sixteen-year-old named David Meurant to get a few innings of work and hopefully keep the game close.

In the seventh the PUC bats exploded against a parade of weak pitchers. In true International fashion, they scored ten runs. Combined with the two they scored in the sixth gave them an 18-8 mercy victory. Meurant had done his job and got the victory, Moggle had driven in five runs and Chiche hit a grand slam. The PUC was on their way to their best finish ever in the European Cup.

Jeff had tried to digest the short lesson Moggle had given him. Basically it came down to shortening his stride by about six inches and driving with his shoulder, and not opening up too soon as he threw the ball. Jeff also pitched with a bit of a short arm which could cause arm problems. The few changes Moggle suggested should prevent that, plus, the little bit of shortarming gave him his outstanding curve ball.

The PUC had lost to both the Dutch Champions Haarlem Nichols and the defending European Champions from Parma. Tonight Jeff would pitch against the Italian Champions from Grosseto and their former big league pitcher Win Remmerswaal, a Dutch born player who pitched for the Boston Red Sox during the 1979 and 1980 seasons winning three games

The PUC had already clinched fourth place with their two victories, but Grosseto needed the victory to go undefeated and win the tournament. The little French team was given no chance against the mighty Italians. Yes, they did have a feisty little American pitcher, but this was not the

Spaniards. What they did not know was that Jeff was not your average little feisty pitcher.

The high humidity was still unbearable as Jeff walked out to the bullpen with Moggle and Dédé to begin his warm-ups. The crowd had swelled to close to ten-thousand to cheer on the hometown squad. The singing and partying filled the stadium with an electricity that Jeff had never felt before, and it helped pump him up for what he hoped would be the ultimate upset.

There are a few moments in a person's life when an event can either change their course in life or simply prove to oneself that there is no limit to what he can accomplish. Jeff felt that one of these moments was here. He knew that even if there was no baseball in his future, tonight would be that future. That very special time.

Slowly he began to throw, concentrating on a shorter stride. The drill he had practiced over the last couple of days became almost natural as he let fly some fastballs. He could feel the extra zip. His new coach was right and the unexpected thrill of knowing that there was more inside of him made him feel good.

He may have been past his prime, and he wasn't exactly facing an offensive powerhouse but Remmerswaal still looked like a magician out there. Changing speeds, moving the ball in and out, he was in complete control as he struck out the first seven PUC hitters on his way to three perfect innings.

"Weak shit," that's all he's throwing. Keep us close Jeff and I'll get you one." Pete Moggle said with conviction and animation. It was the first sign of the inner linebacker that Jeff had seen. For his part Jeff was doing his best to match Remmerswaal. He used his curve a lot and blew some high fastballs by the Italian hitters. It was as if he had a new and improved right arm. The short stride and arm extension made all the difference and through four innings the game was scoreless and it remained that way through seven.

It was the game of the tournament and probably the game of Jeff's life. He thew better than he had ever done at Hobart, and he didn't think that was possible, at least not yet. He had given up a mere two singles and one walk. He had struck out thirteen Grossetto hitters.

Remmerswaal had only allowed a single to Moggle and a walk. He had struck out fifteen PUC players. In the top of the eighth with two outs, Moggle came to the plate and snarled at the former big leaguer as each got set. The belt high fastball sailed deep towards the right center gap just out of the outstretched glove of Grosseto center fielder Bob Pate. Moggle turned his legs as furiously as he could as he rounded second like a crazed linebacker, only peeking quickly to see where the ball was. He was now on a mission as he rounded third making a beeline home. The throw came in to the secondbaseman who fired the relay to the Italian catcher who had but a second to brace himself for the oncoming locomotive. The impact was quick but brutal. Moggle had lowered his shoulder into the unsuspecting catcher, but it was not enough to jar the ball loose, he was out. He stood momentarily dumbfounded as the catcher struggled to his feet amidst the thunderous noise of the hometown crowd.

The score remained tied at nil as they entered the bottom of the tenth. Jeff was still pitching and enjoyed and relished the frustration of the Italian hitters. He induced the third place hitter to ground out and then Bob Pate approached the plate. Pate was menacing. He was big and built like the linebacker Moggle used to be with big forearms and a wide grin which said, nothing's getting by me kid.

Jeff wasn't sure if it was out of luck or skill that he had managed to handle the former Expo, but he had.

Jeff dug in with more resolve as Dédé flashed him a one for a fastball. As soon as he let it go, Jeff knew it was a mistake. The only question was how far it would go; the answer was too far as it sailed almost twenty feet over the left field fence. The game was over, but to the PUC, it had felt like a victory, and even to Jeff and Moggle while it was a heartbreaking loss, it was one they could live with. It was quite a game. The moment had passed and Jeff realized that there was no limit to what he could accomplish.

The Italian crowd cheered on the PUC and Jeff as they shook hands with the Italians. In a corner away from the action Moggle disappeared to talk with a fifty something man. "He needs a little more work," Moggle said "But I think he'll be a fine one."

"I have no doubt Pete, I just don't know how we all let him go. He looks so special out there. I'll be in touch," the man said as he picked up his briefcase and left. Jeff was already on the bus, only stopping for a brief congratulations from Remmerswaal and Pate. The disappointment had already faded.

EIGHT

"What do you see in your future Jeff?" Moggle asked him as they started pitcher number two of Long Island Iced Tea at the Chicago Pizza Factory on Rue De Ponthieu just off the Champs Elysées. It was a rustic looking place with overpriced pizzas and one of the best happy hours around. The ambiance and music was decidedly American with sports pennants and videos of baseball and football games. It was a place where young foreigners and French alike gathered for a good time.

It had been a couple of weeks since they had returned from Italy, and the two Americans had become regulars. Mostly they sat and talked baseball, the PUC and the upcoming European Championships which were three weeks away. Tonight, the tone seemed to be a little more serious.

Jeff had gotten to know Moggle as well as he could since they first met and he realized that he was a complex and pensive individual. But with his complexity, there was a great deal of compassion, warmth, intelligence, caring and inner strength. Jeff knew that he could talk to, and trust him. Pete had sensed that Jeff had some anger and angst inside of him. The young kid, already thinking about giving up the sport he loved and confused about his future, still struggling with the recent memory of the young woman who had opened up her heart to him.

Even with his mixed emotions, Jeff had found new peace on the mound and seemingly new strength and a quicker fastball. Pete wanted to instill the killer instinct in his new friend and to encourage him to continue on his path, so that the man with the briefcase in Grosseto would make all of Jeff's dreams come true.

"What's in my future? Great question Pete." Jeff answered. "Most of the time I have no idea and it doesn't bother me and other times it eats me up inside. I wanted baseball so bad this Spring and I did everything I could and worked so hard for a shot at the pros and got nothing. I'll go back to Hobart and get my degree and maybe go to business school or law school. Sure I'll play ball and maybe some of the things I learned this Summer will make a difference and maybe I will get my chance, but I don't know."

"Jeff," Pete responded, "You probably have the stuff to be a pro, maybe your chance won't come but maybe it will and you have to be ready. There are two main components to succeeding in baseball; talent and desire. Most players have talent, some more than others. It is the desire and the willingness to work and to sweat, when everyone else has gone home that makes the difference. Not everyone has that desire, but that little extra is what it takes to succeed. The one and only thing I regret is that with all my skills and abilities, I did not have that little extra desire, I did not give myself the chance to succeed, because when it's the best against the best, the hard workers will win."

"I will remember that Pete and hope that I get the chance to prove you right." Jeff said. "You know though, I also got that girl Robin I told you about, man I just don't know what to do. She's so precious but..." Pete jumped in.

"Look Jeff, my last lesson for the day will be this: instincts. If it doesn't feel right then it isn't. Maybe one day it will click and you'll know it. But right now it's not. Take care and watch over her, but trust your instincts at whatever you do. Enough lecturing, Let's get another pitcher and see where our instincts take us tonight. It's still early."

That was the truth. It was only 8:00 p.m. but felt much later as they had already quaffed two pitchers and were starting to feel the effects. They chatted up with a couple of Danish bartending bombshells during the slow period between happy hour and the start of the night. Moggle's smile was hard to resist, but it was all in fun. Even if they had a chance, neither one thought they would be able to last until 4:00 a.m. when the two blondes would get off work.

In their jeans and golf shirts, the two sort of contrasted with the yuppies going out after a tough day at the office, but they liked it that way. That was something else the two had in common, they liked to stick out and be different but in a mellow and respectful way, no mohawk hair cuts or earrings, just dignified difference.

"You know Jeff," Pete said, "you've been here before, but this whole Europe stuff is sort of cool. I mean there's a flair to living and experiencing Europe. A certain elegance that you just don't see back home. The Internationalization of Paris is amazing. I mean look we've already talked to Danish, French and American babes. Who knows what's next?"

"You speakith the truth oh wise one. Realizing that and remembering the differences that bring us together, gives us an edge on everyone back home who have no idea and have not been lucky enough to experience what I have and what you now have. And that's my lesson for the day" Jeff answered back with a smile. "I have no idea what's next, but I'm sure it will be interesting."

"Look at that Jeff" Moggle said as he pointed to the TV and the tape of Nolan Ryan pitching. "Look at that power, the use of the whole body and the release point. Man, it's beautiful. It's important to watch and learn from the best, there's no one like him, look at that explosion." Moggle's enthusiasm was accentuated by the Long Island Iced Tea they had been guzzling.

"I know of things more beautiful and explosions much more pleasurable," a female voice interrupted from just behind them. Jeff and Pete turned around to see two gorgeous olive skinned brunettes with tight jeans and white tank tops, no bras and perfectly sized firm breasts. Man it was just 9:30 p.m. and they had already visited the world from Danish blondes to Brazilian brunette babes. It was one of those nights.

The two striking beauties were elegant and sophisticated and smelled like the most exotic flowers one could find. You just wanted to inhale, and remember that smell forever. It would be enough to simply freeze-frame the moment in your mind. It wasn't often that that could happen. Anna and Maria, two Brazilian models had picked the two American ball players for some fun and company. They continued drinking, talking and laughing at Chicago's. A little after 1:00 a.m., they went down the block to the City Rock Cafe and danced.

Jeff had paired off with Anna and Pete with Maria. They danced and made out just like in high school, until the sun came up and the cafés on the Champs Elysées opened for breakfast. The foursome had a great week of fun. Pete and Jeff would run from practice to the small apartment the two girls shared in Odeon, just above the Pub St Germain. There they simply talked and drank. It was a magic time, but it did not last long. As suddenly as they had appeared Jeff and Pete quickly realized the two beauties were caught up in a world of drugs and deception which meant more to them than the two men in front of them. And when Jeff and Pete would not become part of that world, the only thing all four of them would have would be a memory. Hopefully a happy one. When they pecked each other on the cheek that July afternoon, no one had to say it, but they all knew that they would never see each other again. Gone as quickly as it came.

It was now two weeks until Barcelona and the European Championships. The team was improving, but it was not quite where it had to be. With Jeff and Gilles, the staff had a bit of a base to work with, but the offense was weak and the defense shaky. Jeff had even been taking some ground balls at second and first and would probably see some action.

So off to Barcelona for the 1985 European Championships the spunky underdog French team would go, trying to emulate what the PUC had done less than six weeks before riding the wing of an undrafted, unknown pitcher who now had a mission and a goal. In less than two months, he was nurtured and guided by a former Ivy League hippie ballplayer who brought the young pitcher to a height he had never dreamt of and on the verge of something truly wonderful and magical.

The production crew from THIS WEEK IN BASEBALL was doing a documentary on International Baseball and wanted to talk to Jeff before the big game against Italy. It was mostly fluffy stuff and background information. How did he get involved with French Baseball? What he enjoyed about the International game? And then the interviewer asked him what he expected out of today's game? Jeff responded full of confidence that he expected to win.

"But two years ago they beat France 36-0" the interviewer replied.

"Well, that was two years ago and I wasn't pitching." Jeff countered with respect and poise. The interview finished with the famous phrase Baseball Fever Catch It which Jeff said in French: *"La Fievre du Baseball Attrapez La"*.

Jeff went through his pre-game stretching and running, just as he had done countless times before on fields in Virginia and upstate New York. Montjuic Stadium was filling to capacity as almost eight thousand fans crammed into the historic and beautiful Barcelona stadium to watch the underdog French team take on the mighty Italians in the semi-final game. The Italians had won their first European Championship on this same field in 1975 and had a contingency of almost thirty-five-hundred fans who made the pilgrimage from Italy to cheer and sing and support their heroes.

On the other hand the French supporters had swelled to about one hundred, mostly family and friends, but the balance of the crowd was ready to adopt this David as their team, and back them to the hilt. The previous year in Havana, the Italians had beaten the USA at the World Championships and had romped through the preliminary round out scoring the opposition by sixty runs. The French team, expected to finish last in their division surprised everyone only losing to the powerful Dutch team. The spunky French team played solid defense and smart, if not spectacular offense, not their trademarks. But it was Jeff's pitching which made the difference in Moggle's no mistake philosophy to stay close and hope for a break.

Jeff tossed a no-hitter versus. Germany and a five hit one run game against Sweden which France won 3-1. He relieved Gilles Thomas for 1 1/3 innings to get the save against Belgium. With some of the burden taken off Thomas by Jeff, he had pitched better than ever and had vaulted France to the semi-finals. Both pitchers had seen some duty in the field Jeff at second and Thomas at first. They even contributed a couple of hits and steady play in the field. Jeff hadn't played in the field since high school, but he really enjoyed it.

Jeff was now ready to battle. He had scouted the Italians in their previous game against Spain, a few days earlier. He remembered some of the hitters from Grosseto and made notes of how his counterpart, and nemesis Felix Caño had pitched to them. He knew that he had also been scouted by the Italians and Jeff felt that he should alter his pitching pattern a bit in this sudden death semi-final match up. He planned on using his curve early in the count to get ahead, and to be careful with his fastball as his arm was a bit tired with only two days rest. He wanted to use his slider and change later in the count to get the outs. He didn't use these two pitches often but he had confidence in both of them and in his ability to make the pitch when he had to.

As the teams stepped on the field for the national anthems, Jeff felt a certain patriotic pride as *La Marseillaise* played over the speakers. His teammates sang out loud and proud, and although they didn't quite resemble a real ball team, they had spunk and character. Jeff looked to his left and winked at Dédé and then turned to Pete who gave him the thumbs up sign and told him to just go out and have fun, and he did.

The French squad went down in order in the first and when Jeff strode to the mound for the bottom of the inning, all he was concentrating on was getting the first of his twenty-seven outs. Massimo Fochi, the Italian shortstop approached the plate with a cocky strut and a "no little French team's gonna worry us" attitude. Three pitches later, head down and between his legs, he slowly walked back to his dugout after watching a curve, a fastball and a slider zoom by without even lifting the bat off his shoulder. He retired the next two batters as well as the twelve after that. The Italian fans were silenced, as their mighty squad could not score on the team that they had crushed by thirty-six runs a mere two years before.

Jeff had pitched five perfect innings, striking out eleven. David Farina, the Italian ace was equal to the task as the score stood deadlocked at zero. But as in the past, the inexperience and lack of skill overcame the French squad. After a one out single and a booted double play ball, the Italians went on to score three runs. The scrappy French team, as well as their pitcher had no more miracles left and went down silently, yet proud, the rest of the way. Jeff pitched one more inning and left down by five behind a huge ovation and a sense of accomplishment. In the end, Italy won 8-0, but the fans and players knew that the game was much closer and that the spunky little team had thrown a big scare into Goliath.

The Italians would go on to beat Holland and reclaim their European Championship while France turned in a lackluster performance and lost to Spain to finish fourth, their best finish ever.

At the Closing Ceremonies, Jeff was named to the All Tournament team, becoming the first French player ever to receive such an honor at a major International competition. To Jeff the award was nice, but what made him feel even better was knowing how he had rediscovered his love for baseball and the magic it always held for him.

From the time he was a kid, playing pick up games with friends, running and throwing all day, playing stickball and looking forward to the game of the week on NBC or an afternoon in the bleachers at Memorial Stadium; that was baseball. It was a love and magic that he hadn't even realized he had lost. He hadn't thought of baseball in these terms for awhile. For so long it had been win and succeed. At Hobart, the team relied upon him when the game was on the line. And while he relished those times, he often could not understand all the pressure and importance that was placed on him by everyone, including himself. Maybe that wasn't even the case, maybe it was simply his disillusionment with the sport when he wasn't drafted. Those feelings had dissipated, but he now felt a closer bond to the game, a zest and enthusiasm. But no one could have seen what was just ahead.

NINE

The team was getting ready for the long train ride back to Paris when Jeff noticed Moggle chatting with someone who Jeff thought looked familiar. A Spanish official Jeff thought, but he was wrong.

"Jeff," Moggle said, "I'd like you to meet Ben Adams, the Director of International Scouting for the Toronto Blue Jays." It was the man with the briefcase in Grosseto.

After the introductions, Moggle explained that Adams was the scout who signed him with the Indians and that they had met in Grosseto earlier in the summer.

"Jeff, I was impressed when I saw you pitch in Grosseto." Adams started, "and your performance here reinforced what I saw then. You've turned it up a notch. I saw some of the changes that you and Pete have worked on and it has made a difference. In fact, even though you had great college statistics, the fact that you were not drafted, although it hurt at the time, has benefited you. You've gone from a marginal pro prospect, at best, to a potential Major League prospect. The key word is potential. You'll see in the next couple of weeks teams will be after you and you will be offered some solid money. The Blue Jays are very interested in you and when you get back home, we would like to come visit you and your family and to offer you a contract.

You've worked real hard and have a lot to be proud of, now it's time to take it up to the next level and we want you to be part of our family. Now have a safe trip back. I'll be in touch next week and we will get to work on the details." Adams concluded as Jeff looked on in a haze.

The three men shook hands as Adams headed to the airport and Jeff and Moggle boarded the train. Adams was a youthful looking fifty-five year old and had twenty- seven years of scouting experience behind him, most of which was spent with the Yankees, six with the Indians as their East Coast Supervisor and the last two with the Blue Jays and his old friend from the Yankees, Pat Gillick, in the newly created and avant garde position of Director of International Scouting.

Adams' mandate was clear: go anywhere at anytime to search for baseball talent. With the growth of baseball as an International Sport, and maybe one day an Olympic sport, the popularity and growth were spreading. Baseball was played everywhere: Australia, Europe, China, Guam, and Africa. The Latin countries were no longer the only foreign sources of talent.

Adams had no more room on his passport. He had been to advanced countries like Australia, Korea, Taiwan, Japan, Italy, Canada, and Holland many times, but he had also slowly planted roots and made contacts in such far off places as Nigeria, South Africa, Yugoslavia, France, Spain, and Brazil. Wherever baseball was played Adams had been there or had someone there who knew what was going on.

In all reality, he knew that the results of his work were still a few years away, but nevertheless, he had signed two young and raw Australian infielders, a shortstop from Guam, and a pitcher from South Korea. However, in Jeff he saw the possibility of signing a player who could make an impact quickly. He was not the classic player he was looking for, but it was good old scouting just the way he liked it. Unfortunately, he knew that Jeff was no longer a secret. While the world of International Scouting was not well developed, it did exist and the Blue Jays were not alone.

As the Alitalia flight took off, Adams got out his bulky laptop and entered his scouting report, which he would, once finished, compare to the one he had completed earlier this summer, and then to the one that was on the team's database. The Blue Jays used the 20-80 method of evaluating prospects with 60 being the Major League average. The closest you get to 80 was a Nolan Ryan fastball or a Bert Blyleven curve in pitching and maybe Ozzie Smith defense when it came to range. Basically, the majority of baseball players fall below Major League average, especially amateur players, and that was nothing to be ashamed of. The tricky part for the scout is to project, or to attempt to project where that player might be three to five years down the road. That is obviously not easy when you consider that less than seventeen percent of all players who sign a professional contract make it to the Major Leagues for even one game. The odds are not either on the players' or the scouts' side. Now settled in, Adams began to enter his information.

He started with the basics such as name, date of birth, height, weight and school and finally the grades and the comments which were:

"Right-handed pitcher undrafted out of small Division III school. Standout pitcher this summer in Europe. Somewhat on the small side but is a bulldog. Made great strides this summer and has added about 6MPH to his fastball, with more to follow. Curve ball is well above average now with a slider and changeup to follow. If draft were today, he would be a top fifty pick to me. Only fault is that he tends to short-arm sometimes, but is very coachable and should still mature a bit physically. Others are after him. He is a must sign. Would go up to $75,000 signing bonus plus education."

When Adams had finished his report, he realized just how impressed he actually was with Jeff. It happened that way sometimes, players just snuck up on you, and then you realized everything they could do once you put all the parts together. Jeff was one of those players. If Jeff would sign with the Blue Jays, he would receive the highest bonus ever given by Toronto to an undrafted free agent. His scout's instinct, and when it comes down to it that's what a scout must rely on, told him that it would be worth it.

"Was he serious?" Jeff asked Moggle as they settled in for the long train ride back to Paris.

"He was most definitely serious. You know something Jeff," Pete Moggle said, "sometimes when you are too close to something you don't see it, but you have improved a lot over the summer. Sure maybe you should have been drafted, but believe me this will be to your advantage. The Blue Jays are treating you like a high pick which means money in cash and money for you to finish your education. They are probably the finest organization in professional baseball and they will treat you fairly."

"Well, it's so unexpected and sudden at this point, I just figured I would go back to school." Jeff said.

"Look," Moggle said, "most young players never get a chance to live out the dream we all had when we were young. You cannot pass it up; it is almost a duty to go for it. Believe me you are ready to pitch professionally. Besides how wrong could Ben be? He did sign me didn't he?"

Jeff felt excited and somewhat liberated after the conversation and headed to the bar wagon of the train where the team was hanging out and celebrating as though they had just won the World Series. Dédé had a cowboy hat on with a big cigar in one hand and a Krounenbourg beer, obviously not his first, in the other. He might not have been the most talented catcher Jeff had thrown to, but he understood Jeff and helped make him a better pitcher, forcing him to change speeds and to set up hitters. And most importantly, he became a good friend and buddy.

Gilles Thomas was right into it with everyone. The ace of the team, pre-Jeff, had at times a domineering and head above the rest attitude, but he adapted well to playing second fiddle. In fact, the two pitchers often hung out together, talked pitching and brought out the best in each other. Jeff helped Gilles with his curveball and Gilles returned the favor with his changeup.

Chiche, the oversized third baseman, was getting abused as he was downing beer and food while burping and farting. Jeff loved Chiche's zest for life and personality. It was as if he was in his own world. All his baseball skills were due to his lightning reflexes whether it be at the hot corner or turning on fastballs with the best of them. And to think that his little pouch didn't interfere. It was people like him who gave Jeff back his faith in the game.

Thiery Xuereb was in the middle of it all recalling stories of his days working in the Paris Peep-Shows cleaning up booths and hanging out with the schoolteacher who worked there for the thrills and excitement. Like the rest, Jeff listened attentively at the behind the scene stories which were every boy's fantasy. But what Jeff would remember most about Thiery was the time he was playing third base and a slow roller was hit his way and he kicked the ball foul, even though it was still fair, as he had seen on TV once. At the time, not realizing the ball had to be foul to do that.

Through and through, they were quite a bunch of characters who formed this team. This rag-tag team which he came to love and which he apparently owed a lot. He settled in to watch and to partake in the festivities wondering what would become of both him and of them.

TEN

By the time Jeff was back home in North America, after a few days in Paris, it was already August 16th and his mind had been racing for almost a week. He was scheduled to meet with Adams and Toronto General Manager Pat Gillick on the 21st. He was supposed to be back at Hobart on the 30th. Whatever his decision was, it had to be made by September 1st, the first day of classes, or he would lose his current free agent status and be thrown back in the draft next June.

Waiting for him back home were messages from the Expos, Pirates, Dodgers, and Braves. He was no longer a secret, and would soon find out what he was worth. In scouting terms he would find out the dollar sign on his muscle.

While the monetary value of the package would play an important role in his decision, Jeff agreed with his parents that it was most important to find a place and a team where his growth would continue in the best environment. After all, over a span of a career, a few thousand dollars up front would not make a difference. His gut told him that the Blue Jays were the right team for him - young, aggressive and progressive and the first to make real contact and show interest in him. It also meant a lot to Jeff that Moggle believed in, and recommended them as the best organization.

Meetings were set up with the Expos and the Dodgers on the 18th and the Pirates and the Braves the day after. Jeff and his family would then have all their ammunition and information by the time they met the Blue Jays. He realized he was in a unique and somewhat fortunate position. He had what amateur players had not had in twenty years, free agency and teams bidding for his services. Drafted players did not have this luxury. Undrafted juniors had to go back to school with one last chance to prove themselves. Jeff had proved twenty-six Major League organizations wrong in the span of two months.

When his two days of meetings were over, aside from knowing that he would get more money than he imagined, Jeff was not really much closer to knowing where he stood or what to expect from the Blue Jays. The Expos offered $45,000 plus $5,000 for education and a non-roster invitation to Major League Spring Training. The Dodgers' offer was $55,000 and $10,000 for education. The Pirates were on the low end with $25,000 and $7,500 for education while the Braves offered a staggering $70,000 in cash and $10,000 for education. These numbers compared him favorably to a second round pick--he was in the driver's seat and looking forward to meeting with the Blue Jays.

Ben Adams and Pat Gillick rang the Williams' doorbell at 6.30 p.m. sharp and came in for a pre-dinner drink. The two had flown in from Toronto to court the family directly instead of having them come to Toronto. They formed a much more impressive delegation than the other teams who had merely sent the area scout.

Gillick was a big man at 6'4" and he really impressed Jeff. Jeff felt that he and the Toronto GM were alike in several ways. They were both pitchers and Gillick had entered the University of Southern California at sixteen and was barely twenty when he graduated. His intelligence, power of reasoning and memory had become legendary in the baseball world. He had an encyclopedia of phone numbers locked up in his mind. They would range from other general managers' and scouts' numbers to high school fields in California and Florida. For this skill, which Gillick viewed simply as natural, he was dubbed with the nickname Wolley Segap--Yellow Pages spelled backwards.

Basically, Gillick was the best and Jeff could identify with the well-rounded human being that he was, something for which Jeff would always strive. Gillick was known for getting his man, whether it be Danny Ainge or in later years John Olerud and a Brazilian flamethrower named Jose Pett who never panned out.

"Mrs. and Mr. Williams," Gillick started, "we are pleased that you let us meet with you. I know that the last ten days have been quite hectic and that the whole family has a lot of decisions to make, so before we go to dinner and talk in more detail. Jeff, I would like to know what you are hoping to accomplish on and off the field. This way, I will know how the Toronto Blue Jays can help you accomplish your goals."

"Basically," Jeff responded, "I would like two things: first of all a chance to play pro ball and hopefully one day pitch in the big leagues. I want to see what I really have inside of me, how good I am and how good I can be. And second to finish my education. With that in place, the rest should follow."

"Very good" Gillick said, "that's what I thought, but I wanted to hear it from you. Let's go eat."

The phone rang just as the five were about to close the door and head out. Louise, Jeff's sister who had been trying to eavesdrop as best she could handed the phone to Jeff. It was Paul Beeston. Gillick and Adams both had small, almost, undetectable smiles on their faces when they heard that. It was the call that they were anticipating.

Beeston, or Beest as he was known and referred to by most who knew him, was the President of the Toronto Blue Jays. He was the first employee hired by the team in 1976. An accountant by trade, his effervescent personality and perpetual smile became the trademark of the Blue Jays. His respect for people and his desire for doing things first class became the foundation on which the Blue Jays were built into the most respected sports organization in North America, if not the World.

"Jeff, Paul Beeston here," he bellowed out. "Sorry I couldn't join the party, I just wanted to say hi and congratulate you on a great summer and say that I hope to see you in a Blue Jay uniform soon. And make sure Pat picks up the dinner tab."

"Thanks, Mr. Beeston, I really appreciate your call," was all Jeff could muster.

"Any problems with those two, just give me a ring. Take care Jeff." And Beeston hung up with the call having had its desired effect.

After a dinner filled with pleasant and interesting conversation covering baseball, school, and travel, it was time to get down to business. If anything, Jeff's value had risen in Gillick's mind over the last few hours. Between Adams' scouting report and Jeff's poise and intelligence, the General Manager was impressed and he wanted this man to sign.

"Well Jeff, as I'm sure you are aware, we would love to have you sign with the Blue Jays." Gillick started. "We believe that you have the ability, and, more importantly the make-up and determination to be a

Major League pitcher. The basics of our proposal are a signing bonus of $65,000, an educational commitment of $15,000 for you to finish your undergraduate degree and to start graduate classes, if you so desire. An invitation to fall Instructional League, and a guarantee, baring injuries or unforeseen circumstances, a position on a full season team next year" Gillick concluded.

It was predetermined that if Jeff liked what he was told, he could make the decision, without further parental consultation. He knew what he wanted and said. "Your offer is very competitive and appealing, Mr. Gillick, and to be honest, I want to sign with the Blue Jays. If you could boost the signing bonus to $70,000, I will commit right now to becoming a member of the Toronto Blue Jays organization."

And then, with only a slight hesitation, Gillick put his hand out and said "Welcome aboard Jeff," as everyone joined in with big smiles, handshakes and toasts. It was the start of one of the most magnificent relationships an athlete would ever have with his team and their management.

ELEVEN

The plane started its descent over the Smoky Mountains towards Knoxville's Tyson Airport. It had been seven months since Jeff signed his professional contract and it was now time to play for real. No practices, no intersquads, but real games.

He had been a busy person since the end of August. After informing the administration at Hobart that he would not attend classes in the Fall, he had long talks with Brownie, Tim, and Robin. They were all supportive and excited and said all the right things about how they would miss him and for him to go out and show everyone how good and special he was. While Jeff and Robin had continued to drift apart, they would miss each other greatly. He didn't tell them, but he was contemplating taking some classes during the Winter trimester.

Instructional League was an eye opening and intense experience and Jeff's introduction to professional baseball. Surrounded by all the young prospects, Jeff worked hard to prove he belonged. The days started early and often lasted well into the afternoon. He worked on his body to make it hard and to give it the strength and durability he would need to last a whole season. He fine-tuned his skills and understanding of the game under the best instructors. Jeff was curious, always looking for that extra edge and he felt improvement and saw results as the Fall went on. He moved from a tentative rookie to an overpowering pitcher by the end of October. He had opened eyes and looked forward to Spring Training.

It's funny how things turn out, he often thought, as he sat in the locker room at the Engelbert Complex, a mere five miles from the Rodeway Inn and Joe Dugan's where the Hobart squad had called home earlier in the year. He had gone a long way to travel five miles.

As Thanksgiving approached he made his plans to return to Hobart for the Winter trimester which would finish in time to get him to Spring Training. He fit right back into his old surroundings as he settled into a small off-campus apartment on Jefferson Street. The one thing he learned in the Fall was that baseball was now his job, and not a pastime. He budgeted his time between academics and baseball yet still had time for all the fun that went along with college and that included time with his buddies Robin and Tim.

Over New Year's all three, plus another six classmates went down to Orlando to see the Florida Citrus Bowl between Florida State and Michigan. Jeff's brother Marc had decided, against the pleasure of the baseball coach, to walk on to the football squad which he made as a special teams player and seldom-used tight end. For a freshman, it was quite an accomplishment. The two brothers had not had much time together over the last year and they tried to catch up as much as possible.

New Year's Eve was a great time to be in Orlando. Church Street Station, the outdoor amusement area for adults, was filled with bars, live bands, and alcohol. The Hobart contingency partied and drank and danced, as if it was their last chance to be together, and in many ways it was. They were just a few months from graduation when they would all go their separate ways. It had already started with Jeff. They realized that it would never be the same, and that that was the only certainty in the uncertain and real world ahead of them

When midnight came to ring in the new year they all hugged and kissed. Tim and Jeff bear hugged each other like never before and then before Jeff knew what had happened, Robin planted the biggest and best, wettest kiss he had ever had. At that moment the feeling of her in his arms was the greatest feeling. Then the embrace broke and Robin kissed him on the cheek. She gave him a sly little smile which seemed to say that all this, meaning her, could be his. With sadness he realized that it wouldn't happen, at least not now.

Jeff finished up his classes in a breeze and began throwing again in mid-January under Brownie's watchful eyes and with the help of Sherm. They were amazed at how much stronger and better he was throwing, a thought that they could not have imagined last May in Marietta. The time off had given his arm needed rest and he hoped that he could pick up where he left off.

The first few days of Spring Training were mind boggling to say the least. One hundred and seventy five players in minor league camp all fighting for places on minor league teams within the organization. Some clinging on to a last chance and others like Jeff just beginning with a certain naiveté that wears off quickly in a world which can often be dictated by politics and attitude, as much as by talent and results.

He had been assigned to the Dunedin club of the Florida State league which indicated that he would probably end up with Florence of the South Atlantic League once the cuts from Major League camp started pushing everyone down. It was sort of what he expected. It was full season as was promised. His goal was to show that he deserved to be on the higher A club in Dunedin and if it wasn't to start the season, then it would be soon after.

Into Spring Training, Jeff had been pitching well and as the cuts came down, he stayed on Dunedin's roster. Unbeknownst to him the plan was now to move him up to Knoxville, the AA squad, for two starts before the end of Spring Training with the intention of bumping him up instead of down a level.

In those two outings, he pitched solidly and now he found himself contemplating and reflecting as the plane landed, after being named the opening day pitcher in AA for the Knoxville Blue Jays.

Jeff had been lucky growing up as he and his family had done a lot of traveling which had helped cultivate and develop him into the young man he was. He had never been to Tennessee, and was really more worried about how he would fit in on the ball field and in the clubhouse than in the outside environment. In fact he knew that would be the least of his worries.

What he did know about Knoxville was that in 1982 the city hosted the World's Fair which gave the city an economic boost and a now extinct beer called World's Fair beer. Not a large city, it kept some small college charm and college town atmosphere with the University of Tennessee as the focal point of the community.

Jeff was thrilled and scared at the same time as he had always been the best, and always been under control. He had not had the luxury or the experience of the low minors and was entering unknown waters. A year ago he was pitching in college, eight months ago, he was pitching on make-shift fields in the French countryside and now he was playing professional baseball, only a couple of steps from the Major Leagues. This was not Ithaca or the Swedes, not even the Italians. This was the real thing.

To compound some of his anxiety, John Merrill, the manager had named him opening day pitcher, at home against the Greenville Braves. He would be on edge the next two days but he had always managed to channel his edginess and nerves into good performances. Butterflies were natural, normal and a good thing to have. He was glad that he was going to be busy finding a place to live, working out, and getting acquainted with Knoxville.

Instructional League and Spring Training were now over. It was time to really learn what it meant to be a professional athlete. It was time for the games to begin and he was ready; ready to see if he truly belonged.

The plane landed and the team was bused from the airport to the downtown Hilton, their home for the next couple of days. The air was brisk but nice, just a bit cooler than Florida. After checking in and taking a nap, the players got their first look at Bill Meyer Stadium for a late afternoon workout before an evening reception with the local media.

Bill Meyer Stadium was a bit old and a bit run-down. Situated on the outskirts of downtown, it was built in the 1930's and was home for many years to the Knoxville Smokies. Like most old stadiums it had its own charm and personality. Despite the cramped locker room facilities and inadequate concession stands it really wasn't that bad. But ball players always needed something to gripe about and they complained about the locker room and the bad hops from the infield. Basically, they were spoiled, spoiled by the first class Spring Training facilities and the home clubhouse at Dunedin Stadium where most of the players were the previous season.

The K-Jays, as they were more or less affectionately called went through a light hour and a half work out, taking ground balls, shagging some flies and a quick round of batting practice. The pitchers did some running and some threw on the side. At about 6.15 p.m. they hit the showers and got ready to head toward Hooray's, a sportsbar-restaurant-nightclub located in Knoxville's old city.

The old city was adjacent to downtown and not far from the stadium. It had gone through a renovation and a rejuvenation. It was now full of restaurants, bars, nightclubs, and boutiques which catered to all ages. Often they would block it off for street parties and festivals with live music and entertainment. When the University of Tennessee football team was playing, home or away, Hooray's was the place to be, before, during or after the game. It was not uncommon to see the same people sitting at the bar at 11 a.m. as you would see fifteen hours later, long after the game was over. The decor was very college, and open with pictures and pennants on the walls, some pool tables, a huge bar and thirty-foot ceilings with a small second floor where live bands would sometimes play.

For this occasion, the second floor was closed off for the players, staff, and media to enjoy a buffet spread of wings, meatballs, nachos, and salads. Free food was always a good way to attract the media for an event and in this case hopefully get them to plug the team and the next day's season opener.

Jeff attracted a lot of attention because of both his unusual background as well as the fact that his professional debut would be as the Blue Jays' opening day pitcher. He answered some questions for the local TV stations and the radio station that broadcast the team's games.

Bob Steen the Jays' PR Director had warned the players about the sometimes negative reporting which often went on in the local papers, so when Nick Lightner the baseball writer for the *Knoxville Sun-Sentinel* asked to talk to Jeff, the young right-hander was a little apprehensive. The questions were pretty straightforward and Jeff took extra care to answer the reporter clearly and concisely with no room for artistic license by Lightner. But of course, until he saw it in black and white the next morning, he wouldn't know for sure.

Jeff took off a little early from the gathering and went back to the Hilton to rest and watch some TV. He knew it would not be easy to fall asleep. Finally at about 11.30 p.m, he shut off the lights. His mind raced with thoughts of success and ungodly curve balls that caused hitters to buckle, with a victory celebration to follow. He pictured games that he had pitched before: little league games, college games and games he had hurled in Europe. He pooled his memories and his knowledge and hoped to use it all the next day. Finally, he drifted off to sleep.

He woke up at about 8:00 a.m. and went down to get some breakfast. After eating, he went to look at some apartments with Ray Santucci whom he had befriended in Instructional League. Santucci was a scrappy shortstop who was drafted out of Baldwin High School in Long Island, NY. He had progressed through the Blue Jays system and already had three years of professional experience behind him even though he was only twenty, just like Jeff.

Santucci had a lot of Italian-New York in him. He came from a good family, was a good person and cared about people, traits that Jeff could identify with and admired. Also, they got along well and were different enough that they would make good roommates. They had received a list of apartments and were going to check a few out but first Jeff went to get a copy of the *Sun-Sentinel*, to see if the article was in there--it was.

"UNDERDOG WILLIAMS TO MAKE PRO DEBUT FOR K-JAYS"

"The young man sat before me and answered my questions. Not very imposing physically, he spoke in clear concise sentences, trying not to give away too much information, though a bit of anticipation and nervousness did enter his tone but that is understandable. Jeff Williams has never pitched a professional baseball game, yet tonight he will be the starting pitcher for the Blue Jays in their season opener against the Greenville Braves.

Williams is the youngest K-Jay and may also have the most interesting background. "A year ago, I was pitching in College with relatively little chance of being drafted. To start my career in AA, and as the opening day starter, well that's an honor, especially when I look back to where I was last June," Williams reflected calmly.

That's when this young man's story gets interesting. After going 12-1 at Division III Hobart College in upstate New York and leading his team to the National Championship, he went undrafted and decided to go to Paris and take a summer class at the Sorbonne...

So far so good Jeff thought as the story went on to recount how he was discovered and signed. ...."I feel that I can compete and produce at this level and believe that the organization feels the same way, or they would not have placed me here. My main goal now is to work hard and keep on progressing," the young righty said.

Manager Merrill admits that there were some in the organization who felt Williams should have started in A Ball, even after his strong Spring. It was decided however, that because of his performance, international experience and good make-up that there was not a lot of risk to rushing him a bit.

It seems as though that is this young man's story: an underdog who keeps on fighting and winning, no matter what obstacles are in his way. Southern League hitters should soon find out what many before them have."

Jeff and Ray had finally hit the road. At 10:00 a.m. they headed toward the West End where they had the name of a few apartment complexes where players had lived in the past. They settled on the Oakwood apartment complex and got a nice two-bedroom apartment for a reasonable five hundred bucks furnished. The first year salary was $700 a month standard and non-negotiable. It did not leave much room for the extras, or for anything else for that matter.

As they left the leasing office, a stream of ten more players lined up to sign their leases. Tomorrow would be move-in day. Tonight was the opener. Jeff and Ray went back to the Hilton for a short nap. Ray planned on getting to the yard at about 2:00 p.m., some five hours before game time. Jeff did not have to get there until 5:00 p.m., but tonight was opening night and by 3:15 p.m. he was already antsy and took a cab to the stadium.

The nerves were starting to hit him as he realized that tonight was the culmination of all his work and dedication. As he thought more about it though, he figured that was not the case. Tonight was the beginning of his work and the start of something special. When he realized this, he felt much better as he started getting ready for his professional debut.

He put on his shorts and T-shirt and read *USA TODAY* in the cramped confines of the home clubhouse. The rest of the team took the field for batting practice. Jeff would join them later. He grabbed a Mountain Dew from the fridge and finished reading the paper.

He flipped first to the back pages of the sports and found what he wanted. Hobart, led by Tim, the three year All-American and team captain had defeated two-time NCAA Division One champion University of North Carolina and broken their twenty-seven game winning streak.

He felt so proud of Tim and pictured the celebrations and parties on campus. Tim had become like a brother away from home, and he knew exactly how proud and excited Tim was feeling. Tonight Jeff wanted that same feeling and for the parties to continue one more day at Hobart. Tonight they would toast him, but first came the work.

Jeff went out to catch batting practice and soak up some of the atmosphere It was still just 5:00 p.m. and the gates were not yet open. It was a beautiful evening and the weather was unseasonably warm. Greenville was loosening up down the left field line; they all looked big, but the faces meant nothing and only a few of the names were familiar. Jeff liked it better that way, as there was no one to be scared of. He would try to make them scared of him

He went back in the clubhouse and got rubbed down by the team trainer Jim Mercer. Jim had a North Carolina twang and really calmed Jeff down with his down home chatting. Jeff then went to put his uniform on, a brand new white top with number twenty-one. It felt good.

Finally at about 6:30 p.m. Jeff Hearon, the catcher, and Steve Santana, the pitching coach headed out to the field with their starting pitcher. Bill Meyer Stadium was getting packed; in fact they couldn't get them in fast enough as the lines were over one hundred deep.

"When you gonna make it to the pros." A young kid yelled to the two Jeffs who just smiled at the youngster. The two players jogged in the outfield, as the veteran minor league catcher wanted to let the rookie know that he was not in this alone. Hearon did not make a habit of running when he did not have to, but he knew that tonight was important.

The warm weather loosened the muscles as the two players stretched. It was now 6:45 p.m. and Jeff headed to the bullpen as the pre-game ceremonies started. His body and arm felt loose and strong, and with each toss he gained more confidence as he increased the velocity. He realized that he was no longer the inexperienced, yet confident pitcher he was in college. He was now a professional.

He broke off a few flat curveballs. "Pull it down and don't squeeze it, nice and fluid, just like always." Santana bellowed out. Jeff proceeded to break off some hard breaking overhand curveballs which even Hearon had trouble catching, and he knew that they were coming.

"That's the way to throw the deuce, stay within yourself and we'll have no problems. Stay cool and the two of us will get the job done." Hearon said reinforcing the fact that the two of them were in this battle together.

Jeff finished up in the bullpen and headed back to the dugout. He was ready to take the field and pitch. While the walk from the bullpen was only a couple of hundred feet, it felt much longer as the seven thousand fans cheered the start of the new season.

Jeff remembered what opening day meant: the start of Spring, the end of the school year approaching, afternoons in the bleachers, late nights by the radio and playing pick-up in the park. Opening day meant a chance to start fresh and to accomplish dreams which had been dormant all winter. Today Jeff would be part of the lore and the magic of baseball. Children would look up to him and cheer.

As he approached the dugout and looked into the stands he saw the eyes and the smiles of his youth and it gave him a good feeling and a boost of energy and determination to succeed. He stepped into the dugout to the words of encouragement from his teammates and then strode out to the mound and took his place on the field. The Maryville College band played the Star Spangled Banner as the capacity crowd sang with pride.

He thought back to the French team and how they would belt out *La Marseillaise* before every game, and before he had realized it the music was over and he had fired his eight warm up pitches into Hearon. He then stepped off the mound and took some deep breaths as he looked around the infield. Santucci at short gave him the thumbs up while Domingo Martinez, the big Dominican firstbaseman flashed him a big smile of encouragement

It was obvious to all that what happened in the first inning was simply a bad case of nerves. Jeff walked the first three batters on twelve pitches. He was not real wild which made it even more frustrating as he was just missing. Finally Santana came out. "Don't throw scared. Let them hit the ball. C'mon Frenchy throw a double play ball and let's get out of this, nice and easy." The pitching coach said in tone that inspired Jeff.

Jeff knew that his coach was right. For the first time on the mound, he was unsure of himself and what would happen and how hard and how far the ball would travel. He needed the fighter in him to surface and it did.

Chris Beacom, Greenville's big cleanup hitter came to the plate and Jeff quickly got ahead with two strikes. With the cheers of the crowd behind him, the next pitch was a wicked slider which Beacom grounded to Santucci who fielded on two hops and started the 6-4-3 double play. Even though a run scored, there was a feeling of relief and calmness. Jeff was now breathing easier. The next batter flew out to left and both Jeff and the team got out of the inning down only 1-0.

That would be the Braves' only run. Jeff pitched six and two third innings before reaching his eighty-five-pitch limit and led 3-1 on a three-run homerun by Domingo Martinez. In his debut, Jeff had allowed four hits, five walks and struck out five batters. All in all solid first outing. Mike Taylor closed the game.

Jeff felt more relieved than anything after the game. He now realized that he belonged. Jeff, Mike Taylor, and Rick Martinson made their way across town to the Wild Horse Saloon for some opening day celebrations. The line outside was about forty deep, but the three pitchers walked right in. If anything after three years in Knoxville, Taylor knew just about every doorman in town. Not that Jeff was shocked when he walked into the

Wild Horse, but he was a little overwhelmed by the sight before him. On a giant video screen, George Jones was singing with a packed dance floor of people line dancing. Half the patrons were all cowboyed out. The bouncers looked like linebackers as they ushered out two guys who had obviously been fighting.

Martinson went over to the bar and came back with beers and shots of Jack Daniels. A soft throwing lefthander out of the University of Nebraska, he was drafted in the forty-second round three years before as a roster filler, but he kept on getting guys out and continued to move up the ladder.

After only a short while, it was obvious that Mike Taylor had broken a few hearts in Knoxville during his stint in the city. An almost endless line of girls; some young, some old, some pretty and some not, came over to give him a hug and welcome him back into town. Though seemingly stuck in AA ball, Taylor still had the million-dollar smile that graced all the magazines, when he was an All-American quarterback and Heisman candidate at Arizona State University. After a disappointing senior season on the gridiron, he took his frustration out on college hitters and used his lightning rod of a right arm to get drafted by Toronto in the second round. However, this was season number five as a pro, and he felt his career slipping away.

The two veteran pitchers dished out more BS then Jeff thought possible as Jeff watched almost in disbelief as the girls giggled and gobbled it up faster than they could spoon it to them. Jeff started to understand what was meant when others said that it was better being an ugly ballplayer than a good-looking regular guy. Having both on your side was not bad either.

Jeff had seen enough for the moment and crossed the bar to go to the can. When he was done, he stood by the dance floor watching the action in front of him and soaking in his introduction to the Knoxville nightlife. It wasn't quite the same as the parties back at Hobart or even the clubs down in Florida. It was a world all its own and had charm and excitement in a down home but fun way.

The dance floor was huge and in the center of the saloon. The outside walls were covered with bars tended by sexy barmaids in tight jeans. The floor was packed with dancers with many others just standing around, drinking, talking and admiring the show in front of them.

Jeff was transfixed on a couple of beautiful young college girls on the dance floor wondering if this was the type of environment from where Robin came? Was South Carolina that different from Tennessee? His mind was engrossed in these thoughts, his eyes were fixed on the dancers and his body felt the mix of alcohol and the good physical feeling which combines fatigue and pep, the post game feeling that every athlete enjoyed.

"Don't become like them," a female voice said to Jeff. For some reason he recognized the voice immediately--the first time they met, they barely spoke--this time he would not make that mistake as he turned around, immediately in awe of her beauty.

Tracy Cox was the Jays' office manager. She was twenty just like he was and close to finishing up her degree in business at the University of Tennessee. She had worked for the team part time while she was in school, but when the full-time position became available she took it while finishing her studies in the night program.

She was petite and had a slight Southern accent. She dressed conservatively with her shoulder length brown hair pulled back from her pretty face and a smile that reeled him in. Jeff had said hello to her in the office earlier in the day, but he was so pre-occupied with the game he barely looked at her. However, at this moment he got a pang in his heart. He had seen many beautiful girls over the years as he paid attention to such things. To be honest Tracy would probably be called cute by most, but to him she was beautiful with a radiance and magic that attracted him to her at once.

Jeff finally answered back with a weak "excuse me."

"Well," Tracy started firing, "I've seen these players for three years now and most of them are ok guys, but they have the same problems. They generally have no respect for people. They don't care about anyone but themselves and they treat the opposite sex like shit. Excuse my French."

Jeff listened attentively; his eyes fixed on her, inhaling the faint smell of her perfume. He knew what she was talking about. In his short time in pro ball, he had seen things that would make most fraternity parties look tame. It appeared that most of the stories about being a pro athlete were true.

"Look, I don't blame the guys completely, the girls, or whatever you want to call them throw themselves at all you guys. I guess all I ask is that y'all treat people right and care a little about what you do. Jeff Williams, I think you are different and I have high hopes for you." Tracy finished. Saying words that would, just a few years later be made famous by Susan Sarandon in the movie *Bull Durham*. What she meant by that last statement, Jeff was not sure.

They talked at length and Jeff was mesmerized by her. From the beginning, he knew that she was a hold'em girl. To Jeff a hold'em girl was a girl you were happy just holding. The physical and sexual contact was somewhat secondary. Having a hold'em girl in your arms was the greatest feeling in the World. There were not many hold'em girls around.

Soon he found out about her childhood in the Tennessee countryside in a small town called Rugby which was first settled by the British. It had one main street and a few hundred inhabitants -- it was small. Her father was a school principal and her mother a kindergarten teacher. She had two brothers, both younger, one who was a junior in high school and the other a freshman at Tennessee State University. Each word, each look, each move and each smile put a trance on Jeff. He would not disappoint her and the high hopes she had for him, whatever they were.

He was hooked. In turn she asked him many questions about his past, his family, his thoughts about baseball, and his aspirations in life. To some questions he had no answers, to others he entered into long philosophical "Mogglesque" answers.

Tracy soon realized what instinct had told her before, and that was that there was more to Jeff Williams than baseball. His culture and intelligence, sensitivity and knowledge and acceptance of reality were rare traits in ball players for sure, but in people in general. She wished that he would never change.

"We're outta here rook." Taylor and Martinson announced out of nowhere. It was almost three in the morning and they had found their bimbos for the night, nice bimbos at that, Jeff thought with a twinge of envy. They tossed him twenty bucks for a taxi and left.

Jeff refocused on the beautiful sight in front of him. "Case closed." Tracy said as the two pitchers walked out. The last song came on a few minutes later. It was Dolly Parton's *I Will Always Love You.* She asked Jeff to dance and he accepted. He felt like a teenager at a Saturday night party as they danced holding each other in a way that suggested that they had known each other for a long while. It just felt good as they held and danced with each other.

When the song was over and it was time to leave, she offered him a lift home. It was a short ride along Kingston Pike and they remained silent. When she pulled up to the hotel he gave her a big hug and a kiss on the cheek and said good night. Tracy was half disappointed and half pleased that there was no attempt at physical contact on either side. Disappointed because she felt close to Jeff. He was different and special and had just proven it. Pleased because she knew that her chance, in fact, their chance would soon come.

Jeff went right to bed but once again had trouble falling asleep. Indeed he was tired, but it was a physical tired and his mind continued to race as he looked back on the memorable day. Then he was sleeping and his mind danced with dreams, vivid and peaceful dreams, dreams in which he could fly. All his life he had dreams of flying, not high, not fast, he would drift almost as if he was an angel observing the world beneath him. He also dreamt of Tracy. It was a dream in which he married her and held her forever. He never wanted to let go. He never wanted to wake up. He never wanted to say goodbye.

TWELVE

The Knoxville Blue Jays got out of April with an 11-11 record. Jeff did better than that going 3-1 with an ERA of 2.50. His control remained somewhat erratic, but his pitches continued to improve. His two seam fastball became nasty as he learned to jam the hitters, his curveball continued to tighten, and his changeup became respectable by professional standards.

Jeff quickly learned what was expected of him and what a professional season was going to be like, long and grueling with bus rides and hotels from Orlando, Florida to Huntsville, Alabama. For a first year player it was somewhat exciting, but for players who had done it before, the bus rides became torture -- long hours of self-doubt and bad sleep.

Was it all a waste of time? Should I get out of the game before it gets rid of me? How can I support my family? The questions all Minor League players ask as they strive toward the pot of gold in the Major Leagues.

"Jeff," Santucci once told him, "It's a hard life and a hard life to give up. Here in AA it's as if we were playing the lottery and have five of the six numbers and the sixth number hasn't been drawn yet. We've all got to wait around and see what that sixth number is." That sort of put it all in perspective.

Rookies and veterans, prospects and those at the end of their careers, blacks, whites and Latins were all as one on the road, a true team in battle. In battle against others and each other. It was the cruel reality of the Minor Leagues. Sure it was nice to win, and yes it was great to be part of the team, but one of those team members could take your job and steal your career.

It was a game dominated by the necessity for individual performance, sometimes at the expense of team success and that hit Jeff from the side when he least expected it.

It was on a late night, late April bus trip from Jacksonville to Knoxville when Mike Taylor took Jeff aside and started talking. "Look Jeff," he started, "I want you to know that what I'm going to tell you has neither happened, nor may ever happen, but it is always around, especially by the time you get to AA. There is a cruel reality and that is that we are all competing against each other to move up the ladder. You have done great so far man, and I hope it continues. I promise that I am behind you, but others like me have paid their dues and may not be as much of a supporter. So if you hear anything, brush it off and continue to do your work. You must become tough and have confidence in yourself and you will succeed. Hopefully my days are not over yet and we can finish this trip together."

Jeff had never even thought about the make up of the team in that light, but it made perfect sense. The battle was not only against the other teams but seventy-five other pitchers in the Toronto Blue Jays organization.

Off the field, his relationship with Tracy was progressing, albeit slowly, but that was all right. When Jeff was in town, they managed the occasional lunch and late dinner after a game. But even at that pace their bond deepened as they slowly learned about each other. May arrived and suddenly things changed for the better for both of them.

It was a Saturday night and Jeff met her and some of her friends at Hooray's after the game. When Jeff arrived with Santucci, it was obvious that the girls had been drinking and were feeling the effect. Poor petite Tracy, as the alcohol played havoc with her body, she grabbed Jeff by the arm and told him that she needed air. They walked through the old city arm in arm and then he took her home in her car, leaving the rest behind. As he was ready to tuck her in and leave. She reached out to him and whispered to him "Hold me. Please hold me," as she fell asleep in his arms.

Whenever the team was in town, they would fall asleep in each other's arms, simply kissing each other and holding on. The first time they made love it was magical as though they were meant to be one from the day they each were born, and no one had to say it because they knew it and felt it. It had to be love, and they loved it.

His teammates kidded him. They all had seasonal flings and girls in all the cities, even in AA ball. They all said it was a phase, but Jeff knew differently, and would just get bugged more when he would protest, so he stopped. But he knew what he felt, and that was a constant need to be with her, and that was no passing feeling.

You would think that distractions of the heart would affect his play on the diamond but it didn't. Maybe it was the peace of mind or an inner male desire to constantly prove your worth. Whatever it was, he had become one of the most dominant pitchers in the Southern League as he upped his record to 7-1 with an ERA of 2.25. In seventy-two innings he had allowed sixty-four hits while walking thirty-two and striking out sixty-one and his control was coming around.

It was only the beginning of June and there was still a lot of season left. In the span of two starts in early June, Jeff felt tired in his legs and arm, which was not uncommon for a rookie or a veteran in a long season. It was known as dead arm. He took a start off and came back better and stronger than ever.

Marc had just finished up his freshman year at Michigan and got out of the baseball coach's doghouse after having played football. Always the most talented of the two brothers, he hit three seventy-five with eight homeruns and thirty-nine runs batted in. He added two saves on the mound and was named Big Ten Freshman of the year. For five days in June, he felt like a pro, spoiled by his big brother, taking batting practice and ground balls, under the guidance and with the permission of Merrill.

The two brothers had not had time together in a long while and they both enjoyed it. After-game wings and cocktails at Hooters, an afternoon movie, just talking ball. They were kids again, in love with a kid's game that was one brother's job and the other's possible future.

Jeff had told Marc about Tracy, but as Marc told his big brother: "the real package is better than any words. Bro don' t let her go 'cause I'll take her." He said with a big grin.

Marc headed back to Virginia for Summer break and Jeff found his early season form. By June 20th, he had won nine games against only three losses. His ERA was 2.32 and he was about to take a plane.

Things happen suddenly in baseball, sometimes for the good and sometimes for the bad. Bags are packed quickly and plane reservations are made on an hour's notice. Taxis are taken and good-byes cannot always be said, but you go on because you are a ballplayer chasing a dream, trying to win the lottery, and because it is your job.

This sudden and unexpected event was a good one: a trip to AAA Syracuse. It was supposed to be a roundtrip ticket: three weeks and then back. A rash of injuries resulted in the need of an arm and Jeff was the best thing going in Knoxville. Mike Taylor had gone up two weeks before, but the staff was tired and overworked. Taylor had been given the first shot as an effort to put some life back into his fading career and was responding to the challenge. Jeff got the shot because he was pitching well and deserved a few starts against the higher competition. The Toronto staff viewed it as an experience and character builder. However, in baseball roundtrip tickets are purchased one way at a time and there are no guarantees. Fight hard, play hard, do well and that roundtrip ticket can be transformed into a one way trip. The sixth number was closer to being drawn.

As the cliché goes, there are always two sides to a coin, a Ying and a Yang. You gotta take the good with the bad, and they all applied. The joy of moving up was tempered by having to leave Tracy behind, the girl who had become the love of his life, and that hurt.

Tracy was not looking forward to this separation and wasn't sure if the quick yet temporary goodbye was good or bad. She never thought she would cry over a ballplayer but she did as she watched his early morning flight take off from Tyson Airport. She could not know that Jeff was doing the same.

Syracuse, Jeff reflected, back to the Finger Lakes, a mere forty miles away and three years of memories from Hobart. The campus would be empty now, no one to visit, no place to hang out. One thing Syracuse did have was Tim.

The Syracuse Chiefs were in Ottawa, Ontario and that was not an easy place to get to from Knoxville. Jeff zigzagged the East Coast on US Air, from Knoxville to Pittsburgh, to Baltimore and finally to Ottawa. It took almost eight hours for what should have been a two-hour flight. He had managed to call Tim from Baltimore to let him know that his old roomie was back in town and would see him soon.

Jeff arrived at the Ottawa airport at 3:30 p.m. and followed the instructions and took a taxi to the Chimo Hotel and checked in. He then went to see the manager Bob Bailor to let him know that he had arrived. Bails was the first pick of the Blue Jays in the 1977 expansion draft and became their first legitimate star in that first year. In all reality, he was just a ballplayer who would do what it took to win. He had just finished his playing career and had managed one year in Dunedin before his current assignment

"Glad you made it," Bailor said in a straightforward manner and with a smile on his face. He was a true baseball man. "I know it's a day early," he continued "but we need you to start tomorrow afternoon. Give us five innings and we will be fine. Just relax and have fun. Don't change what you've been doing. The bus for tonight leaves in an hour."

"You got it skip." Jeff answered in a tone, which was a combination of nerves, excitement, apprehension, and confidence.

Jeff went to Jose Garcia's room to say hi. Jose was a big Venezuelan catcher whose nickname was "Tongo." Jeff befriended him in Spring Training. Garcia was only twenty-three but this was his seventh year of pro ball, still hanging in waiting for that call to the show. He had made it out of A ball pretty quickly but had then spent four years in AA before making the Syracuse squad this Spring. They talked a mixture of Jeff's broken Spanish and Garcia's sometimes confusing English.

"Look Jeff," the catcher said. "The hitters, they think more and will jump on you mistake, but I know you man, you pitch well, you do well. You must be fuerte; you got it."

"Yo comprendo" Jeff answered in Spanish to his new battery mate. He figured he was lucky that in Knoxville he got to throw to Hearon and here he would have Garcia, two experienced catchers in whom he had confidence and who obviously had confidence in him. It made Jeff's job easier.

Syracuse won a tough one run game that night, and after a spaghetti spread in the clubhouse, Jeff punch drunk from fatigue took the bus back to the Chimo for some much needed sleep after the long day of travel. Even though he needed to prepare for his start the next afternoon he still managed to get a call in to Tracy to say goodnight.

Ottawa Stadium was brand new and the ten thousand seats were filled for every game, and the gorgeous late June afternoon was no exception. Summers in Ottawa didn't last that long so people took advantage of the beautiful days they did have. The joke was that there were two seasons in Ottawa: Winter and the first two weeks of July. As Jeff finished his warm-ups in the bullpen, there was only one place which could be a better place to be and that was with Tracy. Everything else was perfect.

His teammates spotted him two runs in the top of the first and gave him some breathing room for his AAA debut. He felt real good as he took to the mound and it showed as he retired the side on eight pitches.

One of the Ottawa Lynx hitters was Razor Shines, a career minor leaguer who had a cup of coffee in the bigs with the Expos. Jeff had seen him play years before as a member of the West Palm Beach Expos in the Florida State League when Jeff and his family were visiting his grandmother. Razor was a fan favorite wherever he played, with his colorful style, enthusiastic play and warm personality. They had taken two different paths that somehow led them to the same place, at much different times in their lives.

Jeff continued to cruise along through seven innings allowing only one run before being relieved by Duane Ward who shut the Lynx down over the final two innings. Jeff was once again excited and relieved. Excited because he had pitched well and relieved because he did not get shelled facing the more experienced AAA hitters. It was the everlasting paradox which baseball players faced: confidence and self-doubt. It was a delicate balance, but too much of one without the other was a dangerous trait for a ballplayer, even the best of them.

The players loved those rare Saturday afternoon games, and really only for one reason: it gave them a free Saturday night to do what young athletes and young men all over do; go out to drink and chase women. Tonight the boys got an early start. It was barely 6:00 p.m. as the six headed out. There was Jeff, Taylor, Jose, and three other pitchers; Tim Scott, Rick Warren, and Steve Santos.

They headed toward the market area of Ottawa. Ottawa was Canada's capital. It wasn't a really big city, but it was a city with some small town quaintness and charm. The market was the center, full of bars and restaurants. It was the focal point of the city's nightlife. There were young people everywhere from the city's two universities, Carleton and the University of Ottawa, mixed in with the many civil servants out for a fun Saturday night. There really was no summer recess at the two Universities with year round classes and summer jobs in government. There was always action in the city. Ottawa was a bilingual city and was bordered by the city of Hull, in the province of Quebec, just across the river.

The first stop was a bar/restaurant called Schadiak's with a country ambiance. It wasn't quite the Wild Horse, more like a so-so imitation, but it wasn't that bad. The six boys started guzzling pitchers at an alarming rate, as Becky their perky blonde waitress, made small talk and flirted with the six athletes who flashed big smiles and used sweet talking words.

At 7:00 p.m. a couple of ball games came on, one with the Expos and one with the Blue Jays. The ballplayers watched with envy as former teammates and opponents graced the big league fields all wishing it were them. Would their time ever come? They wondered as they ordered two more pitchers.

Sweet talking Mike Taylor didn't need alcohol to talk to the girls, but he was feeling pretty good as he went over to a young blonde French-Canadian. He had been staring at her and vice a versa. She was wearing tight jean shorts and a white T-shirt that clung to her sexy body.

"You have the shiniest legs and you're the most beautiful girl I've ever seen." Taylor muttered out with a boyish smile and a slightly drunken speech. It took him a mere five minutes to get her name and number and to convince her to come to the game tomorrow. She promised she would be there as her friends dragged her out of the bar.

"You see," Steve Santos said in a slight Hispanic accent he acquired growing up in LA. "right there you have the difference between men and women."

"What are you talking about Santos?" Taylor asked.

"Look, it's quite simple. If a guy were talking to a girl, making some progress or just plain getting along well, would his buddies ever pull him away? I don' t think so. But a girl, that's a different story. Her friends get her out of there so fast it's like they're all jealous it's not them. It's like, if they can't get a guy, she's not."

"That does indeed make sense compadre" Taylor answered, but let me ask you something. "Knowing all that you know, how come you or the rest of the clowns didn't go over there to keep her friends at bay while I was working." Before Santos could answer Jeff interrupted.

"It was more fun watching you and seeing the look on your face as she walked out, leaving you only with the memory of her tight little butt."

"She'll be there tomorrow rook, you'll see." Taylor shot back.

"Too bad we leave right after the game, pretty boy." Santos intervened. Before what started out as stupid guy talk got out of hand Jose jumped in.

"I'm with you señor Taylor, let's get out of here and go find some Canadian chicas."

That's all it took, those few words and a big Venezuelan smile and the boys were back on the right track.

By this time it was already after 9:00 p.m. and they were ready to move on. They left Schadiak's stumbling through the market towards Maxwell's, a dance bar where unsuspecting girls would be charmed by the six ballplayers. At least that's what they hoped would happen. It was just a short walk, but it was a fun walk. Taylor and Santos could not help themselves from talking to every girl that walked by, and even some of the guys. It was all fun.

Inside Maxwell's the players were at home as girls were everywhere and flocked to them as they flocked to the girls. A group of young law students came over and surrounded the players and started talking, drinking, and dancing with them. Before they knew it, they were all paired off. Jose paired off with a statuesque blonde who asked him where he was from. In a deadpan voice and thick Latin accent he answered "Mississippi, Alabama." She laughed, not knowing that he thought his answer made perfect sense, or at least some sort of sense. The big catcher didn't mind as he grabbed his young blonde, the type of healthy and buxom Canadian female famous all around the globe. She was a softer looking version of Pamela Sue Anderson. He carried her on to the dance floor and showed her how real men moved.

Warren caught the eye of a petite redhead from Winnipeg with a full set of curls and a mischievous smile. She kept on saying how much he looked like Tom Cruise as she ran her hands through his hair. All that Warren could think was where the hell is Winnipeg and who let her out of her cage? He didn't seem to mind as she led him to a corner and sat on his lap.

Taylor and Scott had done quick work as usual honing in on two sisters from Newfoundland. They quickly disappeared for the night. Santos ended up with the homeliest of the lot, a slightly overweight cutie who was convinced that he was Jewish. He kept on saying that his dad was Puerto Rican and his mother Irish, but she didn't believe him, or didn't want to believe him. In the end, they made their peace with the lot they were thrown, meaning each other and succumbed to having a good time.

Jeff meanwhile ended up with a cute and innocent looking lawyer named Tamara. She was not the most beautiful of the group, but she was the one that he wanted. She had just finished her first year of law school at the University of Ottawa, and kept on flashing an innocent yet inviting smile as she swayed to the music in her white shorts and navy T-shirt that clung to her chest. She moved like a veteran partier and made him forget where he was and whom he left behind. It was like a different world and all he could think about was a romp with his Canadian law student.

When Maxwell's closed down at 1:00 a.m., Warren, Santos, Jeff and their three dates stumbled to a taxi that would take them to the small house the three law students shared and where the party would continue. Eventually all six got what they wanted and once again the ballplayers fell asleep in strange beds in a strange town. No one was proud, it was just part of being young, or so they justified. By the time they woke up at 8:00 a.m., the ballplayers barely had time to make it back to the hotel, pack their bags and hop on the bus to the ballpark for the series finale.

When they got on the bus, they went straight to the back where they joined their three lost comrades and started exchanging war stories. Jose pulled up his shirt and showed the nail marks on his back, mimicking the blonde who had left him injured. "Unbelievable man. I tell you, she claw in to me and yell more! More! And then she scream like a tiger. I no sleep all night. I get three hits today. She come to Syracuse to visit. She want more and me too." Tongo said, not worried what his wife in Venezuela would say about the blonde.

"That's some shit, Tongo." Taylor said. "Shit, all I got to show for my efforts are a fucking eighty dollar Amex bill from the bar and another seventy five for the room. Would you believe it we both passed out. That's right, Mike Taylor passed out with the breasts of a Newfie, or whatever you call people from Newfoundland, in his face. Horseshit Canadian beer, it sneaks up on you like a rattler in the desert. Never again."

They all laughed somewhat in amazement as the stud admitted his failure. At the stadium, Jeff got dressed and looked forward to running, sweating and cleansing his body. He ran his twenty poles in the midday heat and felt his body loosen up from his post start stiffness, as he became drenched with beer and vodka sweat. He might have smelled like a brewery but it felt good and he loved it.

THIRTEEN

It's sometimes amazing what a combination of fatigue, exercise, a hangover, an afternoon sitting in the bullpen, followed by a bus ride can do to one's mind. It really wasn't until he sat down on the bus, getting ready to nap that it hit him.

Jeff Williams had many good traits, and a few bad ones. He had never backed away from a good time and certainly never when a woman was involved. Last night, he hadn't even given it a second thought, but when he closed his eyes on the bus, his mind began to race and an uneasy feeling engulfed him. What he did last night no longer sat well with him. He asked himself how he could one day never want to be separated from Tracy and the next cheat on her without a second thought? Was he the same as all the others? Had he been fooling himself by over stating his feelings towards her or was his hurt real? Was it a twisted way of proving to himself how much the beautiful young woman in Knoxville meant to him? The pain in his heart made him believe that it was the latter. Jeff hoped that he would not lie to himself. He felt closer to the truth.

July 14th, Bastille Day celebrating the French revolution came and went and Jeff was still in Syracuse. His AAA stay was now entering week four with still no return ticket. Through four starts, he hadn't lost a game and was pitching with consistency and confidence. He put his little Ottawa incident behind him and refocused his attention to the mound.

Aside from summer vacation, two years before, Jeff hadn't really been at home. It was easy to forget that he was only twenty years old, and neither talent and luck, nor maturity and elegance can make someone an adult. In Syracuse Jeff had re-bonded with Tim, and with Tim came some stability and homelife. He moved in with the Saunders' and the stability and support felt really good.

It was a modest house in East Syracuse, but it was one full of love and warmth, just like Jeff's. Tim had spent the time since graduation working Lacrosse camps and was now getting ready to start his MBA at Syracuse. That's right, Tim, the innocent young Syracuse boy who had come to Hobart wanting to play some ball was now going to business school, while Jeff was now playing ball for his livelihood. They laughed at the reversal of roles and how much had changed since that September day they first met on the small campus in upstate New York. How they had enriched each other's lives and fostered their development, a re-shaping of each other's mission, dreams, goals and outlook on life. And with all this change, some things remained the same: they still shared a room and did not know where life would lead them.

FOURTEEN

W eek six in AAA found Jeff in Louisville, Kentucky, home of the famed Louisville Slugger baseball bat factory, the weapon of his enemies. It was now July 30th and he hoped to finish the season with the Chiefs. He was six and one with an ERA of just below three. He belonged, he felt good and was continuing to learn and improve. Yes, he did miss Tracy and she him. Sometimes, separation can do people good. Indeed there is pain and hurt, longing and uncertainty, and even a broken heart and tears. And with all this, all you can do is hope, hope that circumstances will change and that two people who care about each other can be together. It is the broken heart and the tears that affirm the caring and the love, and then with separation comes the reassurance, the reassurance that you love someone. Tracy and Jeff realized that day in July that they indeed did love each other.

The tears and hurt don't go away, but they have company. Happiness and fulfillment; daydreams of the future and memories of the past. Each night and each dream brings new hope of a life together, in each other's arm. It was these good thoughts which danced in Jeff's mind as he slept early in the morning at the Old Seelbach Hotel in Louisville.

The Old Seelbach, was indeed old, but elegant with antique furniture and big post beds, just like in Europe. The bed felt good as he slept away with a smile on his face. When the phone rang at 6:30 a.m. it took him a split second to figure out where he was; he had been out of it.

"Jeff, this is Bails" Syracuse manager Bob Bailor said. "Sorry to wake you up so early, but I have to see you right away in my room."

"I'll be right down," Jeff muttered in a daze.

Jose Garcia had also been woken up by the call and realized what was going on. "You take whatever it is like an hombre, you are fuerte. You pitch good here, you be back soon, don't worry." The big Venezuelan catcher told Jeff, at the same time encouraging him and preparing him for the disappointment.

Jeff threw on some shorts and a T-shirt. The elevator ride and the walk to his manager's room was a long one, or at least felt very long. He really didn't understand baseball. He had pitched great up in AAA. He shouldn't have to go back to Knoxville. Sure he had been here almost a month longer than he was supposed to, but it was all on merit. When the reality had sunk in and the anger subsided, he knew that at least he would be back with Tracy. His mind had rambled as he entered Bailor's room.

Bailor's attire was not much different than Jeff's, but he did look more awake. Late nights of baseball did not hamper Bailor's hunting and fishing passion which made him all to used to getting up early. Today, there were no fish or deer, just a face to face with a young man expecting a demotion receiving the best news of his life. There was nothing greater a manager could do then tell one of his players that he was on his way to the Major Leagues.

"Come in" Bails said as Jeff knocked on the door. "Jeff, there are some things that are very difficult for a manager to do and say, and then again, there are certain things that a manager loves to do, and this is one of them."

Jeff's heart started racing as he imagined the unbelievable. "Pack your bags, because you're going to Toronto. I got the call about a half-hour ago and O'Donoghue tore his rotator cuff last night and is out for the year. Right now your stuff's the best we got and they need you there now for the pennant race. They'll probably be using you out of the pen so be ready. You're on the 9:45 a.m. to Toronto through Pittsburgh. When you get to Toronto, take a cab to the Ex." Bailor continued. "I just got one piece of advice for you young man. Take no shit and keep throwing like you are and we'll never see you back here again. Go get' em."

All Jeff could muster was a weak "Thanks skip." He didn't know what to do. He felt numb and in a daze. Like just about every little boy, he had dreamt of this day since he was six years old; he collected baseball cards, played stickball, pretended he was Jim Palmer standing on the mound of Memorial Stadium with the cheers of the crowd behind him and watching, imitating and dreaming of one day being the one who was looked up to and admired. Today he was one of them. Today he was a Major League ball player.

He rushed back to his room and high fived Garcia. Jose, the veteran had paid his dues and while still waiting for his shot did not begrudge his rookie friend. He gave him a big hug and a smile and went back to sleep; it was all part of the game.

Jeff shaved and jumped into the shower, and in his off-key voice, he sang--he sang *La Marseillaise*. It had been almost one year since he lost to the Italians and this was his salute to his French Comrades.

He toweled off and reached for the phone to call his parents. Pierre and Jennifer were never real baseball fans, but they were their children's biggest fans and supported them in whatever they did. There was no one else he could share this news with first. His parents had seen him through the many highs and lows of his youth; his difficult periods in school and his growing pains. He loved them and he now had something to show. His happiness and accomplishments made them happy and that was the only way to return all they had given him.

"Hi mom," he said.

"Jeff, what's wrong?" She asked in her usual alarmist tone.

After convincing her that everything was all right and that he was going to Toronto, her joy was so evident that Jeff began to cry--he had to hold back his tears and keep his composure on the phone. His being happy and successful was the only way to repay his parents and that was all they wanted.

He would have to talk to his Dad later since he was already on his way to work. He hoped to convince them all to come up to his new home and watch him play

He then tried Tracy at home and got her before she left for the stadium. Her enthusiasm was evident, but Jeff picked up a certain uneasiness in her voice which he didn't push. There were only four weeks left in the minor league season and she was looking forward to some time with him. Now Jeff hoped she could come to Toronto, to spend some time with him there and to be a part of his dream.

Tracy's mind raced as she drove to work. She had fallen in love with Jeff in the few months that they had been together. While he was in Knoxville, she was able to be with him; their separation in Syracuse was tolerable, but being involved in baseball, she knew that people, or more specifically ballplayers changed once they made it to the Major Leagues. It was called Big Leagueitis; the money, the perks, the travel, and the groupies changed them all. Very few could keep their sense of reality and values.

Jeff got off the phone somewhat puzzled and troubled by Tracy's tone as the excitement and life that was always in her voice was not there. Still he finished packing and quickly grabbed a cab for the fifteen-minute drive to the airport. The taxi went by the stadium at the fairgrounds where he had beaten the Louisville Redbirds two nights before. He wondered if this trip to the Majors would be a short one, his only shot. Would he soon be back in the minors forever or would he have a long big league career. It was time to prove himself one more time.

The US Air flight from Louisville to Pittsburgh was a short one and Jeff read *USA TODAY* to catch up on the previous night's games. The Jays were only 2 1/2 games behind the Yankees with about eight weeks left in the season. This was the first time in their short history that the Jays were in a pennant race and the city, province and country were in a buzz. Every game was now important, every play and pitch scrutinized. There would be pressure in this intimidating environment. No matter how many times someone would tell him to relax, he knew that this was for keeps. The pressure to produce would be evident.

He made his connection in Pittsburgh and quickly dozed off. Actually, it was more of a trance; he was aware of his surroundings, but he was also sleeping and dreaming. During the flight, he thought back to his childhood, his family, his grandmothers, playing in the park, his fights with Marc, his Lycée teachers, his days at Hobart, and playing ball in France. He was trying to grasp the sum of his experiences and influences as he pondered how he came to be where he was today.

With his past in place, he pondered the future. He tried to put into perspective the fact that he was a Major League baseball player, living out his dream, every boy's dream. However, at the most exciting time in his life his heart and mind were confused. He was twenty, a month shy of his twenty-first birthday. Everything had happened so fast over the past year that he was not sure if he was ready for all that was being thrown at him.

Was he ready for the Major Leagues? He had always succeeded under pressure. His demeanor and ability had never abandoned him. Could he perform and could he do well? He had never truly doubted himself when it came to baseball, but now when he needed all his confidence, he was, and that was not comforting. More importantly, he realized that his ability to fight and compete, and willingness to battle, would contribute to his acceptance and to his future.

He concluded that his on field performance would take care of itself, for better or for worse. He would give his all and that was all he could do, he reasoned, trying to put his mind at ease

His heart was another matter. Tracy had come out of nowhere and now consumed all his thoughts. He had never been in love before, but he was sure that this is how it felt. He now had everything he wanted in life yet he did not know if he could hold on to any of it.

The plane landed at Lester B. Pearson Airport in Toronto and Jeff had no problems clearing customs. As he had been instructed, he took a taxi to Exhibition Stadium, the football stadium on the shores of Lake Ontario where the Jays had played since day one in 1977. The twenty-minute ride seemed like an hour on the suburban highways of metropolitan Toronto. The anticipation was starting to gnaw at him.

Jeff instructed the taxi driver to let him off by the players' entrance, wherever that was. "Visiting a friend on the Jays, eh?" The taxi driver asked Jeff.

"Well not exactly," Jeff responded hesitantly. "I'm a pitcher and I just got called up."

"Congratulations eh, and sorry about the friend remark, you just seemed so young eh. Good luck, I'll be routing for you. Let's go all the way eh?" The taxi driver said as Jeff got his bags and headed into the stadium.

It took Jeff a few minutes, but he did manage to convince the security guard that he was indeed a player, and he was let in. The home clubhouse was deserted as batting practice was just about getting under way.

His first stop was manager Bobby Cox's office. Coxi had come over from the Atlanta Braves and was the person management wanted in place to guide this young team.

The Blue Jays' plan was somewhat simple, yet complicated to achieve. First they found the best young players and then they drilled them and taught them. There was always an emphasis on teaching and that was why they made Bobby Mattick the oldest rookie manager in Major League history. He could teach the young players, which now made up the team's nucleus. Mattick had no misconception of his job: winning was secondary to developing. Bobby Cox was now in Toronto to win. Cox treated his players with respect and in return earned their respect. He was a players' manager.

"Look Jeff," his new manager said. "We brought you up here and we intend to use you, so stay loose, relax and do your best. Learn from your teammates and don't be afraid. Throw the ball like you have all year and you'll be fine. Now get dressed, get out there and remember to work hard and have fun."

The uniform felt as soft as a baby's little butt and the cap fit his head perfectly. It was as though he was putting on a uniform for the first time and it felt better than his first kiss at Camp Olympus when he was eleven years old. Where was Cary Butwin, he wondered? The sparkling white home uniform with number thirty-nine now belonged to him, and he hoped to wear it for a long time.

Finally, Jeff was ready to hit the field. He walked through the tunnel and out onto the turf. He was a child again, walking into the ballpark for the first time, absorbing the sounds and the smell and gazing into the land in front of him. The uncertainties and glories of a baseball field. There was no place like it.

The gates had just opened and the fans started streaming in for the series finale against the Boston Red Sox. The late July sun was just starting to slowly set as he stared around in a daze. Out past the rightfield fence, crowds were enjoying the many rides and games of the annual Canadian Exhibition, as the Blue Jays finished batting practice.

"Time to get to work," a voice bellowed into Jeff's ear. It was Mike Pierce, a veteran pitcher, who the Jays had picked up a month before from the Baltimore Orioles. Pierce had pitched thirteen years for the Orioles and had a Cy Young Award in his closet. Jeff had seen him pitch many times at Memorial Stadium. Once a hard throwing lefty, like Frank Tanana, Pierce had become a finesse pitcher, forced to rely on experience and changing speeds. Toronto had been using him out of the pen, mostly against left-handed hitters.

Just as important, Toronto was looking to Pierce as a leader down the stretch for the many young players who were in a pennant race for the first time. He took Jeff around to meet the players and then volunteered to run with him. Pierce was known for his off-field antics and partying, yet on the field he was a professional and a leader, respected by teammates as well as opposing players. Though he was not the dominant pitcher he once was, he always came to the park ready to play and he always gave the game all he could.

As the two generations of ballplayers ran in the outfield, Jeff looked over toward the Red Sox and saw Jim Rice and Dwight Evans hit line drive after line drive and thought how he might have to pitch to them. The awesomeness of where he was started to set in.

When the game started, Jeff took his seat in the bullpen between Pierce and Buck Martinez, one of the two Blue Jay catchers. Ernie Whitt, the other catcher was in the game. Jimmy Key, the young Toronto lefty, was on the mound and Jeff sat down to watch the game.

"This is where you will do most of your learning and studying," Pierce told his young pupil as Martinez nodded in agreement. "Remember," the old lefty continued, "the players are human, they are not supermen. Do not be in awe. Be cocky, to a point, and don't be afraid to let loose. You must have confidence in yourself and in your abilities."

"Look," Martinez said "we're all a team here, if you get in there, just listen to Ernie or me and we'll get you through it. If you need anything, have any questions, just ask. Don't be afraid and don't show fear," said the future Major League manager.

The game progressed into the middle innings, and Jeff barely had time to soak in the Major League atmosphere as the two veterans guided him through the pitching patterns and thought process. Their collective knowledge was beginning to overwhelm him and it had only been five innings. Their minds had committed to memory scouting reports and tendencies of every hitter.

In the bottom of the sixth, Martinez went in to pinch-hit against Boston lefty reliever Tom Burgmeir and cleared the bases with a double to give the Jays a 7-2 lead. In the top of the seventh, Key walked the first two hitters and the call came down to the bullpen for Jeff to warm up. He wobbled to his feet and made the short walk to the bullpen mound. It was not a long walk but with his jello legs and butterflies in his stomach, it sure felt like it. Finally, standing on the mound, his home, he felt fine again. He took a deep breath and all his strength returned as he started warming up. The next batter grounded into a fielder's choice, but after two consecutive singles, Jeff was called in with a 7-4 lead and runners on first and third.

He jogged out to the mound, the fishbowl surrounded by forty-five thousand people and the weight of new teammates, a city and a country on his shoulders. After a short conference with Coxi and Martinez and some words of encouragement, he started his warm-up pitches. He had warmed up quickly in the bullpen, yet felt extremely loose and strong. His fastball had pop and movement, while his curve was breaking from shoulders to ankles, and his sliders exploding.

When it was time to get down to business, he managed to block out his surroundings and barely heard the polite applause when he was announced to the crowd, just about all of whom had never heard of him. He had felt this way on only a few occasions, a combination of physical and spiritual strength and well being: he was in the zone.

The zone was a term used by athletes to describe a somewhat mystical state where the person and the sport were in unison and operating on almost a supernatural level. For a hockey goalie it would be seeing the puck in slow motion and knowing where the shot was going before it left the opposing player's stick; for a quarterback, it was effortlessly, firing passes into receivers hands, oblivious to defenders and rushers; and for a pitcher it was like having a laser guided missile in your arm with the ball the missile and the arm and body guiding it right to its target. When an athlete was in the zone, he was operating on a different level, almost above the sport.

He had first felt the magic of the zone when he was fourteen years old with batters looking foolish at his curveball and swinging aimlessly as his fastball zoomed by. It was more than pure command, it revolved around inner spirituality and magic. The zone would come and go and it could not be ordered at will. It had to be cherished, protected and embraced when it was there, because it might never re-appear.

Red Sox designated hitter Mike Easler stepped up to the plate and jumped on the rookie's first pitch but only mustered a weak pop-up to the third baseman Garth Iorg. With two outs Jeff took a deep breath as he stared into Jim Rice's eyes. The Red Sox slugger was one of the few hitters in baseball whose presence at the plate brought excitement to the ballpark. Standing in the batter's box, it looked as though he could not miss the ball. Jeff would always remember thinking that when he saw him on television. He was an imposing and menacing figure.

Jeff looked into Martinez for the signal. From the set, the young rigthander checked the runners looked and fired the fastball that Rice launched deep towards the left field stands and, at the last second just hooked foul. Martinez came out to calm the young hurler and help him re-group. The next pitch was a nasty curveball that Rice missed by a good six inches. With the count zero and two, Rice glared into the eyes of the rookie who had just made him look foolish. This gave Jeff more resolve as he fired a fastball up and in just missing Rice. Jeff would not be intimidated. It was Jeff's turn to glare in toward the veteran who was digging in. Martinez called for a curveball and Jeff let loose one of his magical deuces that caused Rice to buckle as it broke over the plate. Forty-five thousand fans jumped up in unison and cheered as Jeff jogged off the field.

In the dugout, Jeff sat by himself and tried to calm down. Aside from a few words of encouragement as Martinez took a seat next to him, his teammates let him be. When he took to the mound in the eighth, his dominance overpowered the Red Sox as he struck out Dwight Evans, Dave Henderson, and Bill Buckner.

He was sent back out to close the game in the ninth with a three run lead. He struck out the first two batters but then walked Rich Gedman and Spike Owen. Wade Boggs, the lead off hitter and tying run, stepped to the plate. This brought Bobby Cox to the mound. With the lefty Pierce ready in the pen, Jeff was sure that he was gone so that a lefty-lefty match-up could be created against the American League Batting Champion. To his surprise, he stayed in. The Toronto manager had seen a quality in Jeff's pitching which radiated confidence and competitiveness. With O'Doughnohue gone for the year, he had found his new closer in the most unlikely place.

Boggs battled Jeff to a full count and then fouled off six straight pitches; wicked sliders, hard breaking curveballs, and a couple of fastballs. It was time to attack from a different angle. Jeff shook off his catcher until he got what he wanted, the straight change. Jeff had not used it yet, but something inside told him it was time. With the crowd on its feet, he reached inside his glove for the circle change grip and then fired. By the time Boggs adjusted, it was too late, and all he could do was muster a weak fly ball to center field which Lloyd Moseby easily tracked down and caught to end the game.

In the clubhouse, reporters from all the newspapers and electronic media gathered around him and fired questions for almost forty-five minutes. They were looking for any tidbit of information and quote about the unknown rookie. The onslaught by the media was more grueling and draining than the game. Finally, when it seemed that the barrage of questions would never end, Pierce broke up the free for all and saved Jeff.

"Look Jeff," Pierce said, "One bad outing and they'll be all over you. Savour the moment, cut out the clippings and save them, and then move on. The game is made up of people and memories, that's what keeps us going, that's what keeps us all going. You did well tonight, real well. The key now is to keep it up and make this a long-running performance. Go get showered and let me buy you a drink."

Fifteen minutes later the two teammates, looking more like father and son, left Exhibition Stadium. Jeff's odyssey continued in his mind, thinking back to a few years ago at Memorial Stadium when he skipped school to watch Pierce, then the Cy Young winner. Now he was walking with him as a teammate and fellow Major League pitcher.

They grabbed a taxi and headed to the Loose Moose, a favorite watering hole and restaurant of many players. It was a three-floor establishment with two of the floors a restaurant overlooking a dance floor that was constantly crowded with rather conservative young professionals, drinking over-priced cocktails and dancing with little rhythm. One thing was always certain at the Moose, the players were treated like kings, and the women, all the women groveled and gawked at them, and generally would do whatever the players wanted, and enjoyed doing so.

It was almost midnight by the time they got there, and like every Thursday night, there was still a line up to get in, even though the prudish Ontario laws resulted in a 1:00 a.m. last call. They circumvented the line and headed to the back door where all the players went in.

Even though the Moose was crowded, Pierce quickly found who he was looking for. Standing in the corner, under the big moose head were a couple of stunning young ladies who Jeff figured to be in their late twenties. The brunette was wearing a black mini dress which was clinging to her tight body, not leaving too much to the imagination. The blonde, with short cropped hair was only slightly more conservative in a knee length leather skirt and a tank top. Both of them had spiked black heels which accentuated their long legs.

In another place and at a different time, they may have looked slutty and cheap, but they had a certain soft beauty that radiated healthiness and sex appeal. They had the perfect mix of sexiness, cuteness, and sophistication and they smelled so good--they were big league women.

Pierce introduced the blonde as Chantal and the brunette as Julie. They were both flight attendants for Air Canada and were in and out of town a lot, just like Pierce, and just how Pierce liked it. It was perfect for him, relationships of convenience with no commitment, just fun.

"Ladies, this is Jeff Williams, and he pitched his first big league game tonight. He's our next great star, so please take it easy on him." Pierce bellowed out with a sly smile, feeling the effect of the four beers he guzzled in the clubhouse.

Pierce ordered drinks and shots three times over as all four toasted Jeff's big league debut. Jeff was enjoying himself and was starting to feel some effect from the drinks, yet he felt somewhat uncomfortable around the "older women". This was not a frat party on campus where a freshman mingled with seniors. The blonde, who he quickly found out was supposed to be "his," was thirty years old, quite a jump for the twenty-year old kid he was, and felt like. In his eyes, appealing as she was, he felt a generation removed, and any sexual urge he may have had disappeared.

And then he thought of Tracy and her youthful exuberance, beauty and love. He did not want to be with Chantal or any other woman; he wanted to hold the woman he loved. His escapade in Ottawa had turned his stomach more than he thought it would. He did not like how it made him feel and he did not want to repeat that mistake. With that mind set, he made an excuse about being tired from the long and exciting day, which he was, and left amid the protests of Pierce

"You don't know what you're missing rook," Pierce said to him with a dumfounded yet friendly smile.

"Yes I do," Jeff shot back.

Jeff strolled back to the Harbour Castle hotel, where he was staying. He was tired and a little buzzed as he walked toward the Lakeshore and gazed into the water and up to the clear and star-filled sky. The city was going to sleep and the excitement and exhilaration of the marathon day began to dissipate. He was coming down off the high and he just sat staring out into the night.

From his seat on a bench, along the water, he looked out toward Olympic Island and let his mind wander. He thought of his grandfathers he never knew. A picture of one with a bat in his big hands and sculptured arms was the only memory Jeff had. He never had the chance to play catch with his grandson or watch him play ball. He couldn't brag to his friends about his grandson the Major Leaguer. Jeff could not give him the ball from his first win, or take him into the clubhouse to meet the guys, or to lunch to just talk. All he had was the picture.

His European grandfather would not have understood the importance of the game and its place in society, nor the status of his grandson, but he would have understood the dream which every little boy has, one only a selected few will ever fulfill. It was that same type of dream of a better life which he passed on to his son, and which his son fulfilled. He would have been proud.

Jeff felt a bond to the grandfathers he never knew through his grandmothers, now too passed away. He would feel badly when he didn't think of them enough. He missed the feeling of hugging his grandmothers and the anticipation of the little boy waiting for them at the airport. He missed the smells when he walked into their homes, but most of all he missed their love. Once in a while he would dream about them, he would talk to them as if they were still here and then he would wake up with a tear in his eye as the visit ended and he realized it was all just a dream.

More and more Tracy invaded his mind. He'd lie awake at night thinking of her and wanting to hold her. She consumed his every moment. He looked up to the stars and saw her smile and felt her soft touch and wished that she was now with him as the best part of his life was starting. He knew deep down that she would be with him and that they would be together for a long time.

Finally, after what seemed longer than the day itself, he went to his room to sleep. He had been awake for twenty hours.

Jeff woke up at 11:00 a.m., still tired and unfamiliar with his surroundings. He had a few hours before he had to be at the stadium and needed the time to relax and re-group. He showered and slowly got dressed. His wardrobe was pretty small, a couple of pairs of jeans, some Dockers, and a couple of suits and a blazer most of which was still in either Syracuse or Virginia. He would have to expand the selection a bit. He settled on a pair of khaki pants and a white polo shirt that was clean and not too wrinkled.

When he was dressed he called Tracy in Knoxville and gave her a first hand account at what she already knew. Hearing her voice put him in a great mood and vice versa. The apprehension that was in her voice yesterday was gone and they were making plans for her to visit once the Minor League season was over around Labor Day. They talked for about twenty minutes, mostly babbling about how much they missed each other and how excited they were about his debut. He gave her a big kiss through the phone, and with a smile they said goodbye.

Feeling much better than when he woke up, Jeff went down to the lobby to get some food in his system. He ordered a couple of eggs, bacon, toast, orange juice, and a Coke. A little bit of a greasy breakfast, but he felt like it. He picked up a copy of the *Toronto Sun* and saw himself in full color right on the cover, an expression of exuberance on his face after striking out Rice. Across the top was a big caption THE NEW SAVE-IOR. He then turned to the sports and read the article with the same headline.

"In the first inning of his Major League career, the rookie accomplished what few other veterans had before him: he made Jim Rice look foolish by buckling at a curveball, and then it got better. Twenty year old Jeff Williams, just off the plane from Syracuse, with less than a year's experience in professional baseball, may now find himself Toronto's new closer as they enter the most important eight weeks in their young history. By now, his story is probably well known...

'He showed great poise and command for such a young man. I really think he will help us down the stretch.' Toronto pitching coach Al Widmar said after the game with a big sly smile on his face, wanting to convey that they might have a big surprise and secret weapon in young Jeff Williams. It has indeed been a worldwind tour for Williams and he acknowledges and admits it.

'No, I would not have imagined that I would make it to Toronto so quickly and in the middle of a pennant race. But I'm glad, ecstatic, and every other good feeling. All I can do now is continue to work hard and hope that every outing will be a good one, and that I can help the team win the division.' He was excited like a little boy, but he carries himself like a man and it reflects on people's opinions of him. Sincerity, dedication and perseverance are words used by members of the Jays' front office to describe him.

Management, fans and teammates hope that this shot of energy from a most unexpected source will be the boost that the team needs to propel them to the top for the very first time. The introduction is now over, let us all see what happens as we start to turn the pages."

Jeff put down the paper and wondered the same thing, What will happen next?

It was a beautiful Friday afternoon and Jeff always loved Fridays. It was his favorite day of the week. He decided to walk to the stadium. It was a twenty-minute walk and a good opportunity to relax and become familiar with his surroundings. As he walked through the Canadian

National Exhibition, more commonly known as the CNE, and approached the stadium through the large crowds, he had to talk to himself to make sure that all that had happened was true. In order to reinforce it he said to himself "I am a Major Leaguer," and then smiled.

He made his way to the clubhouse and was one of the first ones there. He quickly said hello to Ken Carson, the Trainer and Jeff Ross the Clubhouse Manager. He then made his way through the still unfamiliar clubhouse to his locker where he found a stack of telegrams. There was one from Dédé and the rest of the PUC. Moggle sent one which simply said, "I always knew you could do it!" There was one from Tim and one from Robin. Yes, sweet Robin had sent one from El Salvador where she was in the Peace Corps sending all her love and best wishes. His old catcher Sherm sent one as did Brownie and an assortment of old friends from Hobart and Virginia. It was nice to know that he had touched these people and that they cared enough to let him know that they were thinking of him and cheering him on. CNN sure did have quite a reach.

FIFTEEN

Jeff left the Harbour Castle, his home for the past two months, at about 2.30 p.m., more than five and a half hours before game time and probably more than eight hours before he might go to work. He had come to enjoy his walks to the ballpark. It was always a peaceful time, a chance to get away from all the excitement and think. It was time that belonged only to him.

Tonight was game seven of the World Series and everything was on the line. It was a brisk October day and it would be a cold night at the EX, but the stadium would be packed and the fans would be loud. BJ Birdie would display his silly antics. *OK BLUE JAYS* would be belted out in unison by over fifty-thousand fans during the seventh inning stretch, and hopefully, Jeff would have a chance to save his fourth game of the series to give the Jays and Toronto their first World Championship.

Since that first game against the Red Sox, Jeff firmly established himself as Toronto's closer, and down the stretch became one of the American League's most dominant pitchers. He appeared in twenty games and recorded fifteen saves with a one and one record. In twenty-eight innings, he allowed twenty-one hits, twelve walks and an almost microscopic 2.11 ERA. Toronto had chased the Yankees until the final week of the season when they tied them and then won six of their last seven to win by four games.

It was a magical time for Jeff, and he absorbed and enjoyed all that came with being a Major League player; the travel, the money, the status, and the glory of winning. He appreciated it all because it was new to him and totally unexpected.

Deep down he wasn't sure that it would not all be taken away from him without notice, the same way it was given to him. And if it would be, if the Major Leagues would be taken away from him and he would become a one hit wonder, he reasoned that he already had memories that would last and remain entrenched in his mind forever; walking in from the bullpen and pitching at Yankee Stadium, the temple of baseball, shagging fly balls in left field at Fenway Park, with the Green Monster looming behind, getting the save to clinch the division, against his home town Baltimore Orioles and getting the win against the Kansas City Royals in game six, to win the pennant and propel the Blue Jays into the World Series.

Jeff couldn't have written a better script. With the $17,000 he had already earned and his playoff share which would be a minimum $45,000 more, plus his signing bonus, he would have a little nest egg to start his life, a life with Tracy. She had come up for the final two weeks of the season and like the rest of the families and significant others she was joining the players on their odyssey toward the World Championship. If anything became obvious during this period, it was how much they loved each other and how much they wanted to be together.

However, with all his recent accomplishments and his emotional happiness, he was on edge as he walked through the player's gate at the EX at 2.55 p.m.. All that was on his mind was game seven and the St Louis Cardinals. He had to be ready, if and when he was needed to close the door. One thing which helped Jeff as a closer was that by nature he wasn't too nervous and that he realized that as a stopper, there was always tomorrow. But this time, there was no tomorrow. It all came down to tonight, and the whole World would be watching.

The two teams had split the first two games in Toronto, before moving to Busch Stadium in St Louis where the Cardinals won two out of three. Facing elimination in game six, the Blue Jays trailed 2-0 going into the eighth inning when Willie Upshaw hit a three-run two-out homer off the Cardinals' ace reliever Todd Worrell. Jeff then came in for a one-two-three ninth inning forcing tonight's game seven.

In four games Jeff had pitched five shutout innings, but none of that mattered tonight as it was down to a one game battle, a three-hour war, and he was ready.

He still had chills when he thought back to game one and that feeling of excitement and the roar of the crowd as he was introduced. It was just like he had planned it so many times, many years ago, in his backyard with Marc, playing, dreaming, jumping and laughing. He had just turned twenty-one and was on the verge of being a World Series hero. Could he go anywhere from here? The question may have perplexed Jeff, but those who knew him knew that he would go wherever he chose to go.

Time passed painfully slow for the players, waiting anxiously like soldiers to start their mission. Tension replaced jokes and no matter how much the players tried to conceal it, there was no way to disguise that tonight was no ordinary game. By the time batting practice got under way the natural release of hitting, throwing, and running took over as the players started to loosen up and feel better.

The clocks continued to turn slowly. The agony and impatience to start the game became almost unbearable as the emotional roller coaster which had taken over and invaded every player since the moment they woke up continued.

Finally at 8.21p.m., the introductions were finished in the frigid stadium on the shores of Lake Ontario. First Huey Lewis and the News belted out the *Star Spangled Banner* and then Anne Murray sang *Oh Canada*, more beautifully, melodically and magically than she had back in 1977 when she did it for Toronto's first game.

Blue Jay ace, Dave Stieb took the mound. He had won game one and lost game four, but had pitched well in both. It was fitting that the team's first star would be in the spotlight for the biggest game in the young franchise's history. The Cardinals countered with the fiery Dominican right-hander Joaquin Andujar who had opposed Stieb the two previous times.

The game started. Stieb struggled in the first, unable to get loose in the cold. He walked Vince Coleman and Willie McGee to lead off the game. After a Tommy Herr sacrifice, Jack Clark drove in both runners with a single, and in less than five minutes St Louis was up by two. Stieb then settled down and got out of the inning without any further damage, and with a deep sigh of relief, as it could have been worse.

As the game continued, the wind picked up and the cold intensified. In the dugout, the pitchers were wearing parkas and gloves, making trips to the clubhouse between innings to stretch and keep loose and warm. The normally quiet and passive Toronto crowd got a boost of energy from the cold and cheered and yelled like they never had before, almost magically warming up the open-air stadium. Even BJ Birdie, the team's much maligned mascot, managed to turn up his antics a notch.

Stieb's first inning problems appeared behind him, while Andujar was overpowering the Blue Jay hitters as he attacked them with his fastballs and sliders, wearing a short sleeved uniform top. Through three innings, all the Blue Jays had mustered was a single by Willie Upshaw.

In the bottom of the fourth, Jesse Barfield hit a one-out double and advanced to third on a groundout. With two outs, Ernie Whitt hit a sharp line drive up the middle and a roar went up as the crowd anticipated a hit not realizing that Ozzie Smith was extended in mid air, en route to snagging the line drive destined for centerfield. The Wizard of Oz had done it again and the Blue Jays first scoring opportunity went for naught.

Stieb continued to mow down the Cardinals and had not allowed a base hit since the second, keeping the Jays in the game. Finally, in the bottom of the seventh, Toronto scored a run, but failed to capitalize on a glorious scoring opportunity. The Jays had loaded the bases with no outs and after a Jesse Barfield sacrifice fly, George Bell ripped a ball right at third-baseman Terry Pendelton who turned a double into an inning ending double play. With six outs left, the Blue Jays were still down by one.

Meanwhile, in the top of the eighth, Coleman and McGee led off with back to back singles and Cox went to the bullpen and brought in Pierce to turn around the switch hitting Tommy Herr to the right side. Also, since Pierce was a lefty, he would have a better angle at fielding a bunt and gunning out the speedy Coleman at third. Jeff started to get loose in the pen.

Herr settled into the box under the microscope of fifty thousand pairs of eyes in the stands, eighty more on the field and millions at home. This at bat could decide the game. That is how crucial it was. Herr dug in as Pierce peered in and got set. Herr squared around and Pierce fired as the Blue Jays set in motion an unconventional rotation play for the situation, sending shortstop Tony Fernandez to second, Damasso Garcia to first and charging both corners leaving no one to get the lead runner at third. The pitch was a high fastball and the good bunting Herr fouled it off.

Now ahead in the count, the signal from the dugout was now for the more traditional rotation play with Mulliniks holding his ground at third and Pierce covering the left side. The old veteran got set again and fired another fastball, which Herr bunted firmly just to the left of the mound. Without hesitation Pierce fired to Mulliniks for one who in turn, instantly fired to first to nail Herr by less than a step. It was a seldom seen yet beautiful double play.

With the Cardinals' dangerous cleanup hitter and RBI leader Jack Clark at the plate, Coxi signaled for Pierce to walk him, in order to set up the force play. The Toronto Manager then slowly strolled out to the mound and signaled to the bullpen for Jeff to come in to face switch-hitting third-baseman Terry Pendelton.

As he jogged to the mound, he felt strength and power, not only in his arm, but in his entire body. The short jog seemed endless as everything appeared in slow motion before him. His whole life appeared before him, his ambitions, his dreams, his memories, his family, his successes and his failures. This was it. This is what it all was about and this is where he wanted to be.

"Keep us in it." Coxi said with a tone that was a combination of giving an order and a plea.

"Let's do it!!" His catcher Ernie Whitt threw in. As he started his warm up pitches, Jeff's theme song rang through the stadium. It was Rod Stewart's *YOUNG TURKS*. *"Young hearts be free tonight. Time is on your side."*

It was the veteran and mentor Pierce's idea to have these words associated with Jeff. Fans now joined in and fifty thousand voices sang in unison as the newest sports hero in a city with a long sports tradition got ready to keep the dream alive.

He was oblivious to the cold air, which now felt warm, and the thundering roar of the crowd which now sounded like a mere whisper. The totality of his mind and body were focused on one thing, and that was to get Pendelton out. Jeff's arm felt like a rocket launcher as he fired his warm up pitches into Whitt. Jeff had faced Pendelton once before giving up a single on a first pitch fastball. The Cardinal third-baseman now stared in at Jeff from the on deck circle, but Jeff would not give him the satisfaction of looking back at him. He saved the glare for when Pendelton stepped into the box.

The game was now in Jeff's hands, as the Blue Jay bullpen lay dormant. Todd Worrell began to throw for the Cardinals. In both dugouts, the tension was almost unbearable as players and coaches could barely watch as they alternated between cringing and relaxing with every move in front of them.

Finally it was time and Jeff settled into the stretch and got the sign. He then checked the runners. The Ex was suddenly silent as he fired a fastball. He would go right at Pendelton. The stadium erupted in unison as the umpire called a strike. Whitt, an original Blue Jay was pumped as he pointed back to Jeff to keep it up. Jeff got the ball back and walked behind the mound. For the first time, he felt pressure, real pressure and the realization of the enormity of the situation and what the outcome of the game would mean. It all sank in at once. This was game seven of the World Series and the game was on the line and this most definitely was not his backyard.

He took a deep breath and tried to relax. He stepped back on the mound and looked in once again as an eerie silence hovered over the stadium, He checked the runners and fired a fastball up and in, and just when it looked like Pendelton would let it go for ball one, he took a mighty swing and missed the high heater. The crowd erupted again.

Coxi was somewhat relieved by the last pitch, but he could not control his nerves. He needed an out right here and right now for his team to have a chance to win. Whitt went out to the mound to make sure he was in sync with the young pitcher. Jeff knew exactly what he wanted to do and he convinced the veteran catcher to let him go right at the hitter. Pendelton got back into the box and stared out at the rookie pitcher. He would not be made to look bad again. Whitt crouched down and flashed the signals. The crowd was now clapping together anticipating the out. Whitt set up inside. Jeff focused as he gripped the ball in his glove, and then he fired the nastiest and prettiest cut fastball he had ever thrown. It kept tailing and tailing until it crossed the black of the plate and froze the Cardinal third-baseman, who stood dumbfounded as the Blue Jays jogged off the field.

The EX exploded with noise as Toronto came to bat in the bottom of the eighth, but the moody Blue Jay fans went quiet quickly as Worrell set them down quietly in order. Momentum had shifted back to the Cardinals as Jeff took the mound in the top of the ninth. St. Louis was only three outs away from being World Champions and Jeff would have to hold them to give his team a chance to tie and then win.

His part took eight pitches as he retired the anxious Cardinals on three groundouts. Once again the fans roared, backing their heroes, yet unsure if their young team could do it, unsure if they had any more comebacks left. But they would cheer and scream their loudest on this cold October night, on the shores of Lake Ontario, with the eyes of a continent upon them.

Todd Worell, the hard throwing Cardinal closer came back out to try to shut the door against the bottom third of the order, Upshaw, Mulliniks and Garcia. Upshaw, the soft-spoken first baseman, also known as Chuggy, strode to the plate, desperately looking to get on base. Quickly, he fell behind 0-2. He then managed to foul off two wicked sliders as Worrell attacked. The Cardinal stopper came hard at him one more time, but Chuggy managed to get a piece of it and blooped a single just over the outstretched arms of Ozzie Smith. Cox quickly sent Manny Lee in to pinch run.

Mulliniks walked up to the plate and looked down to third-base coach Jimy Williams for the sign. Lee at first also looked attentively. Both saw what everyone in the stadium expected, and the Blue Jay third-baseman squared around to bunt as Worrell fired. Pendelton and Clark charged from third and first as Lee expanded his lead. Mulliniks pulled his bat back as the slider headed towards the dirt. Tony Pena, the Cardinal's catcher got in front of it, but it skipped a few feet to his right and Lee took off for second without hesitation. The rifle armed Pena pounced on it and fired a strike to second. Lee slid headfirst, and with his outstretched left arm, just managed to avoid the tag. The tying run was now on second with no outs.

Cox now took off the bunt sign, as he did not want to give up an out. He had a veteran left handed bat up who should be able to get a ball to the right side, and maybe sneak one through. Lee took his lead off second, fighting for every inch, ready to explode towards third. Mulliniks got set in the box, thinking more of solid contact than pulling the ball. Worrell got set once again and fired. The fastball was belt high and hitable. Razor ripped the ball up the middle for a sure base hit, until, Ozzie Smith, outstretched again snared the ball and fired to first. But this time the slow-footed Mulliniks somehow managed to beat the throw by a step and Lee scampered back to third after a big turn. The winning run was now on first base.

Cox went to the bench one more time and put in Nelson Liriano to pinch run at first. Damasso Garcia, the ninth place hitter stepped in to face Worrell. Damo was hitting a cool .315 for the series and just wanted to hit a flyball. The second baseman worked the count full after falling behind one and two. He then fouled off two wicked sliders and a fastball that was ball four.

The battle resumed one more time as the runners took their leads and Worrell glared in. Pena flashed the sign. The big reliever fired a high fastball up and in. Garcia swung and managed to lift a soft flyball to shallow center field. The hang time was such that anticipation and debate would take place while the ball was in flight. When the ball finally landed in center fielder Willie McGee's mitt, Lee took off like a sprinter. It would take a perfect throw by the speedy, yet weak-armed McGee to get Lee, and it was. Suddenly the Blue Jays were reduced to their last out of game seven of the World Series. Liriano was still on first. An attempt to advance would have been too risky.

The crowd was almost as stunned as the Blue Jay dugout as an eerie silence engulfed and suffocated it. But just before the silence killed the team, Pierce spoke; "Hey boys, this game ain't over until we let it be over. I don't know about the rest of you pretty boys, but I want my ring. A couple more hits and this mother fucker is ours." And like a bunch of high school kids, they responded to their new leader as they jumped and cheered as leadoff hitter Lloyd Moseby got ready for the biggest at bat of his life.

The fifty thousand fans now stood clapping and yelling. This October night was indeed a cold one as the air blew in off Lake Ontario. But in the stadium it was hot. Hot with nerves, anticipation and excitement. Worrell walked behind the mound and took a deep breath. "Shaker" walked confidently to the plate. Liriano on first was ready to pounce. With two outs he would have to score on a double. Clark held him at first and Pendelton guarded the line. The outfielders played back, preventing a ball from being hit over their heads.

And now, after what seemed like an eternity since Garcia's at bat, Moseby got set in the box. Worrell looked in as Pena called for a fastball down and in; he got set, checked the runner, and fired. Moseby pounced on a fastball up over the plate and lined it between Clark and Herr. Liriano made it to third easily as the crowd erupted. The Jays still needed one more hit and suddenly both bullpens got busy. Toronto had John Cerutti start to loosen up, more out of precaution than necessity while the Cardinals got Mark Little and John Fulgham up.

It was now up to Tony Fernandez, the young Dominican shortstop to keep the Jays alive. The switch-hitter stepped into the box as near hysteria overtook the stadium. Worrell quickly jumped ahead with a hard fastball which Fernandez whiffed at; but the quiet Canadian fans would not be silenced as the duel continued. Now two and one Worrell came in with a fastball that Fernandez ripped down the first-base line, foul by inches. Pena wanted another fastball, but this time outside, hoping to freeze the young hitter. With the count even at two, the big Cardinal stopper fired and gasped as Fernandez lined the ball over Pendelton's head at third and down into the left field corner. Liriano scored easily to tie the game and Coleman picked up the ball just as Moseby hit third. Jimy Williams waved him in as Ozzie Smith fired the relay into home, but it was too late. The Jays had won, the battle was over and all of Canada could now celebrate their first World Series.

The champagne and beer flowed. Players poured more on each other than they drank. They screamed and yelled and sang as Commissioner Peter Ueberroth presented the World Series trophy to Beeston and Gillick and then the World Series MVP trophy to Jeff who had collected three saves and the win in game seven. It was great to be World Champions and everyone took part in the celebration. Coxi, Beeston and Gillick were all drenched by the players. George Bell was doing a little conga dance singing *La Bamba*, Pierce lit a stogie with Beeston, Jeff and Martinez took turns drenching each other between chugs while Willie Upshaw just kept repeating " I don't believe we won, I just don't believe it."

Sometimes dreams can come true.

SIXTEEN

It is a strange feeling waking up in the morning, for just about the first time in your life with nothing to do; no school, no work, no baseball, just time, sunshine, and the women of your dreams right beside you. If only Jeff could get rid of his cottonmouth and headache, life would truly be perfect.

The celebration had been fun and intense. The ballroom of the Harbour Castle belonged to the players, staff, employees, and their families. Music, food and alcohol flowed all night. Jeff's parents had been there for games six and seven and had met Tracy. She was at Jeff's side as beautiful as ever and they all got along well. Today they would spend the day in bed, recuperating before a week-long trip to the Bahamas and an attempt to figure out what was next. At this moment, all he wanted was to never let her out of his arms.

He took only two calls that day, both pre-arranged. One was from Louise, who had stayed home in Virginia with the flu and did not make it up to Toronto, and the other from Marc, who starred the day before, catching the winning touchdown against Michigan State, in front of a national television audience. Both victories were shared by the entire clan, separated as they were. Jeff promised to visit each of them once he got back from the Bahamas, and suddenly filled up his schedule until almost Thanksgiving. A wave of panic hit him as he realized Spring Training would soon be here.

He quickly put that thought out of his mind and turned around and kissed Tracy, who had fallen back asleep

It was a glorious week on Paradise Island. The last minute reservations landed them at the Holiday Inn Pirates' Cove. It was tucked in the far corner of the Island, not far from Club Med and a short ride to the Casino. There was a big pool, the beach right in front of them, and a tiki bar built into a boat.

Jeff and Tracy spent most of the week on the beach or by the pool sipping Bahama Mamas, listening to reggae and calypso music and sweating away their hangovers by making love. They found a closeness that both had hoped was truly there, but that they had never truly had a chance to find. It was unspoken and remained that way, but both knew that they had found it and did not want to lose it.

They left Nassau and flew back to Knoxville where Jeff would spend a couple of days before heading up to Ann Arbor to see Marc and catch the Ohio State game. Jeff had decided that it was important for him to go back to Hobart for the Winter trimester and take some classes. He really wanted his degree and was six classes short. He wasn't so sure that he would be as motivated in the future.

It provided perfect timing for him. He would be in Knoxville for Thanksgiving and then head to Geneva and finish his classes right in time for Spring Training, By then, he hoped he would have a clear picture of exactly how his relationship with Tracy would evolve.

The campus at Ann Arbor could not have been a further contrast from Hobart's. From a small intimate family setting of eighteen-hundred students, Michigan was a constant place of activity and rush with large classes and impersonal professors. There was not the same sense of community Jeff had experienced, but Marc enjoyed it. Young Marc was getting more playing time on the football field and had grown into a very strong young man, looking more like an athlete than Jeff did. Unlike Jeff's studies of economics and political science, Marc was breezing through his history and philosophy classes. A young Moggle, Jeff thought. And though Marc enjoyed football, baseball was still his first love and he was looking forward to building on his solid freshman year.

The two brothers who had been apart for most of the past four years had a great few days together. Jeff went to a couple of classes and hung out at practice. It was the first time since the victory that Jeff realized what an impact he had as the Wolverine players and coaches greeted him with awe. In Jeff's mind, he was still one of them and was just about their age. He had to hide his awe for them, as he watched them at practice. Man did he love football.

The Buckeyes beat Michigan in a hard fought Big Ten trench war. Both teams tried to run it down each other's gut in front of the one hundred thousand screaming fans that had packed the stadium. Bo Schembechler had gotten Jeff a field pass where he stood and watched the true savagery and intensity of big time football. Marc played about half the game catching one pass and spending the afternoon trying to block defensive ends and linebackers--it was not an easy task, and he felt the post battle pain, as the two brothers sipped down some cocktails.

Jeff gave Marc all the details about Tracy and how he loved her. Marc peppered Jeff with questions about the baseball season, life on the road and the players. It seemed like an eternity since his brief visit to Knoxville. Jeff kept him transfixed with his stories. They realized how much they had grown up and changed over the last four years as they toasted each other and talked about one day playing on the same big league ball team.

The two brothers helped and nurtured each other, just like when they were young. Marc was a young man full of potential and life, and if Jeff could nurture him by example that would be great. And Marc gave Jeff what he needed, a kick in his butt, putting him back in his place, and not letting his stardom go to his head. It was what brothers did.

The next stop on the tour took him back home to his parents. He hadn't really seen much of them either the last couple of years and after living in a hotel and strange apartments, it would be great to be home. No matter how old you are, where you live or what you do, there's no feeling like going home to the house and the room you grew up in. That's exactly how Jeff wanted to feel, he was sheltered, protected and safe. It was a time for him to relax and momentarily forget about baseball.

His parents hadn't really changed, maybe a bit older, but as loving and understanding as ever. Like Marc, his sister Louise had grown up, almost suddenly, and was now a beautiful young lady, with early admission to the University of Virginia in linguistics. She didn't let Jeff forget that he couldn't get in to UVA and egged him on with her claim of intellectual superiority. In return, Jeff threatened to abandon the shopping trip to the mall which he promised her, thus hitting every seventeen year old girl where she is most vulnerable.

He really didn't do much with his time at home and he didn't care. He slept in, caught up on phone calls and letters and made arrangements for his return to Hobart by renting an apartment on Main Street, just off campus, overlooking Lake Seneca. He spoke to Tracy every day and planned his Thanksgiving trip.

Jeff didn't talk to his parents much about Tracy. It wasn't really his style, but they caught on quickly to how much she meant to Jeff. With his Dad, he tried to get his finances in order. In his time in the majors, he made about $17,000 which after taxes and expenses left him with about seven which he split between his checking and savings account. It was sort of his cash on hand, his spending money. He added that to the ten grand of his signing bonus which he had also split up, and he had a little cushion.

They agreed on a mix for the $65,000 World Series share and decided to split it up in some stocks, stock mutual funds, and tax free municipal bonds, the same mix they had agreed upon for his signing bonus. He was twenty-one and now had $125,000 working for him, with very little expenses. A couple of more solid seasons and he would be on his way to lifelong financial security by the time he was twenty-five. Now that was a great feeling.

They agreed that wherever he was playing next year, Major or Minor leagues he would contribute a monthly amount, depending on his salary to the different investments. His tuition, room, and board was still covered by the Blue Jays, as stipulated in his contract, so that was an expense he didn't have to worry about.

It was a productive and much needed visit, but as he kissed his Mom good-bye on the way to Knoxville, it sunk in that his childhood was now over. He was no longer the little boy who pretended he was Batman, or who would have soldier fights with his kid brother. He was now truly on the path to becoming a man.

The ride to Rugby from Knoxville was a little less than two hours through the winding countryside and hills of Tennessee. To Jeff, it was foreign soil, different from his home, different from Paris and different from the little towns of upstate New York. This was the country. It was like a movie or TV show, almost make believe. As they got closer to their destination, Tracy guided him through the county landmarks, making sure to let him know who lived where and who did what to whom. They drove by the county high school where she once was a cheerleader.

When they pulled up to the home that she grew up in, Jeff felt as though he had somehow been there before. There was a big wooden house tucked away and hidden off the road and a pebble path that led up to it. There was a storage shed almost as big as a barn that sat next to it, and there were big trees and a large yard. It hit Jeff as he parked the car that it reminded him of Walton's Mountain and he liked that. He cherished what Walton's Mountain stood for; family, love, hard work, and support. It was these things that would make him cry when he watched the show growing up.

Jeff and Tracy were the last to arrive and the house was full of cousins, aunts, uncles, and grandmothers. Right away, he felt at ease and at home. It was a good place to be. He had almost forgotten the warmth of a grandmother's hug and the life you felt on a brisk Fall day. He realized how much he missed it and how much it meant to him.

Turkeys were smoking outside while the finishing touches were being put on the Thanksgiving Day feast. Everyone caught up on the family gossip and news as they mixed in talk about Tennessee football and the new school construction. It was almost as though they lived in a self-contained world with the occasional trip into Knoxville as the big adventure. But it was their world and they were happy and content, and maybe it wasn't so bad if you didn't know anything else. Jeff knew what else was out there and was sure that Tracy needed it. It was a nice life, but there was so much more to the world, so much more to do and see, so much more to experience, and they would do it all together.

They feasted on a traditional Thanksgiving meal of turkey, fresh mashed sweet potatoes, green beans, stuffing, biscuits, cornbread, assorted salads, fresh pies, and ice cream. And then, they all sat around the television, stuffed from the meal, and watched football. Tracy took a seat beside Jeff and cuddled up to him. He really didn't know what love was, but he believed that this was it. It felt so good to be near her, to hold her and to be held. He wanted to go on like this forever. It was a feeling that would always remain entrenched in his mind and in his heart, one of those rare moments that you never forget.

In the early evening, they left Rugby and headed back to Knoxville, happier than ever, with a life full of happiness and love ahead of them. Their time together was wonderful, and they were thankful that they were always able to pick up where they left off. But little pieces of time together were not enough, and while both knew that a relationship, a true loving relationship could not go on like this, neither one risked verbalizing it for fear that it would ruin what they had.

Jeff questioned himself and looked deep into his heart to make sure that he truly understood his thoughts and feelings and to make sure that he wasn't pulling another Robin, in his not willing to truly commit. He truly believed that this was different. It had to be; he loved her and wanted her. He knew that sooner rather than later Tracy would be his wife. The only question was when?

SEVENTEEN

Jeff was finishing up the Winter trimester at Hobart and could not wait to get down to Dunedin for Spring Training and what he hoped would be his first full season in the Major Leagues. He was happy he came back to take classes and move a little closer to his degree, plus it offered him a somewhat structured schedule which he needed. The time away from Tracy was very difficult, and while the daily conversations helped, he was more convinced than ever that he loved and needed her always and forever.

He cherished the beauty and magic of Hobart, but missed the faces of his best friends. Tim had graduated and was getting his MBA and well on his way to accomplishing his goals. Sherm was taking care of the family's baking business and Robin stunned her parents, but not her friends, by enrolling in the Peace Corps and was sent off to El Salvador to help the country's children. Those she touched would be lucky.

Jeff made sure he stayed part of the College and the Geneva community by speaking in schools, and helping out for special fundraisers. He still had a few baseball buddies around like Todd Whalen, Brian Reed and Rick Stevens, but he tried to keep his partying to a minimum. He knew that generally what went on at campus stayed on campus, but you never knew what might get out. The days of sliding in beer and having girls ride on his shoulders were probably over. He was nostalgic about the good old days.

Jeff raced through his upper level classes on International Politics and Economics in order to make sure his work would be over in time for him to leave for Dunedin on February 15th, a little before the trimester was officially over. He worked out diligently at Bristol Gymnasium, building up his strength while maintaining his flexibility. In January, he picked up a ball and slowly worked his way up to throwing every other day, so he would be sharp and ready in order to defend his role as closer on the World Champion Toronto Blue Jays. He was confident that his work had paid off.

In the evening of February 14th, he put the finishing touches on his senior thesis which was entitled: *The Olympic Movement: Power, Money or a Uniting Spirit.* As he read the last paragraph, he was proud of his work and the words that he had used. He was relieved to know that he could still use his mind to create and think and that the whole Jeff who he had cultivated was still there within him, not engulfed and lost in baseball.

"The importance of the Olympics is truly to compete, not necessarily to win, and while money and political gain may be won or lost, what truly is at stake is the human spirit and harmony; the willingness to believe in something and to go for it. As important is the ability to sing, dance and rejoice in participation, and to smile watching all of humanity unite. The challenge now is to acknowledge the economic and political realities and to work within these guidelines, to bring out and nurture humanistic and athletic considerations and spirit."

He walked over to Trinity Hall, pausing and reflecting at each landmark on the way. It was a cold night, but he was oblivious to the wind blowing in his face. He made his way through Friendly's parking lot and by Boswell field, home the Football and Lacrosse teams, up the winding road which led him to upper campus and the William Smith dorms. He paused as he looked around at Miller, Comstock, and Hirshon, thinking back three and half years to the day after his eighteenth birthday and his trip to Hirshon to see Robin and thank her for taking care of him. He suddenly felt old and grown up, but he wasn't.

He then went a few hundred yards out of his way, by a snow covered Keg Hill and baseball field, and then by his old dorm room, and the quad. He wished that Tracy were with him to see the majestic beauty of a quiet Winter night on Lake Seneca. He was lonely and he missed her.

Finally, he dropped the paper off and stood on Main Street looking out into the night and the ice covered lake. It was so beautiful, peaceful, and heart-warming. Just what his solemn mood needed right at that moment. He took a few seconds to simply look out blankly and peacefully, thinking vaguely of his past and contemplating his future career and, he felt more certain than ever, his future wife.

What he really needed when it came down to it was to get back to his real life of playing baseball and being with the woman he loved. His real life had once centered around Hobart, and no matter how much he loved the place, he realized that those days were gone, no matter how strong the bond was to Geneva and how much he enjoyed being there. Yes, he would be back, but on different terms.

After about ten minutes, he made the short trek over to Kappa Sigma, just to see if Todd Whalen, Reed, or Stevens were around to go to The Oaks for a couple of cocktails and hang out. No one was around, they were probably all out at some Valentine's Day bash. Jeff decided to cruise by The Oaks anyway. It had been the sight of so many good times, in what now seemed like a previous life. He took a seat at the bar and ordered a seven and seven.

The place was pretty empty and that suited him just fine. As he downed a couple of drinks and started to feel a little buzz, he remembered so many nights staggering home across campus or if he was lucky up the hill. He chatted with the bartender a bit, but pretty much kept to himself. "Did Tim and he actually piss by the Pac Man machine?" He laughed almost out loud and thought back to when a dollar for a drink seemed like a lot and seven dollars was a big night out. It was at that time, sitting at The Oaks alone and buzzed that he realized how much the three full years at Hobart molded and shaped him, how the friends and people he met and learned from helped him develop into the person he now was. It was easy to get caught up and forget, and this upset him. Maybe Hobart and Geneva could not be what it once was, but in what it is now he was able to find what he was looking for, and the fact that he had almost forgot made him sad.

He left The Oaks and headed home. The cool and windy wintry night air sobered him up quickly, as he entered his now bare and packed up apartment. He flopped on his bed and put on the TV, before reaching for the phone. When she picked up on the other end, her voice sent an uncontrollable shiver through his heart. He loved her so and told her with more conviction than ever. They missed each other so much and could barely wait to meet in Florida and hug and hold. Finally, after about an hour they said goodbye and Jeff went to sleep looking forward to the great things that awaited him. His first Major League Spring Training and a chance to be with the woman he loved. He was only twenty-one but he believed that he had all he could ever want.

EIGHTEEN

Jeff felt a sudden surge as the plane landed at Tampa Airport. The warm weather and palm trees let him know that the baseball season was here. The gym work up North had given him the hunger to continue to work hard and improve. He felt invigorated by the Florida sun as he picked up his rental car and looked forward to the challenge of proving himself all over again.

He headed towards Dunedin, over the Courtney Campbell Causeway and up US 19, retracing the route he had done two years previously with Sherm and the boys. He glared over to the Tanga and saw a bunch of parked cars, the same at Hooters. Joe Dugan's was tucked away, but he knew that the Spring crowd would keep the place hopping. US 19 was just as it was last Spring, littered with car dealerships, strip malls, hotels, and restaurants. Not much had changed.

It took him a little over half an hour to get from the airport to the apartment he had rented not far from US 19, just off Main Street in Dunedin. It was in a big complex with a pool and a couple of tennis courts, not that Jeff did much of either but it was nice and about half the price of a condo on Clearwater Beach. He figured that if he could save some of $125 per diem, or at least break even, it wouldn't be such a terrible thing.

By 9:00 p.m., Jeff fell fast asleep. He had a big day ahead with physicals starting at 8:00 a.m., followed by a light workout and then a meeting with Assistant General Manager, Gord Ash, to get his contract done as Jeff was his own agent.

He woke up early, chugged down a Mountain Dew and took the short drive to Engelbert Complex. The welcoming committee and surroundings were a little different from when he had reported to minor league camp the year before. World Series logos were everywhere and a scrum of Toronto, Florida, and national media had invaded little Dunedin for the first day of camp.

Inside the clubhouse, the players quickly unpacked their personals in their numerically assigned lockers. Jeff's looked familiar with his number thirty-nine hanging. There were not many unfamiliar faces as the players and staff greeted each other. Trainers Ken Carson and Tommy Craig set them up with their packets for the physicals. Jeff was greeted by Taylor and Martinson who had both gotten non-roster invites to Spring Training. For Martinson, it was a chance to show that he had pitched himself into a prospect, while for Taylor, it was one last chance to show he had what it took both in his head and in his right arm, after a strong finish in AAA. He then saw old Mike Pierce, who looked in better shape than he had remembered.

The physicals were a pain, but necessary. A battery of tests, X-rays and exams. It all took a few hours. Jeff was happy to find out that he had somehow managed to decrease his body fat, reflecting that his workouts must have overshadowed the Cams pizza he loved so much in Geneva. He was now a muscular one hundred and eighty seven pounds. He had finally developed a true athlete's body.

A little after 11:00 a.m., twenty-one pitchers and six catchers gathered on field one with coaches for a quick workout. The first group of five pitchers threw off the mound for ten minutes while the others long tossed. They ran through their PFP's, known to the common man as pitchers' fielding practice. These were the drills which every announcer refers to during the season as the drills which the pitchers run through from the first day of Spring Training, and it was true, but everyone was probably sick of hearing it.

After that, they did their running and sit-ups. It was true what Jeff had heard; Big League camp was more relaxed than minor league camp. The players knew what was expected of them and they did it without having to be led around by the hand. Also the fact that they were defending World Series Champions permitted a business-like confidence to surround the camp even though it was only day one, and the whole squad was not even there yet.

By 12:45 p.m., Jeff had showered and changed for his meeting with Ash. Most of the others were going over to Hooters for some lunch and Jeff hoped to meet them later. Jeff had spent much of the last couple of days wondering what the Blue Jays would offer him. The Major League minimum salary was $60,000 or about $10,000 a month, but that was for players with no experience and no title of World Series MVP.

With the bulk of his World Series share invested, Jeff's main concern was a one way guaranteed contract which would protect him from a lower pay scale in the event he would have to go back to the minors. In the back of his mind, he had to protect himself from the fact that he may be a one hit wonder. He was scared that he might be another Joe Charbonneau, the Cleveland rookie of the year who disappeared from the Major Leagues almost as quickly as he appeared. If Jeff were to fall quickly, he wanted to take with him as much as he could, so that he would have a nest egg to build his life.

He felt that he should be somewhere in the $90,000-$100,000, A yearly salary he could not have fathomed a mere two years ago, or for that matter one year ago, when he had no per diem for Spring Training and $700 a month in Knoxville.

Jeff walked into the small and barren Spring Training office of the Assistant General Manager. "How's it going Jeff?" Ash asked sincerely.

"Real well" Jeff answered enthusiastically. "I'm ready to go. I feel great and can't wait for the season to get going."

"Good, good" Ash continued. "We're counting on you this year. As you know by letting O'Dougnohue become a free agent, we've cleared the path for you to become our closer from day one. We are confident that you can pick up where you left off Jeff, and contractually that puts us in an interesting situation and I'm sure you've been giving a lot of thought to it.

"Technically," Ash went on "you are still a rookie, yet you've had great success in the big leagues. You will probably be our stopper yet you are not established. With this in mind, we would like to offer you a base salary of $80,000 with bonuses of $5,000 every save over twenty and $2,000 for every game appeared in over forty. On the other side, we would want you to agree to a minor league contract of $35,000. In the event you were sent down."

Jeff did not like that last sentence and Ash could tell, but it was his job to throw it out there.

"Look, Gord," Jeff said after having made some quick calculations in his head and figuring that with thirty saves and sixty appearances he would make $150,000, "I'm conservative by nature and my main concern is a one way contract. Since we both believe I will be in the bigs and do well, that should be a moot point. However, I will concede a little on the money front. With your offer, I should realistically come close to $150,000 and I am willing to split the difference between the $80,000 and the $150,000 and take a one way guaranteed salary of $115,000 with no bonuses.

Ash did not expect his young star to think so logically. He wrongly believed that Jeff would only see the up-side and not take into account the minor league portion of the contract. All the baseball people in the organization were confident that Jeff would pick up where he left off, and in the long run, he would probably save the team some money, but he couldn't give in to the youngster quite so quickly. So after some minor bargaining, they settled on $112,500 and the first creative contract in Jeff's big league career was done.

The two men shook, each equally happy at what had transpired, the building block of a happy relationship, in what both sides hoped would be a long and successful career in Toronto. "Good luck this year," Ash said as Jeff left Engelbert and went to meet the guys at Hooters and enjoy some wings, a few beers and the great sights. It was one of the true pleasures of Spring.

Early on in Spring Training, a couple of things became apparent to Jeff. First, he was no longer just another person, or an unknown Minor Leaguer, he was a public figure and wherever he went in Dunedin, he was recognized. It felt nice and strange. He most enjoyed mingling with the kids, just as he had done in Knoxville and Syracuse. He knew he was now a man, or close to being one, yet he felt close to the kids, and found energy in their smiles, enthusiasm, and joy. He still felt like one of them, wanted to be one of them, but he knew that was no longer possible. Second, no matter what rumors circulated in the off season, the closer's role on the World Champion Toronto Blue Jays was Jeff Williams' to lose.

From the first intrasquad game he was being prepared. Last year he was simply thrown in by accident and let be. This year they would fine tune and make some adjustments. It was mostly the little things, such as fielding his position and holding runners close to first. They pretty much let his mechanics and pitching be. The coaching staff did not want to mess with that. It took his arm a few outings to feel loose as the indoor throwing he did over the Winter was not the same as being outside throwing off a real mound. The work he had done on his body up in Geneva was paying off, as he felt stronger and as resilient as ever.

Tracy had come down to Florida for the last ten days of Spring Training to be with Jeff and enjoy the Florida sun, dreaming of what the future held in store for them. The love between them was there and she did not doubt it, but the geographical distance and the uncertainty ate away at her daily. Being with Jeff and relaxing was a good tonic for her.

Each morning she would drop Jeff off at Grant Field and then go over to Clearwater Beach and soak up the sun before heading to the ball game whether it be in Dunedin, Clearwater, St Petersburg, or Tampa. At night they would have dinner on the beach or relax at the apartment. Each day he spent with Tracy, holding her, looking at her beautiful face, he fell deeper and deeper in love with her, realizing whole heartedly that there was no way of escaping it. Without talking about it they realized that this was the life they wanted, one which they would share together, one in which they would grow old together, have children and grandchildren to love, just as they had always been loved. It was in these terms that their minds worked, though neither one was yet twenty-two years old.

On March 30th, two days before Tracy was to return to Knoxville and three days before camp broke, in a burst of energy and courage, fueled by one too many cocktails, Jeff lifted Tracy up, put her on his shoulders and sprinted away from the Tiki Bar at the Adam's Mark hotel, and brought her out on to Clearwater Beach. Just as the magnificent Spring sun set over the Gulf of Mexico he threw himself at her feet and said to her.

"Tracy, my love, you are the most beautiful woman in the World. I love you very much and would like to ask for your hand in marriage, so we can share our lives together."

She could barely muster a yes as she broke down in tears of joy as she hugged and kissed Jeff. There is nothing in the World like the feeling of true love and if anyone looked in the eyes and hearts of Tracy and Jeff, it would be clear that it was there. The only damper would be in the midst of all this joy, they would be separated once again; but this time it was easier, made easier by the fact that they now knew that they would soon be together forever.

The news spread quickly to friends, family and teammates, all ecstatic and supportive. They planned on waiting until the season was over and figured that the middle of November in Knoxville should be fine. Jeff could now concentrate on his official rookie season and helping the Blue Jays defend their World Series Championship. He would let the rest fall into place and let the women relish in the planning.

As the Blue Jays broke camp, the team had not changed all that much. Whitt and Martinez were still behind the plate. Fernandez and Garcia up the middle and the Iorg and Mulliniks platoon at third was joined by rule five draftee Kelly Gruber. The outfield remained the same. The big change came at first where the beloved Chuggy Upshaw was traded to Cleveland to make room for two young sluggers who would platoon, Cecil Fielder and Fred McGriff. The pitching staff featured a rotation of Stieb, Clancy, Key, Cerruti, and Mike Taylor who mysteriously found command and control to go along with his 95 MPH fastball.

The bullpen had Jeff who would be set up by Pierce, back for one more year. Free agent veteran Steve Dunbar who was signed away from the Dodgers, and two hard throwing youngsters in Duane Ward and David Wells. It was the mix that all General Managers tried to put together: veterans, youngsters, lefties, righties, speed, and power. The Blue Jays headed up to Detroit, confident they had what it took to repeat as World Champions.

NINETEEN

Toronto picked up right where they left off winning four of their first six games on the road against Detroit and Cleveland. Jeff saved two games and felt great and full of confidence. Major League Baseball now had a different feel to it. The excitement, the joy, and the fun were still there and he loved every minute of it, but the reality of the situation had sunk in. He had felt pressure last year, but it was more of a pressure he put upon himself - nothing was expected of him. This season he was expected to perform, to save every game and to get the job done day in and day out. Inexperience could not be an excuse. The subtle reminders of making or breaking every game were around him, in the press and within the team. Jeff did not mind nor did he truly worry about this responsibility. He had just never really given much thought to it and to what would happen if he failed to be an effective pitcher.

As always, he missed Tracy enormously, but now he had some peace of mind and it made it easier to get through the day, yet the temptation which awaited him and every other Major League baseball player, every day, at every ballpark, and at every bar and restaurant in every city, would attack him and from time to time get the best of him. Jeff honestly felt that he was a good human being, devoted to his family and true to himself, but in the early months of the season, he gave himself one last hurrah, or so he reasoned as a way of justifying it to himself.

His downfall was probably deciding to share an apartment with Mike Taylor, whose million-dollar smile and athletic California body worked just as well in the show as it did for so many years in Knoxville. At first

Jeff tried to resist the many beautiful young girls who waited for them and at first he managed to do so. But for a two-month period he resisted nothing and ate up big league life and all he thought it was. The guilt was suffocating him. The only place where he found peace and relaxation was at the ballpark, where he took out all the anger at himself against the opposition and went through a twelve game stretch were he saved eleven games and did not give up one run.

It finally hit him one day in Baltimore, back home in early June with his family and fiancée who made the trip up, that his period of wildness must stop. The closeness and love attacked him deep down in his heart and broke it. It was now time for him to mend it and for the real Jeff to resurface.

Taylor the friend, Taylor the womanizer, had too many years of this life behind him, and in Jeff had found a partner, yet he saw what it was doing to him and somehow knew that he was partially to blame, and the big former football All-American felt badly. "Jeff," he said, "I'm sorry I've encouraged you to go out and party. Look I've got an idea, why don't we each get our own place, man we got the dough. Why don't you have Tracy come up for a while. I think it would do you both some good."

"I think you're right Mike, but don't blame yourself for what I did. I knew what I was doing and I have to live with it and have to make peace with it. I have to find a way to look at the woman I love and not break her heart like I have mine. I just hope it can be done."

Tracy had noticed some small changes in Jeff in Baltimore, he was a little more aggressive and not quite himself. The last night though when he asked her to come to Toronto for awhile, she could see the Jeff she knew, the caring loving and compassionate young man. But she had been around baseball, and she knew why he was doing this. Neither one had to say anything, as they fell asleep crying in each other's arms.

When you're not quite twenty-two, it's sometimes hard to understand that you have a long life ahead of you and that time can heal the many wounds which life inflicts. It would be a lesson that Jeff would have to learn on more than one occasion.

Jeff had found the peace and tranquility he was looking for with Tracy and the wounds started healing as he entered the All-Star break. Toronto had opened up a ten game lead over the Yankees and placed five players on the American League squad for the game in Montreal. Along with Jeff, who already had twenty-five saves, were Dave Stieb, Tony Fernandez, Jesse Barfield, and George Bell.

It was a glorious three days, built on the great tradition of baseball, family and fun. Jeff was truly in awe of the great players of whom he was now one. Nolan Ryan, George Brett, Gary Carter, Cal Ripken, and on and on. Jeff pitched one scoreless inning in an American League loss, but it didn't matter to Jeff. The highlight for Jeff was the re-creation of the Olympic plaza were the All-Star gala was held, outside Olympic Stadium in Montreal where the 1976 games were held.

Jeff had always loved the Olympics. No doubt his dual continent upbringing played an important role. He imagined what it would be like to walk into the stadium with every country in the world represented and participating in the greatest festival of them all. He had already participated in the greatest festivals baseball could offer, the World Series, and the All-Star game, but he believed that the Olympics were something completely different. He felt lucky to have come this close to the feeling.

The dog days of summer had little effect on the Blue Jays as they started running away with the AL East. On September 1st, the lead was up to fourteen games with both Barfield and Bell clubbing their thirty-fifth homerun. Stieb had fifteen wins and Taylor was the closest competition Jeff would have for rookie of the year as he had twelve wins and only five losses while averaging a strike out per inning.

Jeff, however, was magic, unthinkable magic when you consider where he was two years ago, but he already had thirty-seven saves and an ERA of 1.38. Tracy was spending more time in Knoxville preparing for their November 17th wedding, but her presence had the soothing effect Jeff was hoping for back in June, and Tracy had been just as happy.

When they clinched the division on September 18th, it gave them two weeks to prepare, set the rotation, and wait for the Twins and Angels to battle it out. Then they would try to do what no team since the Yankees a decade before had done and that is repeat as World Champions.

There are two schools of thought in sports: clinch early and get ready or take it down to wire and stay as sharp as possible. The Twins with their makeshift pitching staff had clinched the division on the second to last day of the season and attacked the Blue Jays with a level of zest and enthusiasm that they had not seen in a while. But Toronto's talent did manage to shine through and silence the upstart Twins. It took Toronto six games, and it wasn't easy, but the bats of rookies Fred McGriff and Cecil Fielder proved to be the difference. Jeff got in to only two games but saved them both.

Toronto was now off to the Big Apple to face the Mets who had easily disposed of the Dodgers in four straight games. They had a scintillating young pitching staff led by Dwight Gooden and Ron Darling, and a potent attack with Gary Carter, Keith Hernandez and Darryl Strawberry. The Blue Jays and their coaching staff did not feel comfortable going into this series after their performance, albeit victorious, against the Twins. They seemed to have lost their edge and sharpness--they were in a funk. That is as much as a funk you can be in when you make it to the World Series, and it showed from the first inning of the first game at the EX.

Even the crowd didn't show the same excitement they had the previous year against the Cardinals. It was as if victory was inevitable, but it was the contrary, for some inexplicable reason, the Blue Jays were destined to lose and they did. It was not easy for the Mets, but the outcome of the Series was never in doubt as the Mets celebrated after a game five 5-1 victory.

It was a bitter ending to the season for a team that had won one 102 games and romped through their division, and it was the first real taste of losing for most of these players. For Jeff, his career had pretty much been one success after another. Now both he and his teammates had a long off-season to contemplate what it would take for them to get back on top to where they all wanted to be, to where they had to be again, and to where they belonged.

It sometimes takes a step back in life to be able to go forward and surpass where you have been before. It takes the knowledge of what it feels like to lose, to be able to once again win. And to win again as a team is what they all wanted.

PART TWO

"I would do anything for love
I'd run right into hell and back
I would do anything for love
I'll never lie to you and that's a fact....
But I'll never stop dreaming of you
Every night of my life-
No way"

Meat Loaf and Jim Steinman

TWENTY

APRIL, 1989

It was one of those perfect early season West Coast trips. The weather was warm but not suffocating. After three cold and rainy games in Cleveland in cavernous Municipal Stadium, also known as The Mistake By The Lake, the players were all looking forward to a free Saturday night in Southern California following the afternoon game against the Angels.

The past year and a half had flown by for Jeff and Tracy. After the disappointing World Series loss to the Mets, they concentrated on finishing the preparations for the wedding. While Tracy relished in it, Jeff too found some pleasure and escape.

The wedding was beautiful, a true celebration and party, just the way they wanted. They incorporated Southern charm with Jewish tradition. Famiily, friends, and teammates who had come in from such places as Paris, Virginia, and Toronto had been able to celebrate with them. It was quite interesting watching Tracy's Uncle Bill from Memphis try to converse with Jeff's Aunt Dora from Paris while Mike Taylor listened and watched with a big grin on his face

He was perhaps most happy to see his two Hobart friends who had helped mold him into the young man he now was. Tim had come to Knoxville with his fiancée from Syracuse where he was working in the New York State Small Business Development Office. It was what he had wanted and he got it. Robin had driven in from Columbia where she was back home studying for a Masters degree in clinical psychology at the

University of South Carolina. Even with all the love Jeff had for Tracy, seeing Robin's smile touched him in a small place in his heart that he had reserved just for her, just as he had told her the night she fell asleep in his arms after celebrating the national championship at Hobart.

It was not easy for Robin to see Jeff marrying another woman. She still loved Jeff but tried hard not to show it. Tracy seemed lovable, likeable and pretty, but Robin was jealous and it hurt. It hurt her more since she was still alone and she felt old, much older than the first time that Jeff had kissed her. But she wasn't old, because if she were old she would know that at twenty-three her life had barely begun.

Tracy and Jeff went to France for their honeymoon. She had never been abroad and it was a chance for her to meet the rest of Jeff's family on his father's side, and to discover Paris, the city of love. Through Tracy's youthful, inexperienced and exuberant eyes, Jeff rediscovered Paris in all the beauty, charm, magic, and spirit in the City of Lights.

The brisk November weather did not prevent them from roaming the streets of Paris, up and down the Champs Elysées, avenue Foch, Montmartre, St. Michel. They shopped in the famous Galleries Lafayette, gazed at the Pompidou Center, took a night time boat ride on the Seine in a Bateau Mouches and even strolled through the wall to wall hookers on rue St Denis. Downtown Knoxville Paris was not.

Jeff took his young bride to the wooden building on rue Basfrois in the eleventh arrondissement where his father had grown up. The toilet was in the courtyard and the small two-room apartment was three floors up. It had housed up to seven people. Amazing that his Dad had grown up there, even more amazing that this building was still standing and that people still lived there.

They spent three days visiting the Loire Valley and the magnificent castles which Jeff had learned about back in fifth grade at the French Lycée. The castles were one aspect of his history classes which had captivated him, but in all his trips to France had never managed to visit. They spent three days visiting Blois, Azez-Le-Rideau, Chenonceaux and the grand-daddy of them all, Chambord. Hand in hand they walked and gawked at the magnificent structures. Jeff was a ten-year-old kid again with the memories of his history class now alive in front of him. He was in awe and it showed on his face.

The day before they headed back to North America, Jeff had managed to meet up with Dédé, Chiche, and Gilles Thomas for a quick lunch and some reminiscing. It had been almost two and half years and they hadn't changed much since Jeff left them soon after the European Championships in Barcelona. They were still playing, as were most of the PUC and the National team, and while they had not quite been able to duplicate the success of that magical summer, they assured Jeff that French Baseball was improving, and if ever he wanted back in, they would try to find him a place on the team.

When it was time to go home, their home was now Oldsmar, Florida, in a brand new house they had bought in a country club community, about twenty minutes from Grant Field, the Spring home of the Blue Jays. It was big and spacious but not extravagant, with a small pool and a backyard that overlooked the eleventh green. They used the off-season to set up a home and start their life together. Jeff enjoyed the free time of the off season. He took a course at the University of South Florida, inching closer to his degree, worked out with many of the other Blue Jay Major and Minor leaguers in the area. He was reaping the benefits of being a professional athlete and the life that went along with it. In early January, he signed a two year $1.2 million contract. He was a millionaire at twenty-two.

The 1988 season proved to be a transitional and disappointing season for the Blue Jays. Garth Iorg retired, Rance Mulliniks, became a pinch hitter and Kelly Gruber took over at third. Jesse Barfield missed most of the season with an injury and the team struggled to find a designated hitter.

The starting rotation had remained intact, but was inconsistent. Taylor was unable to regain his outstanding form of the previous season and bounced between the rotation and the bullpen before being sent back down to AAA where he pitched well before a September call up; but when it was all said and done his contribution was minimal. Big lefty David Wells had moved in from the bullpen to assume his spot in the rotation and pitched well. Steve Dunbar, the free agent who had done admirable work in middle relief the previous year struggled early and underwent shoulder surgery in June, creating a void in relief. With the team ten games out and in third place on August 15th, Mike Pierce was released, and replaced on the roster by a Venezuelan lefty flame thrower, named Miguel Perez who had cruised through the system striking out over a batter an inning. The team was reloading some guns and looking ahead to the following season.

The release of Pierce got to Jeff and he was mad. Mad at the Jays' for releasing him, mad at Pierce for not pitching better, and mad at himself for reasons he did not know. Maybe he thought back to watching the former Cy Young winner in an Orioles uniform, dominating hitters and controlling the game, or taking a young green kid under his wing and teaching him what it was like and what it took to be a Major League pitcher. Jeff was losing a friend, a teacher and an idol and he did not like the feeling. The old lefty had a long and great career and it was time to move on. Perhaps, Jeff saw the eventual end to his career, or perhaps it was something else. Whatever it was, it made him mad.

"Look Jeff," Pierce said "Don't worry about me and for sure don't feel bad, I lost whatever I had in my left arm, the team has treated me great and they've been patient. There is a moment, and it will come for you too, when it is time to move aside and make room for some young blood, some young cocky son of a bitch who throws smoke. It's in many ways what makes baseball great, it's like passing the torch, a sort of rebirth of the game that keeps the tradition alive, just like Spring Training. You're still young and you got a few hundred saves left in you, but one day you will do with others what I have tried to do with you, Wardo, Key, Cerutti, and Boomer. It's what makes baseball great; you must always care about the game. On top of that I'll still be around from time to time, you ain't getting rid of me that easy."

And so Jeff and the rest of the team pushed on, finished in third and for the first time since the early expansion years the organization was happy that the season was over. Through all the turmoil and disappointment Jeff had still managed to save thirty-seven games. The nucleus of a great team was still there and that gave everyone hope, hope that 1989 would be different.

The off-season was once again spent in Florida, living the Florida lifestyle that both Tracy and Jeff now enjoyed, the slower pace of life and time together. They even talked about starting a family and the thought of little kids crawling around and enriching their life excited them. They traveled to Rugby for Thanksgiving, made a quick trek to Toronto to rent a condo for the season, and over the Christmas holidays, they joined Jeff's parents and sister out in California to see Marc play in the Rose Bowl against the University of Southern California. Marc was now a senior and starting tight-end for the number eight ranked Wolverines. His future still rested in baseball which was his true love, but he derived an almost intellectual joy of football, with the preparation, the detail and the importance of every component of the machine needing to work in harmony, to achieve the end result: victory.

Marc had been drafted by the Oakland Athletics in the ninth round after his junior year. However, he was not overly impressed with their offer of $12,000 and their refusal to allow him to leave early at the end of the season for football. So he went back to school vowing to improve on his all-conference baseball season and get closer to his goal of following his big brother to the Major Leagues.

And then, once again before Jeff knew it, it was time for Spring Training with all the hopes and aspirations, fun and sweat that it brings. It was his third big league camp, and as he looked around the clubhouse at Engelbert Complex and the fifty players who had assembled, he realized that he was no longer the new kid on the block. He had moved up the experience chart. The new players in camp, some of whom were older than he, others whom he had crossed briefly in the minors were now looking up to him. He was still only twenty-three but becoming what they call in baseball terms a young veteran and he enjoyed such a role on the team. It was a role in which he blossomed while at Hobart and was thrust into while in France. At the professional level, he had never been in such a position.

It was with this outlook on baseball, and peace of mind in his personal life that he embarked on his third full Major League season, now almost a month under way and going along great. Cito Gaston had taken over from Bobby Cox, who moved on to the Atlanta Braves, and the team was responding well to Cito's laid back style with an 18-9 record.

After two blown saves in his first three outings, Jeff had saved nine straight giving him ten in total a mere twenty-seven games into the season. He was basking in the California sun in the visitor's bullpen as the rejuvenated Blue Jay line-up was pounding Angels' starter Chuck Finley when the phone rang and as always was picked up by bullpen coach John Sullivan. No one really paid much attention to the fact the call was taking longer than usual, nor to the pained look on his face. When he hung up, he went over to Jeff and told him that Cito wanted to see him.

From time to time Cito would ask Jeff into the dugout to ask him how he felt and if he needed more work, and after three days without getting into a game, he figured that would be the subject. But when Cito ushered him into the clubhouse in the middle of a game, he feared the worst, especially when he was met by Pat Gillick, his old battery mate Buck Martinez who was now a team broadcaster, and travelling secretary John Brioux who were all there. He figured he had just been traded, but it was much worse than he could have imagined.

"Jeff," Gillick said sorrowfully, but to the point. "I'm afraid Tracy's been in a car accident on the Gardner," referring to one of Toronto's main highways, and she's in bad shape. We don't have many details as we just got the news ourselves. John has got you on the next flight back to Toronto tonight and Buck will take you back to the hotel to get your stuff and take you to the airport. I'll be in touch and if there is anything we can do let us know."

Jeff quickly discarded his uniform and took a quick shower in his dumbfounded haze. The call to the hospital didn't shed much light, as all the doctor would say is that she was in critical condition and that she was hit by a drunk driver. He encouraged Jeff to get there as soon as possible, which was what he was doing.

He called both sets of parents before making his way to the airport with Martinez. After what seemed like hours, he collapsed in his first class seat hoping that the sleeping pill he took would get him some rest and knock him out for the cross continent flight. He settled into a restless and shallow sleep. There was no way of him getting the picture of Tracy lying in the hospital, helpless and hurt, out of his mind. He wanted above all to think of her smile and her laugh, her touch and her warmth, her life and energy, not her pain and suffering, both their suffering.

The Air Canada red eye touched down at Pearson Airport at 5:45 a.m. and Jeff quickly jumped into a limo which would take him to Toronto General. The ride down the 427 and then up the Gardner was moving in slow motion for Jeff as he wondered if he had just passed the accident site. Finally, he knew they were close as they passed the EX and then their soon to be new home, at SkyDome, but baseball was the farthest thing from his mind.

By 6:45 a.m., Jeff was in the elevator making his way to the sixth floor intensive care unit. Dr Allen Gross, the Blue Jay's team doctor had been contacted by Gillick and had met Jeff at the hospital. "Jeff," Gross said compassionately, "I want you to realize that she is in very bad shape and it is touch and go. I don't mean to scare you but be prepared for a bad sight." All Jeff could muster was a nod.

He was not prepared for such a diagnosis, and the doctor's words did not sink in until he saw the love of his life, lying there with casts and bandages, unconscious with tubes hooked up to her. He looked at her beautiful face which looked so peaceful, and felt so helpless and hurt that all he could do was cry.

It seemed apparent that Dr Gross was preparing Jeff for the worst, but the young man could not accept it. He needed her and loved her and was afraid that he would never hold her again. At about 8:30 a.m., he fell asleep holding her hand and dreamt of the first night they met at the Wild Horse back in Knoxville. His mind filled with pictures of that first dance and first kiss. It suddenly felt like a lifetime ago.

By 11:00 a.m., both Jeff's and Tracy's parents had arrived at the hospital, and just as Jeff had been, they were in horror of the sight in front of them. The vivacious and loving young woman with all of life seemingly stripped from her, as she lay limp and lifeless. Jeff was too drained and wiped out to cry anymore. No one knew who should support whom and who should try to lift whose spirits. There was a lot of silence.

From the gloom in the doctors' voices, it became apparent that the inevitable, yet unspeakable and unthinkable decision may have to be made, but no one was ready to even discuss that. However, after a week, there was no progress. In fact, if anything, the doctors had agreed that Tracy's situation was even worse, if that was possible. Worst of all they agreed that it was irreversible. She was so helpless, still beautiful and peaceful, but stripped of her life. It was now time to say goodbye.

It has to be the hardest thing for any parent to do, to outlive a child and for Jeff the thought of saying goodbye to his only true love was too much to fathom, but each person made their peace as best they could and realized that the decision had to be made. At twenty-three Tracy was too young to die and at twenty-three Jeff was too young to be a widower.

TWENTY ONE

The small church in Rugby was packed on the sorrowful occasion with many of the family and friends who celebrated Tracy and Jeff's wedding, such a short time ago. The Blue Jays charter had detoured to Knoxville on their way to Texas. Mike Pierce traveled up from Dunedin where he was now a minor league coach. Tim flew down from Syracuse, and Robin drove over from Columbia where she was still studying. It was really Robin's smile and hugs that gave Jeff the strength to stand up and talk.

He slowly made his way to the front of the room, straightened his tie, cleared his throat and looked out at those gathered and attempted to find some of the poise and confidence that made him the best relief pitcher in baseball. In a low voice that resounded in the silence he began.

"From the first time I saw Tracy's smile, I knew that she was special. I didn't know that she would become the most special person in my life, my wife and best friend, but she did. She had that effect on everyone, wherever she went. She was sunshine, pure and simple. I know that the happiest moments in my life were when I was with her. Without her, there will always be a part of me that will be empty, and that will never ever be replaced. Her kindness and beauty were taken away from all of us much too soon. She had so much life left in her, so much more to give." Jeff choked back tears and continued on.

"I remember the first time I held her, that amazing feeling brought warmth to my heart and a tear of joy to my eye, and now when I say goodbye and hold her one more time it will have the same effect, and I guess that will make me a lucky man. Goodbye my love, may you be watched over and may you watch over us. I will always love you."

Nothing more had to be said. It was short and sweet, full of emotion and love. The only thing left to do was to have one big cry, and they all did. When it was over, he sat alone in the dark with his eyes shut and tears streaming down his cheeks. He missed her so much. He doubted whether the hurt would or could ever go away. He would never let his beautiful wife's memory fade.

The music rang out in his mind and a picture of her magical smile and her soft touch played tricks with him. He pictured them dancing in the sand, holding each other, never wanting to let go, but it was over and nothing could change that. He had the love and support of his family and the ability to sink himself in his profession, his sport, his game. He was lucky that he was not alone, yet ultimately it was up to him to push on forward and continue his life, to regain his emotional strength and become the man he knew he could be.

TWENTY TWO

JANUARY 1991

On the balcony of his spacious condo on Clearwater Beach, sipping his morning Mountain Dew, and overlooking the Gulf of Mexico, Jeff sat down groggy eyed just like every morning, a childhood habit he would never outgrow. He looked out on the beach, a young man's habit he wished had never started and didn't know if he wanted to end. He looked down at the spot where he had proposed to Tracy. He looked down there every morning he was there, not sure if it was a habit he wanted to break or one he never wanted to give up. It had almost been two years and he had not been able to start letting go. He couldn't wait for his fifth big league season to start so he could get lost in it, get lost in the Game and all of its' magic and not the cruel bitter reality which he had now come to despise. It was so unlike him to be bitter. It was untrue to his personality and unfair to himself.

At 10:00 a.m., he jogged down Mandalay Boulevard, passing the snowbirds, early Spring Breakers and the tourists on their way to the beach. He arrived at the 7-Eleven and picked up a copy of *USA TODAY BASEBALL WEEKLY* and stared at the big color cover of himself in his white uniform, on the mound, pensive and sweaty. The caption surprised him, but it was there for everyone to see: THE BEST EVER! The cashier did not make the association as Jeff threw his dollar bill down.

He made it back to the condo, flung off his shoes and headed through the den, dodging his clothes, old newspapers and other stuff until he made

146

it back to the balcony. He started reading the feature story by Lisa Winston, the Minor League beat reporter who had followed Jeff's career from his first Instructional League. She lobbied hard for this story which would normally have gone to one of the Major League reporters and she got it.

"Sutter, Fingers, Smith, Gossage, all great relievers, but now when you talk about stoppers, there really is just one name and that is Jeff Williams. At just twenty-five and four plus seasons in the uniform of the Toronto Blue Jays, his numbers are not only unparalleled and unprecedented but almost unimaginable: 169 saves, 24 wins 4 losses and an ERA of 1.53. Over that span he has pitched 282 innings and struck out 299 batters. Simply put the best numbers ever, and he is getting better.

If you ask those who know and love him, you find out quickly that it is not his pitching which truly makes him unique, but his heart, his compassion, his drive and as Williams says himself, his unwillingness to forget, both good and bad how he got where he is today. That place is his balcony on Clearwater Beach looking out on to the Gulf of Mexico, looking for answers or a sign. Yet for a man so confident in his profession, he is not sure to what questions he needs an answer, or what form that sign may take, but every morning he looks out there. "It's my quiet time, my thinking time and my remembering time. It's very important to me."

His path, just like he is, was unique. His on field battles and off-field tragedies turned him into a man when he was still a boy. "The first time I saw him pitch, I knew he was a special pitcher. The first time I talked to him, I knew he was smart, smarter than most, but it is his way with people and the good feeling people get around him that make him so special," said Ben Adams, Toronto's International Scouting Director who signed Williams as an undrafted free agent when he was playing in Europe. While scouts are sometimes biased, these sentiments are echoed by others.

"No one knew who he was, so I figured I'd try to help him out a bit, maybe take him under my wing and show him the ropes, just like the veterans did for me in Baltimore. You know baseball is like that, you gotta nurture the young and show them the game. Jeff wasn't even twenty-one when he got called up, but you wouldn't know it from his poise and his willingness to learn. He had confidence, but not the cocky confidence you often see in young players. I was old enough to be his Dad and I hope I taught him something about baseball and about being a big leaguer, but I know he taught me more. He showed me how to be a friend and a good person. He's the best." That was former Cy Young winner Mike Pierce, a teammate of Jeff's with the Blue Jays.

It was early in 1989 that his life changed. No rookie of the year award or World Series ring could help him or make him feel better. At twenty-three, his young bride Tracy was fatally injured in a car crash. "I think it was the most devastating thing that could have happened to me," Williams said recently looking out into the Gulf of Mexico, with an empty stare. "I still can't sleep at night," he continued. "She is always on my mind and my heart is still broken. I really don't want to feel sorry for myself, but sometimes it's hard not to. Without my family, her family, my teammates and the Blue Jays' organization, I'm really not sure where I would be. The Blue Jays have always worried about Jeff the person over Jeff the player, and it is probably because of that, that I have been able to keep my game up and pitch so well."

Great is probably a better description. In 1989, despite the tragedy and missing three weeks of the season, he still recorded fourty-four saves and helped lead the team to their second World Series Championship. Even though Toronto missed the post season the following year Williams was not worried.

"Believe me he said, I love winning, it is a great feeling, but so is doing something I love everyday. We had a great run and I know we are ready to come back this year. We are a young team and there is plenty of time for more success."

It is often hard to remember that he is only twenty-five years old. Thrown into a World Series at twenty, widowed at twenty-three, but he is still a kid at heart and his younger brother, a minor leaguer with the Phillies, echoes this. "Sometimes, when everything is perfect, it's as if we turned back the clock twelve years and we're just playing catch and hacking around like kids with no worries just having fun. It is at those times that I know my big brother is ok and will be fine, because it is at that time when I see Jeff, the real Jeff. It is at that time that I cry and hurt for him."

"I know how people feel by the way they look at me, and on one the hand I appreciate it, yet on the other hand I have to get on living. I am still young at heart, I still feel like a kid. I have plenty of saves left in my arm and a full life ahead of me to live."

It is refreshing to hear these words, as a biased fan, which a reporter should not be. I want this young man to come back off the field, to be happy and get what he desires. There have been rumblings that he was getting ready to walk away from the game, to leave it as quickly as it found him.

"Am I planning to leave baseball?" "No," Williams answered himself a question which was not asked. "I love baseball and what I am doing," he continued. "But I know and believe that there is more to life than what goes on between the white lines. I know that there is a lot more for me to accomplish outside the game. While playing professional baseball was always something I dreamt about, I never though of it as my destiny or my calling. It is something that I will always cherish, but when the time comes for me to leave, whether it be after this season or ten years from now, I know that I will be content and happy."

The article was pretty much what Jeff had expected. He was still a great pitcher and loved the game, but he felt there was more to life, but he wasn't quite sure what. Love-- yes, but could he and would he love again? He hadn't even tried and really did not want to get close to anyone. He continued on with the article.

"It was weird, but we were like best friends from the day we met. I mean I was a little apprehensive, being from the inner city of Syracuse," said Tim Saunders, Jeff's roommate in College." I sort of expected a D.C preppie-boy type. You know everything I wasn't. And aside from being an athlete, he was sort of everything I wasn't but he was also everything I could have asked for. He was tolerant, giving, smart and brought everyone he came into contact with up to another level. When I watch him on the field or read about him, I can see that he still does it. It is with complete certainty that because of the way he helped me look at things that I am where I am today," said the youngest city councilman in the history of the city of Syracuse.

"That's my boy," Jeff said out loud as he attacked the last paragraph.

With Spring Training ten days away, the Blue Jays are looking to get back to the World Series and need their young stopper to help them get there. "We are hungry again." said Williams. "I can't wait for the season to start." The excitement in his voice was evident, as the young superstar seemed to have found an enthusiasm for the game which even he didn't realize he still had.

When you're twenty-five, a widower, and a Major League closer, it could be easy to forget who you truly are, but Jeff Williams has not forgotten. He is true to himself, true to his family and friends, and a joy to anyone who meets him. I can vouch for that."

Jeff took a deep breath as he put the paper down, looking out on to the Gulf of Mexico. For the first time a smile was mixed with his tears and then he whispered. "This one's for you Tracy."

One thousand miles away, on a big oak rocking chair on the balcony of an old Southern Mansion, a young woman surrounded by big willow trees, clad in jean shorts, a t-shirt and a Blue Jays' cap, sat crying as she too put down the article, just as unsure of her future as Jeff was. She was crying for every reason and no reason. She still loved Jeff and knew that their bond could never be broken. There in Columbia, South Carolina, Robin looked into space and cried just as Jeff was doing in Clearwater, Florida.

TWENTY THREE

As he approached the twelve foot high sliding players' gate at Dunedin Stadium, the early morning spring sun was shining down on this magical little place, the small piece of heaven were Jeff always felt great. He said hello to the elderly security guard as he drove his blue Honda Accord into the players' parking lot. He then signed autographs for the fifty or so fans who were already waiting outside at 7:45 a.m..

Then he went into the clubhouse, put on his warm-up shorts and t-shirt, grabbed a donut and Mountain Dew and headed out to the empty stadium to read the paper. Florida in March and the charm of the small stadium, with the beautiful green grass tucked away in this sleepy residential community, gave him peace of mind and relaxed him.

Camp was breaking today and the clubhouse was busy with the packing and loading of the two big trucks that would head up North with equipment and personal items for the season. Traditionally the last items to be loaded would be the street hockey nets and sticks that were used for the afternoon pick up games in the players' parking lot.

The team was now in place as they got ready for opening day. Pat Borders was entrenched as the starting catcher. John Olerud, the wonderkid with the sweet swing and quiet personality would be at first, Ed Sprague would be at third, getting his first full shot at replacing Kelly Gruber. Roberto Alomar and Manny Lee would patrol the middle infield. The outfield was solid with Joe Carter, Devon White and Candy Maldonado while Dave Winfield was brought in to be the designated hitter that they had so desperately been missing the last two years.

The pitching staff had only subtle changes. The starters would be free agent Jack Morris along with Jimmy Key, David Wells, Todd Stottlemyre and rookie fireballer Steve Karsay. The bullpen had Jeff being set up by Duane Ward, rookie Mike Timlin and lefties Tony Castillo and Pete Duvall. There were only a handful of players left from the first World Championship team of five years ago. The transition had been slow, piece by piece until a new team, with a new nucleus was formed; and so was the world of professional sports, continuous transition and change.

For someone who so enjoyed people, Jeff cherished these quiet moments. There would not be many more over the next year and a half. Sitting down the third base line, everything seemed so clear and simple in the empty little park. There was sun, there was a beautiful green field, an old fashioned wooden fence with a Coca-Cola and Sonny's BBQ billboard mixed in with about thirty-five other signs. The half field adjacent to the stadium, where pitchers worked on their fielding practice was empty. But amidst the tranquility and beauty, there was an underlying fact, and that was that It was now time to get to work. It was time for the grueling one hundred and sixty-two game season to start. It was time to win.

TWENTY FOUR

PITTSBURGH, PA

OCTOBER, 1991

The small section of Blue Jay Fans, mostly family and front office staff, wearing big foam bird heads, that had become all the rage in Toronto, stood and clapped. They were a blue oasis in a black and gold desert of the hometown Pirates' crowd. They cheered as their Blue Jays came to bat in the top of the twelfth inning of what would be the greatest World Series game of all time. It was game seven and the score was tied at two. It had been that way since the third inning almost four hours ago. It was now 1:12 a.m. when Devon White bounced the first pitch up the middle and into centerfield off former Blue Jay Jim Gott, now in his third inning of work. Roberto Alomar followed with a hit-and-run single that put White on third.

The boisterous and chilled Pirate fans fell silent in cavernous Three Rivers Stadium as Joe Carter stepped to the plate. He took two mighty swings and fell behind quickly two strikes. The Pirate infielders took a small step back, still ready to nail White at the plate, but that didn't matter. Carter sailed the next pitch deep to left field for a three run homer. The World Championship title was almost on its way back to Toronto.

Jeff Williams took a deep breath as he strode out to the mound, three outs away from the World Championship. It was his fourth inning of work, the longest outing of his Major League career and the culmination of his best season yet. The mental and physical rebirth he had experienced in the

Spring carried him all season long to this point. He had recorded fifty-two saves, had three wins, no losses. In sixty-eight innings, he had an ERA of 1.46, gave up just forty-three hits, walked seventeen and struck out seventy-nine.

Of everyone, Jeff was probably the most amazed person at what had transpired over the last six months. As he took his place on the mound, he felt good and he felt confident. It was the most natural place for him to be. The outcome of the game was not in doubt to Jeff, but to know where to go from here was. It was going to be the time to fulfill a childhood dream more important than being a baseball player. He just needed to make sure the time was right.

Before he knew it, Jeff was under the pile of his teammates. Barry Bonds was barely out of the batter's box after striking out on three pitches. The Blue Jays were once again World Champions, but this time Jeff was not the young wide-eyed phenom, he was their leader, the star of the team and perhaps the best pitcher in the Major Leagues. It would soon be time to test the World.

TWENTY FIVE

"Un carnet s'il vous plait," Jeff said to the Métro worker. Then armed with his most important tool, his Métro tickets, Jeff could get on with enjoying Paris. Taxis were sometimes quicker but to really feel Paris, you had to take the Métro. For his whole life, Jeff would have engraved in his mind walking up the Métro stairs at Place Voltaire as a five-year-old, and seeing all the lights, the cafés and the people, on his way to his grandmother's house. Twenty-one years later, that was the Paris he remembered. It was the Paris of his childhood.

He had landed at Charles De Gaule earlier in the day and went to his Aunt's apartment where he attempted to sleep off some of the jet lag. He took a late afternoon run along Ledru Rolin and around Place de La Bastille passing over the Seine and in front of the new Opera. This got his body going again and then, still jet-lagged and out of whack, he headed out into Paris as he continued his re-birth.

The Métro was the same as he remembered it. An amalgamation of races, classes and ages. Some going, some coming, some happy and some sad. In one corner there was a group of teenage girls dancing and singing the *Hokey Pokey* as if it was some new fad that no one else knew about yet. On the other end of the car, by the door, a drunk was lecturing to everyone about the benefits of anarchy as he cracked open another Kronenbourg beer. This was Paris and Jeff loved it.

He was not quite sure where he wanted to go. He had thought about getting off at Odéon, in the Latin Quarter and getting a bite and a cocktail at the Pub St Germain, just like he had done on so many occasions with

Moggle. The area was always full of life with students from the Sorbonne and tourists. It was also next door to where Anna Leudi's, the Brazilian model's apartment was, and this brought back memories that Jeff almost didn't remember he had.

However, in mid route, he changed his mind and headed to the Champs-Elysées. There was nothing more breathtaking or inspiring than the Champs at night. The lights, the people and of course the Arc de Triomphe coming into view as the escalator made it's way to street level from the Franklin D. Roosevelt Métro stop. It was amazing. Jeff had walked down the Champs many times, but each time was like magic, a jolt of energy. For some reason this time, it meant even more.

He walked up the Champs as his mind wandered back to the last pitch in Pittsburgh and the World Championship he had so much wanted to taste again. He had accomplished more at twenty-six, than almost any pitcher had accomplished in a career. Three World Championships, one World Series MVP, Rookie of the Year, four All Star game appearances, one Cy Young and a league MVP. It was surreal and unbelievable to the young man who still viewed himself as a seventeen-year-old wide eyed freshman at Hobart College.

He made his way up the famous boulevard, just near the Arc itself and entered the American Drugstore, a place his Mom had often taken him and his siblings for burgers and shakes. He peered in and saw baseball hats being sold for thirty bucks a shot. He made his way inside to the newsstand where he picked up a few postcards and out of the corner of his eye spotted the *Sports Illustrated* with him jumping into Pat Border's arms. He chuckled and purchased a copy.

The Chicago Pizza Factory was just off the Champs-Elysées on Rue de Ponthieu. Not much had changed inside since his days with the PUC and hanging out there with Moggle. The girls were still beautiful, the food overpriced and the music and décor very American. Sporting events were still piped in on the televisions in the bar area. The only big difference now was that he was there on the screen pitching in the World Series as they replayed the games, but no one seemed to make the connection and he for sure didn't care.

Even with the crowd settling in for a Friday night of fun, he found a seat at the bar and ordered a vodka and 7UP. He felt several sets of eyes upon him, and they were. At just under six feet and one hundred and ninety pounds, Jeff was not huge, but there was no mistaking his athletic body. With his faded blue jeans and white golf shirt he stuck out, in a nice way, from the more trendy Parisian fashions. His only bit of glamour was his first World Series ring, which when he wore it, he wore it proudly-though he generally stayed away from jewelry. One thing which did stick out was his Big League swagger, which no player can unlearn and most don't realize they have.

The mix of jetlag and vodka gave Jeff a strange yet good sensation as he flicked through the pages of *Sports Illustrated*, checking out the pictures, not bothering to read the words he had read so many times before, just told differently. He took a few more sips and looked around at the girls and guys partying and it made him feel good. He felt like one of the crowd and hoped to forget about baseball for a few days. But they wouldn't let him.

"Hey, you're the guy who beat my Pirates," a stunning bartender with short auburn hair and flashing plenty of cleavage came over and said to Jeff, as she pointed to the TV, "and that's you up there."

Indeed it was. The seductive look and moves said it all, but Jeff didn't really want to talk to her and for once the part of his brains not located in his pants might just win out. He had seen her type so often, and at times indulged, but not right now. He made some small talk, copped a few peeks at her breasts, which she did a poor job concealing in her tight minidress, as she plopped down a double and told him she'd catch up to him later.

Then a family from Toronto came up and asked for some autographs and took a few pictures. He took a few minutes to talk to them. He really didn't mind that much as he felt it was important to be accessible to the fans, as he wanted it that way growing up. Tonight though, he sort of just wanted to be left alone to drink and soak up Paris. He wanted to have fun on his terms, with no constraints or obligations.

He had been at Chicago's for about an hour and a half and wasn't sure if he wanted to stay. He felt a combination of fatigue and adrenaline, a dangerous mix. He decided to get up, stroll around and case out the joint. It was now 8:30 p.m. and the place was crowded with drinkers at the bar and eaters in the restaurant, with a line-up to get in. Jeff felt good about the place and about the night. Things were happening. He quickly made up his mind to stay and enjoy, even if that simply meant drinking and watching the girls. He could think of worse things to do and worse places to be and since his trip was only a week long, it would be a shame to sleep it away.

Jeff found a corner from where he had a pretty good vantage point. He ordered another drink and decided to make himself comfortable. He found a certain joy in the situation, being out by himself in relative anonymity, drinking and calmly carousing. He had found the joie de vivre that he had started to recapture the previous Spring and to fill some of the emptiness which had overcome him since Tracy's death. He could never stop thinking about her, and believed deep down that she was still close by. And now as the alcohol started to set in, he toasted her and went on to have the fun that he wanted and that deep down he knew she wanted him to have.

At the table to his right, he noticed three American girls speaking a pretty good College French to a couple of Parisian guys. They were no more than twenty-one, cute in a preppie type of way trying to break out of their shell in Paris. Jeff knew this type well from Hobart. They were the same girls who wore turtlenecks and sweaters around campus, and would then, during Spring Break take part in the wet t-shirt contests at the Candy Store in Ft Lauderdale in order to prove their maturity, independence and in some way their sexual awakening. Paris was filled with such Yanks.

Such Yanks like him who came to Paris to discover a new World. One filled with dreams. One filled with potential. A World where all is possible and the enthusiasm, exuberance and determination of youth can accomplish anything.

He felt like judging them, but he could not. He felt like talking to them but was not sure if he should. He felt like walking over and hugging the young blonde who looked as though she had just walked out of *Seventeen* magazine with her short black dress and tighly pulled back hair and telling her not to change. To stay young and playful. But who was he to do so. For a split second her eyes caught his. Tracy!! He almost yelled out. She smiled and turned back to her conversation as if she had read his mind.

"May I stand here?" An elegant and striking young woman asked Jeff in almost perfect English. Jeff had noticed her earlier. She was with a group of about ten professional looking young French and Brits who were out enjoying a Friday night. Though she was not beautiful, she carried herself in a beautiful way. She wore a pair of tailored black pants and a black sweater, both of which accentuated her curves as her jet black curls cascaded below her shoulders. She did not have a model's body or face but her "tenue" as the French would say gave her a certain magnetism.

Jeff asked her a few questions, protecting himself from her inquisition and trying to learn more about this intriguing young lady. Her name was Farida and she was also twenty-six and was born in Algeria, moving to Paris when she was five. She had traveled extensively through the U.S, hence her perfect English. She now worked for an American Law firm just off the Champs.

It was now her turn to get answers.

"Who are you?" she asked bluntly yet affectionately as Jeff realized he was dealing with one tough cookie who was probably unimpressed with him, but he didn't care, in fact it was refreshing. "All my friends noticed you when you walked in." She continued, but no one recognized you. You were just sitting there, minding your own business, yet people kept coming up to you asking for an autograph or a handshake."

"Well, Jeff answered, I guess to some people, I'm sort of a celebrity and simply showed her the *Sports Illustrated* cover that was beside him. They pressed each other for more information and listened attentively as though they were old friends. The conversation alternated between French and English. Jeff brushed up on his French which he was glad he still mastered and Farida was impressed by an American who spoke real French.

They mingled with the rest of the group and Jeff took his turn buying the pitchers of Long Island Iced Tea. He never liked to flaunt his wealth. He remembered his Dad's background, plus he simply was not that kind of person. Back home everyone knew how much he made, but here he was just one of the gang and he was having the most fun he had had in a while. Part of him wanted to buy rounds for everyone all night. In his jeans and shirt, no one really could imagine that he made more in two weeks than the rest made combined in a year.

The music blasted with the soundtrack from Grease and as the waitresses danced around in their poodle skirts, Jeff and Farida, belted out an alcohol induced version of *Summer Lovn'* as the rest of the group sang back up. Here, in Paris, he could, and would do as he pleased. He was not under the Big League microscope of Toronto where a couple of players had been shipped out because of their antics at the Loose Moose. Tonight, he felt like he was back home or at school with the guys, a return to innocence where fun was the only concern.

Suddenly he looked around and could not find Farida. An uneasy feeling came over him, just like when he was first separated from Tracy. His feelings were not of lust but of caring. He knew right then that she was a hold'em girl. She soon reappeared and returned to his side. A sense of relief came over him. Together, they continued their own conversation and mingled with the rest of the group in between. The night progressed and the alcohol continued to take hold of them. The two newfound friends found a corner where they sat and kissed until two in the morning. They left and found a hotel room on one of the quiet streets just off the Champs. They simply fell asleep in each other's arms.

When he woke up at 6:00 a.m. she was already gone. Jeff left the hotel with a sad and empty feeling. He walked up the almost deserted Champs Elysées toward the Métro. He thought about how many people came in and out of lives never to be seen again. He remembered Anna Leudi the Brazilian model he spent a week with and then one day she was gone. People he met in bars and airplanes, gone. He remembered a night in New York when he met two lovable Irish girls who sang, smiled and danced. They were simply doing "the crack" as the Irish called it. They asked him to stay and party but he left. He was gone. There were hundreds of people. Did they ever think of him? Did Cary Butwin, the first girl he ever kissed when he was eleven at Camp Olympus think of him? He thought of her. He thought of her as well as so many other friends. Sometimes it was a dream, out of nowhere or simply a memory of a long lost friend who he never thought of then boom, they were back in his life. Farida was now part of these memories. He entered the Métro and went back to his Aunt's. He was alone again.

TWENTY SIX

The Café De La Gare was already crowded and noisy at 7:00 a.m.. Jeff munched on a couple of croissants and a Cacolac, the French equivalent to Yoo Hoo. Before him, Paris was waking up. It was still dark but the buses were full and the stairs descending into the Métro were jammed. Inside the cafés Parisians were reading *Le Figaro, Le Monde* or *L'Equipe* as they got ready to battle an other day in La Capitale.

Jeff finished his breakfast and walked across the street to the Gare de Lyon to catch the 7:30 a.m. train. The Gare de Lyon was his favorite. It was close to his Grandmother's old apartment, as well as the Bastille, and since the new Opera opened had become a trendy neighborhood. It was unlike the Gare de l'Est or Gare du Nord which were located in more run-down and dangerous parts of town. Montparnasse may rival in some respects, but the area, while historic and beautiful had been invaded by McDonalds and Burger King as well as flashy movie theatres alongside the famous La Coupole and Roger La Frite.

Jeff had fond memories of this old train station as it was from where the PUC and National teams had left and returned to on their trips to Grosseto and Barcelona, what seemed like so many years ago. Several years before that when he was nine years old, he took a one day trip, the same one day trip he was going to take today.

Mr. Noue had passed away some twenty years ago, but Madame was still vibrant at ninety-seven. Her five children, fourteen grandchildren and thirty-eight great-grand-children all lived in St Cyr, a small French village about sixty miles outside of Paris. Jeff wanted to visit with these heroic people, these heroic and simple people whose actions some fifty years ago had saved his father's life and thus in Jeff's mind saved his. To Jeff they were true heroes, not the type of hero he was often said to be. In their minds they simply did the right thing.

Jeff's mind was etched with stories of the Noue's protecting his Dad from the Germans who searched houses door to door looking for hidden Jewish children; the allied bomb which mistakenly fell into the town square and the American soldiers liberating the village and trading bubble gum for cigarettes. And there were always humorous stories about the family pig Zezette. There was a Zezette there seventeen years before when Jeff last visited. A real live pig, which mesmerized Jeff, Marc and Louise and brought to life all the stories they had heard since they were old enough to listen.

He was welcomed into their home just as his father had been. He tried to picture what life was like in the French countryside during the war for a young Jewish boy separated from his family, but he couldn't. He could not imagine what life was like for a young boy in hiding.

The Noues still had pictures and he saw his Dad as he had never seen him before. As a kid, but not a kid like today's kids. Maybe he was with good people, but he was still alone. He was a young boy living in a troubled and cruel world, and he would never see his father again.

They sat and talked for hours. The Noues had stayed in contact with Jeff's Aunts in Paris and knew of Pierre's son the athlete and even saw him on television once. Two young boys André and Serge, aged eight and ten listened to every word Jeff said curled up next to him. After dinner the three new friends took a walk then sat in the yard and talked. Jeff had touched them but not as much as they touched him.

"I don't know if you realize why I'm here." Jeff started. "Many years ago my father came to live with your family when he was in a lot of danger, but your family protected him and took care of him. They are very special and I am here today because of them. Remember that because it is a part of your past, a past which you may not know much about, but a great past that you should be proud of."

Jeff sat and talked to them for another half-hour, attempting to give something back to the two young boys whose family had given so much to him. The three buddies went inside where the rest of the clan was still gathered. They took pictures, told some more stories and they laughed. When it was time to go, Jeff put André and Serge to bed. They all hugged each other tightly. Jeff was overcome with emotion and tears, tears difficult to contain. The day was very emotional, fueled by the fact that he was coming to yet another crossroad in his young life. He shut the light and put an envelope on the dresser with $2,000 in it. It was such an unfair trade.

He then went to say goodbye to the rest of the clan, having to catch the last train to Paris. Madame Noue was last and Jeff hugged her with his strong athletic arms. They both cried as he headed out the door.

Jeff's French getaway was almost over and as he sat on the almost empty train looking out into the nighttime sky of the French countryside, he let his mind wander. He let himself dream, To dream of all he wanted in life, all he wished to accomplish and all he had lost. It was there in front of him, right there in his imagination, the idea that would consume the life of Jeff Williams for the next ten months.

TWENTY SEVEN

Jeff knew the route well. First a croissant and a Cacolac at the Mairie D
'Ivry Métro stop, then the 325 bus to Vincennes and then the five Métro
stops to Liberté. In all it would take about half an hour. At 10:00 a.m. on a
Tuesday the Métro was pretty quiet as rush hour had long finished, and this
section of the Métro line was not heavily traveled by tourists. He read the
International edition of *USA TODAY*. Football season was in full swing and
the baseball teams were busy shuffling their rosters for the upcoming off-
season and Rule Five Draft.

At Liberté, Jeff could never remember if he should take the front or the
back seat. Once again he guessed wrong, adding a few hundred yards to his
half-mile walk to the Bois De Vincennes. It was not as colorful as some Paris
strolls and even though the surroundings were peaceful, his mind became
active and started to race.

Jeff walked into La Cipale, which at one time served as the finish to the
Tour De France. Back in 1985 it was his home away from home, the Fenway
Park of Europe. Now there was a real ballpark and training facility in Paris,
but to Jeff French Baseball was La Cipale.

Today, he was there to think and to remember, to ponder whether he
could give up, or at the very least delay the $10 million contract which awaited
him for a dream that most would say was unattainable. Could he risk what he
already had? He sat in the stands and stared out at the field. First he saw in
his mind Chiche taking a pee behind the makeshift dugout, as Dédé laughed
and mocked him. Then he saw SkyDome filled with fifty thousand people

screaming and cheering for him. Then he refocused and saw the cyclists practicing, going around and around as the coaches yelled encouragement.

Jeff needed some help on this one. He needed to talk to Pete Moggle, the only man who Jeff felt could help him through this dilemma, and perhaps the only man, aside from Jeff, who could make this dream a reality.

For a while Jeff and Pete had kept in close touch. They would get together when Jeff was in New York and Moggle made a couple of trips to Toronto. After Moggle graduated from Columbia, he got a job with the State Department and was assigned to Oslo where he worked in the Embassy. They corresponded for about a year, as Jeff would often kid him that he was a spy, but then they lost touch. Jeff figured that if anyone knew where to find him it would be Dédé his old catcher and Social Director of the PUC.

The TGV high-speed train made it from Paris to Nice in a little over five hours. From the Gare de Lyon the train zoomed into Marseille in a mere three hours followed by a little over two to Nice at regular speed. It was the first time Jeff was on the high-speed train and it was a nice way to travel. He took a taxi to the Hilton and checked into a beachfront room. He had never been to Nice, but like many European cities, it was full of life, glamour, noise and was a bit seedy just the way Jeff liked it.

He quickly showered and changed. He tossed on some khaki shorts and a Hobart baseball t-shirt, both of which would do fine for the occasion. His destination was only a short walk along the beach past the beautiful sunbathers and tourists. The golden women were topless and in G-strings or t-backs as they were called in Florida, and thongs as they would be called ten years later. This was a nice place to be.

And then it was there before him, the Blue Dog Lounge. He first looked in from the outside and saw pennants from American schools and pro teams. The decor was simple and made him think of Key West, even though he had never been there. It just seemed like a perfect Jimmy Buffet song. He walked in through the big wooden door and quickly noticed the waitresses in short tight "Daisy Duke" shorts and tight white t-shirts that barely covered their navels. They too were a great sight.

The place was already crowded at 3:00 p.m. with a mix of locals and tourists. The patrons served as good camouflage as Jeff approached his target who was wearing a colorful Hawaiian shirt, baggy shorts and a straw hat. All of which surrounded the body of a linebacker. He was making drinks with the skill he had demonstrated in everything he had ever tried.

"A pitcher of Long Island Iced Tea" Jeff bellowed out making sure he had the element of surprise.

"Holy shit!" Moggle screamed out as he jumped over the bar to give his old friend a bear hug. He got a waitress to cover the bar as the two men headed to a corner booth with their pitcher, ready to reminisce and to re-hash how they had gotten to where they were today.

"After Oslo I knew the Foreign Service wasn't for me so I came back to Paris and got a position as Marketing Manager for Coca Cola France and stayed there for two years. The money was great and I loved Paris, but had no life outside of work. I was on the job seventy hours a week and always on the go. I guess I had grown up and didn't like it so I started looking for a way out. I stumbled across this old shack on one of my trips to visit the local bottler and the rest is history.

"Anything for a buck!" Jeff said.

"Hey, I did learn something at Yale." Pete replied.

"Very funny," Jeff said as the two long lost buddies started pitcher number two of Long Island Iced Tea.

"To be honest," Jeff continued, "In some ways the things that brought you here to Nice have brought me here to see you. I feel that I'm at a crossroads. I have accomplished more than I ever thought was possible and have, and will, make more money than I can spend. However I find myself both happy and sad, pensive and impatient, content yet empty, and I'm not sure exactly why."

"I can sympathize with that, Jeff, but I cannot fix it. I don't know what is missing from your life," Pete responded.

"Well, the first thing I am missing is Tracy. I still haven't been able to completely accept that she is gone forever, and I don't know if I ever will. The other thing I need is a challenge, an adventure, something new and I have one in mind, but I need your help and support," Jeff told him.

"Now you've peaked my interest," Moggle told him as the drinks started to take effect.

"Have you ever thought of coaching again?" Jeff asked.

"Not really," Moggle replied not sure where this was going.

"I want to" Jeff started in an excited and slightly drunk tone, "I want you and I to make a new French team and go all the way to the Olympics. To form the greatest underdog team and have them over achieve like no team has, to start from scratch and re-teach them the game, to build a team from nothing and watch them grow, to appear out of nowhere and take the World by surprise, just like I did. That's what I want, and I want you to do it with me."

"Do you realize what you are saying, what you are giving up for a pipe dream?" Moggle answered back dumbfounded.

"Yes, but it is my dream, something I want to do Pete. It is a great challenge, something new, and something never done before. Don't you see?

"I see, but I just don't know," Moggle answered back with little conviction.

Jeff started in again. "You are the one who taught me how to dream and how to fight for what I want and believe. What is there to lose? You have your gold mine here. I will have another contract. At the very worst, we play a little ball for a couple of months, travel a little and help French Baseball. And at best, well that would be like a never ending wet dream."

Those words hit the Yale grad in his heart and sealed the deal. The two young men toasted their decision, a decision that would eventually rock the sporting World.

TWENTY EIGHT

Jeff now had to communicate his decision to the Blue Jays. He had to explain his rationale and his plan to Paul Beeston, Pat Gillick, and Gord Ash, the men who helped and guided him during his professional career.

"I think Jeff has a surprise for us," Ash said. "There was something in his voice. He wasn't mad or upset but almost reserved and nervous. I don't think it had anything to do with money. I think he has something to tell us, I wonder if he decided to retire."

"Well, I just hope the boy's alright," Beeston said as he puffed on his Cuban Cigar in the Blue Jays' suite at the Fountanibleu. "He's a hell of a kid, straight shooter, intelligent and talks for himself. We've been lucky to have him on our side."

"He should be here soon," a pensive Gillick said. "We will know then."

Jeff rented a car at the Miami Airport and made his way to the beach. It was much different than he remembered it from fifteen years ago. Today, it looked almost run down. The Eden Rock and the Doral looked plain. The Fountainbleu, where the Winter Meetings were being held, was still the crown jewel of the beach but did not still hold the magic and the awe that he had remembered as a young boy. Now the glamour had moved a few miles down to South Beach which was now one of the trendiest locations anywhere.

Everyone in the baseball world was there; executives from the low Minor Leagues to Major League General Managers and owners; Agents, scouts, the media, and free agents. As always Max Patkin, the Clown Prince of Baseball, was holding court in the lobby bar still talking about his role in *Bull Durham* three years before. Old Max loved baseball and baseball loved him. It can truly be said that at one point in his life he came in contact with just about every professional baseball player, coach, and executive. He was a true legend who never met a Red Lobster Restaurant he didn't like. Jeff walked over to give him a warm hug before checking in and quickly headed up to his room before being bothered or noticed by too many people.

He had one hour before his scheduled meeting and decided to lie down for a half-hour to think about exactly what he wanted to say and how he wanted to say it. He closed his eyes and drifted off, more peacefully and easier than he thought he could. After a shower and a Mountain Dew, he headed up to the suite to meet the three men.

Most players on most teams would have felt intimidated and overmatched and so might have Jeff in other circumstances, but the three men were fair and always treated the members of the organization well. He was always talked to and not at, and that was something that meant a lot to him.

They were his bosses but they were also his friends.

Beeston greeted Jeff at the door with his traditional big smile and handshake. He would make anyone from janitors to players feel like they were part of the team. He could give you the worst news and make it sound ok. He was a true leader and a respected man.

The four men talked for almost twenty minutes about everything but baseball. They talked about the weather, about Paris, even about the cute young lady at the registration desk in the lobby. Finally they started talking about baseball and a new contract.

"Jeff," Gillick said. "You have been a very important part of the Toronto Blue Jays and their success. I hope you know that we want you to be a continuing part of it."

"Thank you," Jeff said. My goal is to finish my career as a Blue Jay, but there is something which I need to say which will make a difference in our negotiations."

"Look" Beeston said, "before you say anything you may regret you should be aware of our offer. The numbers are these: $13 million for three years plus an option year at five."

Jeff was flabbergasted at the numbers. A total of $18 million dollars, eight more than he had imagined. While he was slightly thrown for a loop, he was not deterred.

"Those numbers are quite staggering and honestly more than I expected. However, when I was in Paris after the World Series, I spent a lot of time on my own thinking back to my childhood and things I wanted to accomplish. I thought about the people I loved and what my future had in store. I asked myself what would make me happy? I remember my first game as a pro in Knoxville and the butterflies and excitement. I remember jogging onto the mound at the EX and striking out Jim Rice. It was all so great."

The three men listened attentively, not knowing what words would come out next from their young star's mouth. "I still have the youthful enthusiasm for the game and I love playing for the Jays, but ever since I was young, I have had a dream."

The Orioles, Gillick thought to himself.

"And now I have a chance," Jeff continued "most would say a slim chance, to fulfill this dream, a dream to play in the Olympics. I am planning to go back to France in January to start working out and forming a team in an attempt to qualify for Barcelona. This is very important to me."

"Well," Beeston said dumbfounded and shocked, we have never stood in the way of our employees and this is definitely an exciting adventure, but what happens if France does not make it. Where does that leave us, you, and the team?"

"I have given this some thought and here is what I would like to propose: that we agree on a two year contract extension and an option year starting in 1993 and that a 1992 contract be agreed upon based on the following scale and reporting time frame.

If I report between February 15th and June 30th I would receive a pro-rated contract of last year's salary plus fifteen percent. If I report between July 1st and August 10th, my contract would be a prorated at half my last year's salary and finally if I report after August 10th, I would receive the Major League minimum.

"Where and how did you come up with those figures?" Beeston asked.

"The way I look at it," Jeff said. " No matter what happens and when I report this year, I'm screwing you guys. This is an attempt on my part to make it a little more palatable and to thank the organization for letting me do this. I hope."

Jeff looked to Gillick for his reaction, because while Beeston gave his blessing, Gillick was truly the one who held his baseball future in his hands. Finally he spoke.

"To be honest, Jeff, the idea thrills me less than Beest, but I will not stand in your way and I prefer this to you pitching for someone else, so let's get the deal done and shock some people."

The media room at the Fountainbleu was packed for the 11:00 p.m. news conference which was being fed live to TSN in Canada and ESPN in the States. First Howie Starkman, the Blue Jays' PR Director would read a statement then Gillick and Jeff would answer some questions.

Starkman started to read. "The Toronto Blue Jays and Jeff Williams are pleased to announce that they have agreed upon a two year contract for the 1993 and 1994 seasons with a club option for 1995."

There was a buzz in the room at the apparent mistake but Howie read on. "The two parties have also agreed on a conditional contract for the upcoming season based on days of service." The buzz grew louder and engulfed the room.

The PR man continued once the noise died down a bit. "Jeff plans to take advantage of the new eligibility standards in the Olympics and will attempt to help France qualify for the summer games in Barcelona. The Blues Jays fully support Jeff in his endeavor and will welcome him back at any time during the season." The buzz had now turned into a scramble as reporters hurried to phones and started scribbling madly.

"Jeff now has a brief statement and then he and Pat will answer a few questions," Starkman said as the noise died down waiting for Jeff to speak.

"First of all, I would like to state that this decision is in no way a result of any unhappiness with my situation with the Blue Jays. In fact, I owe them a great deal for allowing me the latitude to pursue this dream and still welcome me back. Being part of the Olympics has always been a dream of mine and I am looking forward to the challenge ahead and helping both France and the Blue Jays reach new heights of success. Thank you."

Hands and shouts inundated the briefing room with everyone trying to ask their question. Starkman took control and gave *Toronto Sun* writer Bob Elliot the go ahead. Elliot directed his question to Gillick. "Are you planning now to go out and get another closer or using what you have?"

"That's a tough question as we don't know how long Jeff will be gone but I believe we have arms in the system that can do the job. This is not to say we will not miss Jeff, but we have Duane Ward and youngsters like Mike Timlin and Jesse Cross who we feel will contribute."

Next was Peter Gammons from ESPN and the *Boston Globe.* "Jeff, this seems like a great idea but it's not like you are going to play with Team USA or Cuba. Do you honestly feel that you have a chance at making the Olympics and if you do, winning a medal?"

"Yes and yes." Jeff answered with a big smile. "Look I wouldn't do this if I did not think I could accomplish what I want to. Will it be easy? No. Spain will be getting an automatic birth as host country. Europe will have one other qualifier from the European Championships. Basically we have to beat Italy and Holland and take care of the other teams as well. I think it can be done. Baseball in France has come a long way since I first played there. I have confidence in the people who will help me make this happen. As far as the Olympics, my main goal is to participate. At that point winning will take a back seat. Maybe," he added.

"One more question." Gammons followed. "Pat, do you think that this will start a trend with players?"

"Honestly, I don't think so. First you need someone who believes in all the Olympics stand for. Second you need a country that would welcome a pro, and third and probably the most difficult is to find a player willing to give up the kind of money that Jeff will be giving up and a team willing to let him try."

Steve Milton of the *Hamilton Spectator* got the last question in. "Will you announce the terms of the contract?"

Gillick responded, "There are still a few details that have to be ironed out as far as language and liability but basically this year's terms are based on last year's terms with sliding amounts pro-rated as the season goes on. After that Jeff will be the highest paid closer in baseball, which he deserves to be."

TWENTY NINE

On January 10th, 1992, Jeff Williams returned to France with a big dufflebag full of equipment, another full of clothes, and a heart and mind full of dreams, memories, excitement and fear. Fear of what, he did not know.

He took up residence at INSEP, the French Olympic Training center, in the Bois de Vincennes on the outskirts of Paris. When he first came to France, they practiced on the soccer field, but now there were indoor facilities with a batting cage and pitching mound. His home was now a small dorm room, but he got his three meals a day. It was a setting where he could thrive and which would provide the discipline and structure needed to mold a team from players who were not accustomed to working to improve and learn as much as possible in the allotted time.

Jeff had given himself ten days in Paris before the real work started. The first five days, he spent as much time as possible with his aunts, uncles and cousins, visiting and getting over jet lag. The next three, he spent on his own at INSEP, writing and thinking. Thinking how best to attack the monumental task before him. He would sit in the main track stadium, watching the workouts of the young French Olympians with a pen and a blank pad of paper.

By the end of the third day, he had accomplished two things. Two things which he had not consciously set out to do, but which really helped him. One, he was relaxed, completely relaxed and at ease. And two, he developed a huge crush on a hurdler named Lydie Joncas, who he stared at for hours in the surprisingly warm Parisian January, as she practiced in her skin tight track pants and top.

She had long athletic legs and short brown hair that decorated her exquisite face that emanated warmth and compassion. Just looking at her gave him energy and youthful spirit. He felt young again, because for some reason, at twenty-six he had felt old, very old. Admiring from far was all he needed and for the time being all he wanted.

Moggle arrived on the 19th and they got down to planning the next eight months, breaking it down in stages, setting goals, anticipating problems, preparing themselves for the worst, while dreaming for the best.

They met with the Paris area players to lay down the plans and what would be expected of them. On March 10th, they would take between thirty and forty players to Florida for four weeks. They would come back to Europe with a working roster of twenty-five who would form the team until the European Championships on June 1st at which time they would have to trim the roster to the International limit of twenty.

From the start they identified their two biggest problems: quantity and quality of arms and power. For the European Championships they could feasibly play ten games in thirteen days. This gave Jeff up to four starts, but he needed at least two more arms to go along with his and Gilles Thomas who was aging but still effective. There were a couple of youngsters with good arms but neither Jeff nor Pete were ready to count on them.

For power Jeff had a plan which could also, if successful, solve some of the pitching problems, but he would have to get to Florida, before he knew if it could happen.

Moggle and Jeff spent January criss-crossing the country looking at known and unknown commodities. The last week of February, they held a Training Camp in Nice for fifty players, choosing the thirty-four that they would take to Florida. They had no idea how good they were but they had the kind of mix they wanted as there were both experienced players and others with raw athletic skills. They had speed, real speed, decent defense, three quality arms including Jeff and a weak offense, but that was no surprise.

While it was the mix they were looking for, it was still somewhat uninspiring, and that could make it difficult to get through the Europeans and on to the Olympics. But as usual, when things could have seemed gloomiest, the Florida sun shone brightly on the little French Baseball team.

Just about every great baseball success Jeff had could be traced back to the West coast of Florida, so there was never any doubt in his mind that was where they would hold camp. He knew that the Blue Jays would support his venture, and he also believed, and this somehow made him feel better, that it was in Florida every March that hope was eternal, phenoms were born and teams were built.

Jeff also had a secret agenda which he had not shared with anyone, and would not, until he knew if it could happen, and it did. Jeff found his power and his number two pitcher so close to home that it was almost comical that no one else had thought of it. Jeff had managed to convince Lee Thomas, the General Manager of the Philadelphia Phillies to let Marc Williams, who was scheduled to be the starting double A thirdbaseman in Reading, take a mid-season leave to play with the French team. Voila, he got a shortstop, cleanup hitter and number two pitcher.

A second move was to bring in another coach, and for this he looked to Mike Pierce, his mentor, who was loaned at no charge to the National Team by the Blue Jays. The benefits of his presence would be immense, not only with the pitchers, but also in the atmosphere and aura. Moggle welcomed him, and Jeff could concentrate more on his playing.

By their last week, the results were no less than amazing. The bats were quicker, the young arms stronger and the team closer. The last week they played some college and low minor league teams, and managed to hold their own. There was now a glimmer of hope.

Securing Marc, gave them a reason to believe, and while he was their best all around player, their biggest and unexpected coup came on the last day before camp broke. During practice, a 6'2" giant of a boy made his way toward Jeff who was standing outside the locker room waiting to take the field. The kid had curly brown hair, broad shoulders and a great big smile. The kid confidently began to talk.

"Mr. Williams." He said. " My name is Bruno, Bruno Lawton, and I think I can help your team."

"Oh really." Jeff answered in tone of surprise more than contempt. "How is that?"

"Well" the teenager replied. "I could just show you, but before I do that let me give you some background and information. As I told you, my name is Bruno Lawton, I'm sixteen years old and I live in Montreal. Similar to you, but a little different, my Dad is American and my Mom French. Anyway, last week I read about your team and knew that I could and should be part of it, so, somehow I convinced my parents to let me take the car and here I am. I also possess something which I know that you can relate to and that is lightning in my arm and bat speed that you gotta see. I just think that it's time to let the World see it."

Jeff was transfixed and mesmerized by every confident word of the soft-spoken young man. If he was all he claimed to be, he could end up being the missing link that this team so desperately needed.

Bruno started again, "I figured that my only chance was to come down and prove it in person, so here I am. If you have a few minutes I would appreciate the opportunity to throw for you."

"Let's go" Jeff said as he led his gentle giant to the back bullpens of Engelbert Complex with Pierce, Moggle, and Dédé.

It probably took them less than ten throws for them to realize that they had caught lightning in a bottle and that the Olympic gods must be looking down on them as the balls exploded out of his arm. They then took their newfound protegé to the back field where Jeff took over and started throwing to the young gentle giant whose hitting prowess matched his pitching. Thus, out of nowhere, the best pitcher, possibly in the World, found hope and rebirth in a young sixteen year old boy who appeared on his doorstep and brought him that much closer to fulfilling his dream.

By the time they left Florida, the team roster was pretty much set, even if it was not disclosed to the players. That could wait a little longer. Moggle, Pierce and Jeff were upbeat as they entered their European preparations.

They had six weeks before they headed to Italy for the Olympic qualification tournament. Marc and Bruno would join them about two weeks before the first game. It was now time for the most serious and structured part of their task. It was time to fine tune and to work on all the details that made winning teams. It was now time to instill the needed mindset in every player who would go forward in battle, to a battle of proportion that not even the three leaders could fathom. It would be a battle and a war that would be more intense, more nerve-wracking, more emotional, more memorable and uplifting than anyone could have imagined or dreamed.

With two weeks to go, the team was set and the results encouraging. Long ago it was decided that they would not play any European competition before the tournament and thus keep an element of surprise. They concentrated on playing touring American and Asian teams. Surprisingly, at first, they were competitive, but more importantly, with Jeff on the mound, they cruised. All facets of the game were improving day by day. Execution was outstanding and slowly momentum was building as Bruno and Marc arrived to round out the team. The pitching staff still had Gilles Thomas and David Meurant who had matured and developed into a fine pitcher and leadoff hitter.

The anticipation was replaced by real excitement and confidence when the team gathered for their pre-departure meal at the Chicago Pizza Factory. They were truly a team, a mix of young and old, veterans and rookies, just as they had planned.

The five pitchers were surrounded by a cast of characters. Chiche could still hit and would play third. Gommy could still run like the wind and would play left. Jean Pierre Millot, a fleet-footed twenty-year old second baseman discovered by Moggle in the small Southern town of Argeles had won the job after having only been playing baseball for a year and a half. First base was unsettled and Jeff, Thomas and the thirty six year old veteran from Nice, Stephane Clementi, would all see some action. Clementi made the team as the last member due to his experience, decent bat and arm that could still hit eighty miles per hour, but most important of all he was a leader and an insider. He, like Thomas, paved the way for the young players. The two of them would be looked upon to both reassure, calm down, and, if needed, kick the butts of their teammates.

As he munched on his pizza and drank his Coke, Jeff looked around and saw his life up to that moment clearer than he ever had. He saw family with his brother next to him. He felt his childhood, his love for his parents, brother and sister, their love for him and the memories of being a little boy, carefree, fun-loving and warmhearted.

Recalling the conversation he had with Moggle his first baseball summer in France, a mere twenty-five feet from where he was now sitting, he remembered doubting himself, doubting his abilities and so unsure of what would become of him.

He then felt his heart beat and he thought of Tracy, his love and how much he missed her. It almost hurt too much to think about it. He felt her there, in his heart, giving him the strength he needed to get through every day, encouraging him to keep battling, guiding him forward, guiding him toward his Olympic dream. Thinking of her so close and in those terms put a smile on his face and tears in his eyes. He was ready for battle.

THIRTY

It was a beautiful Paris morning as the Air France 747 took off from Orly Airport into the majestic blue sky. Flying high, everything seemed so peaceful. Jeff always enjoyed flying as it made him feel closer to Tracy and he liked that.

Nevertheless, he had a very uneasy feeling in his gut, one he had never truly experienced this way. It was a real terrible case of the nerves and of self-doubt. But why? He wasn't a college freshman or a Major League rookie anymore. He was possibly the best pitcher in the World, and that is precisely what scared him. Up until that moment, eyes closed at thirty thousand feet, he had never seriously considered what it would be like if the team failed, if he failed.

Then almost magically his nerves disappeared. How could he think like that? This was a trip, a truly *Magical Mystery Tour* that was waiting to take him away. He had to look around, and take into account those around him, those who had nurtured him and those who he had nurtured. He had to remember the spirit and the reasons why he had attempted this. It was time to get down to the basics of having fun, staying loose, but also being focused and ruthless in the quest for victory and a trip to the Olympics. It was time to get it on.

It took but two days and two games for the mighty French Baseball team to take the European Baseball world by storm. It took only two games for the mighty French Baseball team to overcome any doubts about their ability as a team and to show they were more than just one player.

The first game was against the Spanish Olympic team and they certainly could be called an Olympic team because as host country, they would be there. Moggle and Pierce sent young Bruno to the mound to face Jose Caño, the Caño who the French had faced since Jeff's early days in Europe. Cano had lived up to his early success and was regarded as one of the top five pitchers in Europe as well as a power-hitting first baseman who indeed was Spain's Babe Ruth.

He had not lost to a French team since Jeff beat him back in 1985. But when your team does not score, you cannot win. Bruno pitched seven brilliant shutout innings, before being relieved by Marc Williams who closed the door for the final two innings. The Southern neighbors had never seen such arms from their Northern adversaries. Marc hit a two run homer to seal the 2-0 shutout.

While the victory over Spain could be classified as an upset, it was not until the next day when the true magnitude of what was going on became apparent, and by then it was too late for anyone to do much more than curse and point fingers. The Italians had been arrogant knowing that Jeff would oppose them. They were quoted as saying that the French should not waste their best arm against them and that his pitching style might have problems against aluminum bats.

The game was really over in ten minutes because that's how long it took the French team to score the only three runs of the game against Italy's number four pitcher. Throwing him out there was perhaps the gravest mistake Italian baseball had ever made. To be honest though, it may not have made a difference as Jeff was almost perfect allowing only one bunt single and striking out fifteen. In two hours it was over. The fate of the Italians was now out of their hands and the favorites now needed things to go their way to make it to the Olympic Games. The French meanwhile were closer to their day of destiny, but only a little closer as there was still a lot more baseball to be played.

What should have been the easiest game was next against the upstart Russian squad, but it was not. It became a true European slugfest. Thomas got rocked for seven in two innings, followed by Meurant who pitched four. Finally, in the bottom of the sixth, the French exploded for eight runs and took a 15-9 lead which expanded to 17-10 by the time Marc got the last out in the ninth.

They were in first place with three straight wins and now had a day off before they confronted in succession Sweden, Holland, Belgium, and Germany. They now had to delicately balance their strategy while managing their resources and still not look too far forward. They still had to take one game at a time as everything could unravel quickly if the wrong pitcher was on the mound against the wrong team.

Surprise was no longer on their side. The other teams were now running scared of them, the once laughable French Team. The mighty Dutch and Italians now wondered what it would take for them to beat Jeff when it was all on the line. They truly did not know if they could.

If the French were going to ride Jeff's arm to the Olympics, the schedule was now on their side. Bruno would come back against Sweden, Jeff would go after the Dutch, Marc available for relief for those two games would take on Belgium, and Thomas would finish up against Germany, a team he had always had much success against.

Three more wins would most probably get them into the final while four would clinch it. With the rotation set up as is Bruno and Jeff would be ready to start the final games against the winner of the Holland-Italy game. The way the tournament was set up, the round robin game would count for the first game of the best two-out-of-three finals, so if it were Italy, France would already be up one game due to their prevous victory.

The Swedes were pretty good hitters. Most hit lefty just like they shot in hockey. Jeff remembered that they hit fastballs well but had trouble with breaking pitches. Bruno had a fastball that could overpower them, but when he needed the strikeout he went to his hard curve.

The lack of depth on the Swedish pitching staff was glaring. They had used their top pitchers in their first three games and did not want to bring them back too early against the French team which was now a contender. By the fifth inning France was up 8-0 thanks to Marc and Bruno's two homeruns apiece. In a bold move, the French took Bruno out from the mound and brought in seventeen year old Patrick Martel, who had never pitched in any game that was not for his junior team back home. The decision was made for two reasons. One was to get the kid in a game and this appeared to be the best time to do it and secondly, to save Bruno's arm for the upcoming games.

Martel struggled but the kid plugged through three innings until Dédé hit a two run double in the bottom of the eighth to give France the 13-3 mercy victory. They were one step closer with the mighty Dutch next.

The crowd was surprisingly large for a non-Italian game. The Olympic implications created electricity in the stadium that was felt by all. The Dutch truly had a formidable team led by future Major Leaguers Robert Eenhoorn, the slick fielding shortstop and Rikkert Faneyte, the fleet footed power hitting outfielder. The Dutch would not make the same mistake the Italians had by putting a rookie on the mound. They would start Bart Volkeryk who had pitched just about every big game the Dutch had played over the last ten years including the one which got them to the Seoul Olympics four years earlier. They would not take Jeff and his French comrades lightly.

Volkeryk struck out the side in the first, humbling the French bats. Jeff matched him striking out the first two, but then Faneyte connected on a belt high fastball and launched it way over the left field fence. Jeff was mad. Mad at himself for missing with the pitch and mad that his teammates realized that he was not unhittable. Or was he?

By the time they got to the seventh inning nothing had changed. It was still 1-0 and while the Dutch ace continued to stymie them, there were signs that he was tiring slightly. Jeff had indeed been virtually unhittable, striking out thirteen while only giving up three hits.

With two outs in the top of the seventh, a gift which could only be given to a team of destiny was received. Dédé scrounged a walk which brought Bruno to the plate. With two strikes, he hit a routine ground ball toward second and just as the fielder went to pick it up, it hopped over his head after hitting a pebble. Runners were now on the corners and Marc was up. He had been made to look foolish by the Dutch ace twice already, but this time he would hit one for his big brother, he was sure of it, so sure that by the time it happened, there was no surprise. He had already seen the homerun three times on his walk to the plate. The only difference was that the actual one went farther. The game was now in his big brother's hands which meant that it was over.

Destiny was now in their hands. Three more games and they were on their way to the Olympics. It was finally close enough to taste. The Belgians and the Germans went so quietly that it was alarming. The Italians and Dutch battled twelve hard innings in a truly great game before the Italians scored two, and won 4-2.

The game had taken an emotional and physical toll on the Italians. Their best arms were tired and their minds full of doubt. The French meanwhile were reminded by Dédé, Thomas and Clementi of the 36-0 drubbing the Italians had given them in '83. It was time for revenge, to eliminate them on their home soil. It was time for a meeting with destiny. Zeus would have to be looking down on them. They had come too far, learned too much, bonded like a family. All they needed was one more win, just one more.

The question which was on everyone's mind had actually been answered two days prior, but only a few people knew about it. Jeff, Marc, Pierce and Moggle had decided that Bruno would start the first game which was actually the second game of the finals. He had one more day of rest than Jeff, and had thrown a lot less pitches. Jeff would be ready to close if need be, and if not who else would they want on the mound for a deciding game. They had discussed changing the strategy to put Jeff up against the number three Italian pitcher but decided they liked their shot with Bruno.

The June heat and humidity was suffocating as the teams took batting practice at Florence Municipal Stadium. The gates opened at 7:00 p.m. for the 8:30 p.m start. An hour before game time, the twelve-thousand-seat stadium was full with singing, screaming and flag waving Italians encouraging their beloved team. Even with the heat, Bruno spent some time on the field getting acclimated to the noise and the crowd. But Bruno was not nervous, he relished the atmosphere and soaked up every minute as he searched the stands for every pretty girl. At sixteen, he was mature enough to realize that this could be the pinnacle of his baseball career and he wanted every second etched in his mind for eternity.

By the time he took the mound in the top of the first, the butterflies finally hit him, and after striking out the Italian leadoff hitter, he relaxed and settled into his usual rhythm. The game quickly turned into a battle. The teams exchanged a run in the second. Marc doubled in Dédé in the fourth and the Italians replied with two in the fifth as Bruno struggled with his control. Jeff did not want to go more than two innings and only with a lead, so in the sixth, down by one, Marc came in to pitch. He mowed them down in order in the sixth and seventh, and pitched out of a jam in the eighth, but the French still trailed by one.

Championship teams are indeed teams, not individuals. And while it cannot be denied that the underdog French team would be nowhere without their big three, it is also true that without their supporting cast they could not win. This was never more true than in the bottom of the eighth. Chiche singled, Gommy sacrificed him to second, and old man Stephane Clementi ripped a double to tie it up, as the boisterous Italian fans fell silent for the first time in four hours. The Italian players could not help but notice Jeff accelerate his pitches in the bullpen and feel their Olympic hopes fade slowly.

Meurant then walked and Dédé singled to load the bases for Bruno who had stayed in the game in the outfield. The gentle young giant battled the Italian closer Bianchi to a full count, fouled off three pitches and then, fooled by a change-up blooped it over the infield to score two runs. Marc popped up, but it didn't really matter as the damage was done.

Jeff trotted in from the bullpen to do what he had learned to love and what he did better than any other person in the World and that was closing baseball games. He hadn't been in this position where everything was truly on the line since the World Series. It felt sort of strange, and it felt sort of natural, but most of all it felt good, like coming home after a long trip and getting a hug.

He finished firing his warm up pitches and stood behind the mound cherishing the moment and relishing how close he was to accomplishing his dream. He looked over to his kid brother at shortstop and pointed a finger at him which was a childhood code meaning let's do it. And then, in a move that only his brother saw and only his brother knew the meaning, Jeff gently blew a kiss up to the sky.

The rest was magical and awe inspiring. Nine pitches, nine fastballs, three outs. He threw harder than he ever had as if a lightning bolt energized his arm. He fell behind the mound and cried, drained of all energy. He wept uncontrollably and was not sure why, but there was no one reason, nor one explanation. It just happened. Marc came over to hug him amidst the celebration. The Italian fans stood and clapped as the two teams shook hands.

Jeff's tears were now smiles. They had accomplished what deep down no one believed possible ten days before. Now they were on their way to the Olympics. Jeff let his mind wander. He glanced over to Moggle and Pierce and then to Marc, all of whom quickly realized what that look meant. The sparkle in his eyes and the determined grin. The three others smiled back. Jeff Williams wanted an Olympic Medal. He planned on leading this crew on one more magical journey.

THIRTY ONE

The music rang out into night and up to the sky, reaching high toward the stars, touching the hearts of those looking down to the Earth just as it touched those lucky ones who were there in the small piece of paradise called Montjuic Stadium. The Opening Ceremonies of the games of the twenty-third Olympiad. It was amazing, mystifying, overwhelming, glorious, stupendous, and tear-jerking.

The French team marched in three hundred and twenty five strong and circled the stadium. Jeff and Marc looked up searching for their parents and sister but could not find them so they simply waved all the way around, stopping only to talk with Hannah Storm, the NBC sportscaster. As they took their place in the infield, Lydie made her way to Marc's side. The tall brunette hurdler had found her love. Jeff could only look down, smile and shed a tear, once again looking out into the night and remembering.

Across the ocean in a big old house, a young woman looked out into the night and cried, then picked up the phone and booked a flight to Barcelona. At that precise moment in time Robin knew that Jeff needed her and Robin knew that she needed to be with him.

It could have been easy to forget that there was work to be done. It could also have been easy to claim victory in simply participating, to rejoice in the Olympic spirit and magic and forget that there were games to be played. If any group of athletes could be forgiven for doing so it would be the French Olympic Baseball Team. As much as Jeff, Pierce, and Moggle wanted to win, they knew that they could not apply pressure nor take away any of the once in a lifetime experience from the squad.

They would shoulder whatever needed to be shouldered. They would be the rocks for the rest to lean on. They had made their livings being under pressure and relished it. No one else needed to feel anything but joy and energy when they started playing.

For now though, it was enough to get entranced by the ceremonies and to soak up every second of every minute and look on in amazement as the archer fired his lit bow into the Barcelona night to light the Olympic Flame. There was no need to think about tomorrow or the day after, or the game or the pitch, or anything other then this amazing moment Jeff had dreamed of since he was eight years old.

Then as they marched out of Montjuic Stadium to the buses that would take them back to the athletes village, the euphoria slowly faded and the focus in all the athletes' faces changed to a more serious competitive look. It was now time to go to work.

Life in the Olympic Village was exciting and stimulating as over eight thousand athletes from one hundred and fifty countries were represented. Some superstars like the US Dream Team stayed in luxurious hotels away from the common athletes. Jeff was in their status, but that would have defeated the purpose of his journey, the odyssey and the struggle his team had endured. The beauty was being a common athlete among the Mexican gymnasts in the dining room or the Angolan basketball team in the weight room. It was a United Nations of youth which Jeff would not have traded for any luxury hotel. He felt sorry for Air Jordan and his crew as they did not realize what they were missing.

During the two days prior to the opener against Japan, Jeff took it relatively easy. He spent time with Marc, Pierce, and Lydie and others on the track team who had formed a kinship with the baseball squad at INSEP. There was a short workout mixed in. However whenever possible he tried to be alone and to rest and to visualize being on the mound pitching and winning. Once again, Jeff spent time reflecting on his past and future. This moment in time meant so much to Jeff Williams. It was a metamorphosis, a transition, and a cleansing of negativity. He would use the energy around him, the energy of youth, the energy of athletics and the energy of love. He would rediscover his inner peace and push on.

Jeff felt at ease, focused and determined as he strode to the mound to face the mighty Japanese in the first game of Division B. The Tournament was split into two divisions. In the A division was Cuba, South Korea,

Spain, and Canada. In the B division was Japan, Nicaragua, the United States, and France.

He was high on Montjuic in the refurbished baseball stadium that he had last pitched in seven years ago. So much had happened since then. He had lived so many lives. He had always found escape, refuge, and companionship on the mound; it was his home. But for the first time he could remember, he felt alone as if no one could know how he felt. He felt anger and meanness, emotions he had never encountered on the mound and most troublesome was that he did not know why, nor how to control them. Was his mind telling him that this was a war, his battle to win, or was there more?

The first batter from Japan, Ichiro Suzuki dug in. The young man who would one day be a Major League Batting Champion and Rookie of the Year like Jeff, barely escaped as a fastball zoomed past his head. He then struck him out on three straight pitches. He repeated the same pattern on the next two hitters. The results were good, but he felt uneasy, something was wrong. He didn't know what it was and he never would.

When he took to the mound for the second inning he relaxed, took a deep breath and remembered back to his not-so-distant past, to his youth and to his days at Hobart, and to Keg Hill over the third base dugout. He looked up into the crowd at Monjuic picturing that perfect piece of heaven in upstate New York when he saw the beautiful sight he was subconsciously dreaming of. It was almost too corny to be real. It was like Robert Redford looking up into the crowd in *The Natural* and seeing Glenn Close, but what he saw was true and it was real, not the movies.

First, he saw the smile, then the pain, and the warm expressions, then the beauty as he remembered it and how he must have always loved it. Robin had arrived and was there for him and he loved her for it. If he was not so touched he would have been surprised. Now he could place himself in simpler times as she smiled at him knowingly in her Hobart baseball T-shirt and her Blue Jays cap with her shoulder length blonde hair peeking out.

It then became easy and fun to pitch again. He was young again, he had no worries, no memories and no goals. He just pitched. He showed the Japanese why many regarded him as the most complete pitcher in the World, and Marc showed them why he was on his way to joining his brother in the big leagues. Together they beat the team from the Orient. The French had two hits, two homeruns by Marc. The Japanese managed one unearned run off of Jeff as he struck out an Olympic record twenty-two batters. He had to do it by himself and he did.

The forty-five minutes it took him to pee in the bottle for the drug test, answer the media questions and shower seemed like an eternity. He knew that if this was a dream he would soon find out, but she was there, outside the gate waiting for him with open arms and a big hug and kiss. They did not speak, they just cried. They cried because they were happy and they cried because they were sad. They cried because they missed each other, and they cried because they had demons they could not totally shake, but most of all they cried because they were best friends and they loved each other.

The place in Jeff's heart and mind that he had always saved for her was suddenly not enough. Robin, who Jeff had first described as cute, had become beautiful. Her blonde hair flowed wildly past her shoulders like a blonde Julia Roberts and her blue eyes and perfect smile would put any Miss America to shame. Her tanned body was so beautiful and healthy that he did not want to let go of her. She was indeed a hold'em girl.

When Jeff tried to talk no words would come, but his look said it all. Robin talked. Jeff's women always did more talking, and he preferred it that way.

"Jeff, I missed you. I've missed you for a while. I know you don't want to hear it, but I also felt bad for you. It really started last Spring when I read the story in *Baseball Weekly*, and just snowballed since then. I know you Jeff Williams, better than you think, and you have been trying to liberate yourself. You have been here living day to day, but you have also been on a different plane. I could tell by your words, your actions and the looks on your face. It all came together when I saw you parading in the stadium during the Opening Ceremonies and the emotional look in your eyes. I knew that I had to be in Barcelona. I had to be with you right now right at this moment. I knew you needed something and I thought it might be me."

Jeff hugged her tighter and cried. "Thank you. Tomorrow you are mine toots!" Jeff said as he got on the bus in the midnight heat of Barcelona.

They were carefree teenagers again, strolling hand in hand through the hustle and bustle of Barcelona. Such a lively city in normal times, magnified during the Olympics in such a positive way. They relived Jeff's eighteenth birthday and the magical place that Geneva was and the magical times they had. Jeff was not ready to open up too much and Robin did not press. For today it was enough to simply enjoy.

Sitting at the outside café with a magnificent view of the famous Magic Fountain built for the 1988 World Expo, Jeff's mind wandered again, this time to his honeymoon and to his beautiful Tracy. Was she looking down on him and was she smiling? Was she telling him to enjoy, to have fun and to be with Robin? With all the joy he felt being next to Robin, he did not know what to do or how he was supposed to feel. He could not just let himself be.

At 8:00 p.m., they met Pierce, Moggle, Marc and Lydie at Villadecans Stadium to watch South Korea play Cuba. Any medal would have to go through at least one of these two teams. Jeff had a hard time concentrating on the game with Robin by his side, but she talked and gossiped about the boys with Lydie and didn't seem to mind as the men worked.

Jeff stayed close to Pierce as they took notes, talked and analyzed the hitters. They realized that the Cubans would be a formidable opponent, but the two men also realized that they were free swingers not used to Major League pitchers. With this said, there were easily four starters including center fielder Orestes Kindalen and nineteen year old slugging thirdbasemen Omar Linares who could step into the lineup of almost any Major League team. If Jeff had a chance to face them with an Olympic medal on the line, he would use their eagerness to prove themselves versus him to his advantage. He was convinced he would beat them. He would have to.

A late dinner was followed by Jeff escorting Robin back to her hotel and then back to the Olympic Village for some, much needed sleep, as young Bruno would face a veteran and tenacious Nicaraguan team.

The Olympic Village was still dormant when Jeff made his way to the cafeteria at just after 5:00 a.m. He couldn't sleep any more and he was nervous. He was surprised to see that in the far corner, his baby faced giant was reading a book and sipping a Coke.

"Bruno baby, you OK?" Jeff asked.

"Just a little nervous I guess," the young man replied.

In the few months that the two had known each other, Jeff had forgotten how young Bruno was. Just a sixteen year old high school junior, pitching in the Olympics. Bruno too had forgotten, but the magnitude had now hit him. The pressure had finally reached him, and his desire not to let Jeff and his teammates down overcame him.

"Bruno," Jeff said as he put his arm around the much larger youngster, "nerves are good, you just gotta channel them properly. Look at the way I started against Japan. I was way out of control. That is not good. Controlled nerves are great. Just like in the book".

The book Jeff was referring to was *THE POWER OF ONE* that he had given Bruno to read for the inspiration and perseverance, the overwhelming power of human spirit and goodness.

"Remember Peekay?" Jeff said referring to the main character. "Use your heart as well as your mind to guide you and to show the way. Remember what is most important is to hold your head high and do your best, respect yourself and respect others and you will be fine."

"I'll try" was Bruno's response. Jeff too got a Coke and looked at the special young man next to him and they continued to talk as the village woke up.

The crowd was sparse for the 3:00 p.m. start, under the blistering Barcelona sun, but those who were there saw a battle. Bruno fought and clawed through six innings, battling Nicaraguan players, men some twice his age, pitching like a veteran, pitching like a champion full of heart and determination.

By the time Marc took over in the seventh, the score was tied at four. It remained that way through nine innings. In the top of the tenth, Marc walked the leadoff hitter and Jeff came in. On the first pitch he got a double play ball that the infield turned flawlessly, but Jeff did not see it. He was wincing in pain as a twinge shot down his shoulder, every pitcher's nightmare and something Jeff had never experienced.

But with one out left in the inning he was determined to push on, to finish the job and lead his team to an Olympic medal, but his next pitch bounced halfway to the plate. He could not continue as the pain persisted. What had happened to his arm? Was it all over? Like a fighter he waited on the mound for Thomas to come in. Jeff gave him the pep talk of a lifetime. Just like every player on the field, in fact like every Olympian, this moment was the culmination and high point of their career, Thomas was no different. This was his one shot and he rose to the occasion striking out the batter and pitching one more shutout inning before Marc homered to give the French team the win, the win that put them one game closer to an Olympic medal.

Three hours after the game, Jeff's arm started to feel better after the massages and the ice treatments. It was diagnosed as a freak cramp, but it still hurt as he went to bed. When he woke up the next morning, he reached for the tennis ball by his bed and squeezed it, then he got up and, stepped out into the corridor in a T-shirt and boxers and threw the ball. There was no pain. Jeff was back. He hoped.

With two days before they played the USA, Jeff rested. He would have to beat the Collegiate All-Stars. He could realistically pitch three games in seven days if a medal were up for grabs.

The first off day was spent with Robin before she went back. They would meet again soon. On the second he focused back on the task at hand. The young Americans would be gunning for him, but they would also be scared of him. The fright overcame their talent and Jeff mowed them down with ease. The French team even scored three runs thanks to Chiche's three doubles, each of which scored Marc who was intentionally walked every at bat. The odyssey, The *Magical Mystery Tour* was starting to get most interesting.

THIRTY TWO

"Turn around bright eyes, turn around.

Every now and then I get a little bit lonely and you're never comin' round.

Every now and then I get a little bit tired of listening to the sound of my tears..."

Jeff sat alone in his room waiting for the bus to Montjuic and listened to Bonnie Tyler belt out the words he knew so well. Back in Paris, in eighty-five, he would open the windows to his Aunt's apartment and study in the afternoons before practice while the song belted out from the courtyard. He loved the words and melodic progression and being alone listening and thinking.

Today he was thinking of the biggest game of his life and the first woman he had ever loved and how he would never be with her again.

"And I need you now tonight, and I need you more than ever.

And if you'll only hold me tight, we'll be holding on forever."...

And Jeff remembered holding Tracy and how she felt in his arms and what he wouldn't give to hold her again, for her to be his.

"Once upon a time I was falling in love

But now I'm only falling apart

Nothing I can do

A Total Eclipse of the Heart

Once upon a time there was light in my life

But now there's only love in the dark

Nothing I can say

A Total Eclipse of the Heart"

And Jeff left with tears in his eyes to accomplish his lifelong dream, to rediscover the light in his life and to finally say goodbye to Tracy.

Two hours before game time and the stadium was already buzzing. Jeff remembered the rag tag bunch of players that started both his personal journey and this odyssey some seven years before. There were still a handful of those characters with him now and he was glad.

It seems that wherever Jeff went, a hoard of media hounded him and today it was much worse. He put aside fifteen minutes to answer questions and then an hour and a half before gametime he walked onto the field to relish the Olympic Spirit and energy one more time before he went to work. He knew that today, more so than for any other game he had ever participated in, he would have to do most of it on his own. The Cubans looked more like the Oakland A's than the Korean team he and Marc had shut out two days before.

In the crowd he noticed some familiar faces: Ben Adams, Pat Gillick, and Al Widmar. Apparently they were in Barcelona trying to sign Cuban third baseman Omar Linares, the best player in the world not playing in the Major Leagues. Jeff went over for a quick hello knowing they would talk later.

After stretching and running, Jeff took the new ball and went to the bullpen with Dédé to get loose in the warm ninety-degree heat. The adrenaline was pumping too hard and quick so he tried to calm himself down. His arm felt a little tired and he didn't seem to have his best stuff, but that didn't upset him as he hated leaving his best stuff in the bullpen. However, as he took his final pitches, he let loose some of his trademark nasty curveballs and he knew that he was ready for the Gold.

"Good afternoon ladies and Gentleman, this is Bob Costas along with Buck Martinez for what may very well be the greatest sports story of all time. Two time World Series MVP Jeff Williams is leading an underdog French team into the Gold Medal game against the mighty Cubans. This is the real Dream Team of the Olympics. This bunch has taken away the spotlight from Magic, Michael and Larry. Who could ever have imagined? Only in a dream, Jeff Williams' dream."

"Bob," Martinez said, "underdog may be an overstatement, but if anyone can keep the Cuban bats under control, Jeff is the one."

"You caught him." Costas replied. "What should we look for?"

"First of all Jeff is a competitor and a fighter and he has been that way since day one and I loved to catch him. He'll probably go right after the Cubans with his fastball and great curve. And since they are free swingers, I look to him to use his changeup more than usual."

"Well folks, the scene is set and we'll be right back, here at beautiful Montjuic Stadium with the first pitch in the Gold Medal game between France and Cuba," Costas said enthusiastically.

The game started much like the Italian game in eighty-five. Rafael Palean the 6'5'" righthander struck out the first six batters he faced. The Cuban ace was built like a linebacker and had the threatening look of an oncoming locomotive. He threw the ball ninety-five plus with a deadly slider. It would not be easy to score a run. Jeff got through the first two innings allowing only a two-out walk to Linares.

In the top of the third Gommy battled for a walk. Somehow he managed to foul off three nasty pitches before laying off a slider that was just off the plate. It was a truly amazing at bat that changed the game. The young Jean-Pierre Millot managed to lay down a sacrifice to move Gommy to second.

Millot was young and a tireless worker. He had learned so much baseball in the last four months that he probably forgot the long hours Moggle and Pierce spent with him in Florida working on his bunting and baserunning on the backfields of the Blue Jays Complex. It had all been worth it seeing him square to Palean and then fighting with all he had to get the ninety seven-mile an hour fastball down. He was greeted like a hero in the dugout.

Palean chocked the next slider and the catcher could not handle it as it bounced in front of homeplate. Gommy was now at third with the ninth place batter Franck Didot at the plate. Didot, like Millot, and like every batter in the French lineup, except maybe Marc, was overmatched, but he got his bat on the ball and lofted a shallow fly to left. Moggle had a split second to make up his mind. There might not be another opportunity.

"Pacheco is under it. Gommy is going to tag. Here comes the throw. It's going to be close, he is ...safe!!! What a slide 1-0 France!" Costas bellowed out.

"As you watch the replay, look at the slide." Martinez commented. He beat the tag, the only way he could as he slid by the plate away from the catcher and touched it with his hand. A real heads up play."

After four and a half innings, France clung preciously to their one run lead, as both teams remained hitless. In the fifth, Jeff got into trouble by walking the first two batters. Much to Jeff's delight they did not sacrifice. He struck out the next batter and then a hard hit groundball was turned flawlessly by Marc and Millot.

"Well fans, what a game. Through five innings France leads Cuba 1-0 with neither Palean nor Williams giving up a hit. What an amazing game." Costas said enthusiastically.

Meanwhile, at SkyDome in Toronto, the Jays were getting ready to play Milwaukee and were in a tight pennant race tied with Orioles for first. The players had gathered in the clubhouse to watch the game and cheer on their teammate, friend, and leader who would soon be back with them for the stretch drive.

"Here in the bottom of the eighth, the top of the order is up for Cuba as they attempt to get on the board. Even though he has walked five, Williams has struck out fourteen and still has not given up a hit."

"You know something Bob," Martinez interjected, "He seems to be getting stronger and he has the look in his eyes. A look that I've been on the other side of many times. He is ready to take the game and close it. I would not want to be a Cuban hitter."

With that said he struck out the side and the fans stood as he left the field.

Back in Toronto, the players cheered. "That a way Jeffrey," yelled Alomar.

"Keep on chucking old boy," bellowed Borders.

And then like kids they started chanting in unison "three more, three more, three more" as Jeff took to the mound in the bottom of the ninth with his one run lead.

"Well folks, some may compare this to the Miracle on Ice, but this could go beyond that. Think of a high school baseball team with one ace pitcher beating the New-York Yankees for the Wold Series and this would be it" Costas said with enthusiasm and hope.

The fans rose to their feet rooting, willing the French squad on as Gonzalez stepped to the plate with one out. They quickly fell silent as he walked on four straight pitches. Omar Linares, the Cuban slugger was next. Williams fired a first pitch fastball right at the knees but the slugger reached down and lined it to center in front of Gommy. Suddenly the no-hitter was gone and runners were on first and third.

"Well Bob," Buck said, "Jeff has been here before and I don't know if there is anyone better in this situation. Of course usually he wouldn't have already thrown one hundred and thirty-five pitches, but I'd still bet on him."

Jeff took a deep breath, stepped off the mound and looked over and smiled at his younger brother at short. Although he was focused on the task at hand, that smile, captured by the cameras for the whole World to see said it all. It showed his desire to capture the moment, his love for his brother and the enjoyment and love of the game and maybe his chance to purge his inner demons.

"Just came in time to close it," he whispered.

"Now go do it," he yelled silently to himself.

Costas took over: "Pacheco is set in the box. Williams glares in, strike one as he froze Pacheco with the curve."

"Get him." yelled Cito Gaston back in Toronto.

"Williams sets and fires. Pacheco swings and pops it up. Marc Williams is under it. Two down."

"One more, one more, one more..." Came thundering from his Blue Jay teammates as they were once again fans cheering on their favorite player.

"Allez La France, Allez La France, Allez," could be heard throughout the stadium as the French fans sang their rugby fight song led by double silver medalist, Lydie Joncas and the rest of the track team.

"Let's just watch and listen," Costas said.

Jeff needed just one more out for one of the most unbelievable and heartwarming wins in sports history and he was ready to do it. Just a little more. Even he wasn't used to closing six games in one and that is what the Gold Medal game felt like, but this is what it came down to and this is what he loved.

Ramon the big Cuban first baseman stepped in and Jeff was ready. Ramon had an eerie resemblance to Barry Bonds and Jeff liked that because he owned Barry Bonds and he would own Ramon.

The twelve thousand fans were on their feet yelling and screaming for the victory.

Jeff fired a fastball on the inside corner which Ramon took for strike one. Jeff knew he had him and he would take him out on his terms just like Bonds. From the set, he checked Lineres at first and let go a curveball that Ramon swung at aimlessly. Jeff stared into Dédé getting the sign he was looking for; the back door slider.

Jeff got set ignoring the runners, focusing on the pitch and then stepped off. He was clenching too hard and he knew it. It took only a few seconds for him to toe the rubber again and get set. As he released the ball, time stopped for a split second and then joy. He had done it, but then again had he not done it the moment he marched into the stadium and saw the Olympic Rings.

"Folks, look at the Cuban team out of their dugout clapping and saluting the great pitching performance. Nine innings, one hit, six walks, eighteen strikeouts and one gold medal. They realized that they have been part of history.

In Toronto, Jays players were high fiving and yelling. They wanted in their own way to celebrate the accomplishment of their teammate and friend who went out against all odds and realized his dream, his way.

On the field the French squad was going crazy. Jeff, Marc, and Dédé hugged and high-fived each other. Clementi and Thomas, the two veterans, just looked at each other in disbelief while the rest just piled on. Pierce just stood by clapping.

In the stands a rare scene, noticed by none was the fact that Gillick, Adams and Widmar were on their feet applauding, a rare act for baseball men. For the first time they could remember they were simply fans.

Pierre, Jennifer and Louise made their way down to the field and hugged the two boys.

After about twenty minutes things calmed down and the medal ceremony commenced. *La Marseillaise* rang out loudly into the beautiful Catalan sky. The Greek Gods indeed were smiling down on the little team that could. Jeff and Marc held hands like little boys on top of the podium as the rest of their teammates sang out loud.

Afterwards, Jeff, Moggle, and Pierce made their way to the media room first. They would later be followed by Dede, Marc, and Thomas who would handle more of the French Press.

"Jeff, put this in perspective with a World Series win."

"Well most would say that there is nothing like winning a World Series, yet this is more magical and more special. On the one hand, it's baseball in its purest form, yet it is also the biggest event in the World. I have always been fascinated, even obsessed with the Olympics, but I never thought I could be a part of it and I was. That is something I struggle with every day to put into words.

"When you stepped off before the last pitch, what were you thinking?"

"I just wanted to relax take a deep breath and make sure I remembered the moment. I wanted to look over to my brother and say hi, which I did. I knew it was time to end the game and I just wanted to make sure I was ready."

"What's next Jeff? Where do you go from here?"

"Well first thing I want to do is savor this moment, this Golden Moment. I want to enjoy the Closing Ceremonies then go back to Paris for a couple of days, before heading to Toronto and hopefully back with the Jays for an another World Series run.

"Pete," finally someone asked Moggle a question." When you look at this team and what it has accomplished, what do you think? What can you say?"

"First I want to thank this crazy man next to me for coming up with this idea and carrying it through. It was not that many years ago that young Jeff Williams was a boy not sure where life would lead him, well let me tell you, let me tell the whole World, Jeff WIlliams is a man, a man of character and determination. He is a man who is loyal and honest. He is a leader and perhaps best of all an incredible friend."

"He was indeed the key to our victory, but as he has always done, he helped bring out the best in his teammates, and without their support, we would not be here now. This was an awesome mind blowing experience," said the former Ivy Leaguer.

The questions finally ended and Jeff and Moggle returned to the locker room celebration and watched the joy and exuberance of the team. The team that had become a bigger story than Magic Johnson and the DREAM TEAM.

THIRTY THREE

Jeff knew that what he had just done was special, more than special, some would say it was miraculous. He knew that he would never forget Tracy, and this wonderful achievement would not change that, but he did know that enough time had passed for him to get on and continue to live off the field.

More than ever he realized what he needed was a friend and a partner and as he sat in the middle of the clubhouse, drenched in champagne, he felt at peace and at ease for the first time in a long time. Yes he would go back to the Blue Jays, but more importantly he would go back to life. He smiled as he thought of Robin, his best friend. He knew that they were now meant to be together. He knew that it was with her that he should now be.

And with that realization, he grabbed a bottle of champagne, guzzled most of it, doused Marc with the rest and hugged his little brother. He then toasted his team and cried as they toasted him back. He did not know if he could ever top this, or if he ever wanted to.

THIRTY FOUR

He looked down one more time at the beautiful Stadium. It would soon be his time to march in and dance but for now he closed his eyes and let his mind wander. He was perhaps at the most perfect place to be in the World. The eyes of the World were focused on the party yet he was in such a peaceful place, privileged and alone.

He now focused upwards to a place he had never been, and he flew faster and higher than ever, through the clouds and around the moon, until he started to slow down, guided by someone else's controls, music from the stadium faintly in the background.

Finally he stopped, and then he saw what he hoped was there, what he had dreamt for so long and what he wanted more than anything, a chance to say goodbye.

"Jeff, I think it's time." Her sensitive and wonderful voice echoed in his ears and heart.

He approached and took a moment to look at her. She was so beautiful, so magical and so real, just as he remembered her. He hugged her so tight. This time he would protect her. Then he heard the words he so much needed to hear.

"Push on Jeff, because I will always love you, just as I know that you will always love me." And as quickly as she appeared, she was gone vanishing in his arms.

When he opened his eyes the tears were uncontrollable, but the burden was lifted. The emptiness was slowly filling up. He knew now that she was looking down on him and wanted him to go on. And Jeff had finally managed to say goodbye.